WHAT IS "PSYCHIC"?

To be "psychic" means that you exhibit more ESP—extrasensory perception—than most people. Extrasensory perception is knowledge gained without using the normal means of reception—touching, tasting, hearing, smelling, and seeing.

For years laboratory experimentation has attempted to prove the existence of ESP. Today, much new research is being done on various mind-control techniques. Spontaneous instances of ESP, where psychical phenomena may occur only once or twice—usually to those who least expect them—are not accessible to scientific observation or study because no repeatable experiment involving them can be devised. But they occur so frequently to such a great number of different people that they cannot be ignored.

Someday, as more and more study is given to the subject, there is little doubt we will realize that all such conditions are perfectly normal; they just operate by laws as yet unknown to us. As Saint Augustine said long ago, "Miracles are not contrary to nature but only contrary to what we know about nature."

HOW TO DEVELOP
YOUR ESP

by
Susy Smith

PINNACLE BOOKS • NEW YORK CITY

HOW TO DEVELOP YOUR ESP

Copyright © 1972 by Susy Smith

A Pinnacle Book published by special arrangement with
G. P. Putnam & Sons.

This edition has been completely reset in a typeface designed
for ease of reading. It was printed from new plates and contains
the complete text of the original, high-priced edition.

First printing, October 1973
Second printing, December 1974

Printed in the United States of America

PINNACLE BOOKS, INC.
275 Madison Avenue
New York, New York 10016

Other Books by Susy Smith:

The Mediumship of Mrs. Leonard
The Enigma of Out-of-Body Travel
ESP for the Millions
More ESP for the Millions
A Supernatural Primer for the Millions
Haunted Houses for the Millions
Out-of-Body Experiences for the Millions
Reincarnation for the Millions
Adventures in the Supernatural
World of the Strange
Susy Smith's Supernatural World
ESP
Widespread Psychic Wonders
Today's Witches
Prominent American Ghosts
Ghosts Around the House
Confessions of a Psychic

Contents

How pure in heart, how sound in head,
With what divine affection bold,
Should be the heart of him who'd hold
An hour's communion with the dead.

—HENRY WADSWORTH LONGFELLOW

1: INSTANT ESP

IF you wish to acquire the talent for ESP quickly, there are several ways it can be done. You could fall on your head from a thirty-foot ladder and fracture your skull, as Dutch psychic Peter Hurkos did. Or you could contract a fever like Los Angeles healer Charles Cassidy, who first became clairvoyant after a bout with malaria when he was stationed in North Africa during World War II.

Ronald Edwin, widely known as Mr. ESP, had a bad spill when he was nine years old, and immediately afterward he saw his first psychic vision—a ghost sitting on his mantelpiece. When the man known as Italy's most famous healer, Achille d'Angelo, was in his twenties, working as a circus tout on stilts, he fell and suffered a concussion. After two days he awoke not only healed but clairvoyant.

Charles Cassidy had a very high temperature with his malaria. He told me, "During my recovery period I noticed that when I closed my eyes, I saw pictures very clearly inside my head. Most of these pictures didn't mean anything to me, but some of them proved to be precognitive flashes. I learned in time how to control these pictures. If I looked for some specific coming incident, such as the outcome of a sporting event or a political election, I could get the picture of what actually was going to occur in the future." It wasn't until years later that Cassidy learned he was also a healer.

11

Imagine Hurkos' surprise when he came to in the hospital after his precipitate descent from the roof of a house he was painting and discovered that he knew what everyone around him was thinking. He'd never had that ability before, and he found it most disconcerting. He asked his doctors to help him return to normal, but they, too, were puzzled.

"Even a psychiatrist worked with me and tested me," Hurkos reported in an interview in *Psychic* (April, 1970). But no one knew how to help him. Despite many X rays and medical examinations they could not discover what caused his odd new condition.

"Since the doctors could do nothing to take it away, I gradually had to learn to live with it," Hurkos says. Now making a very good living with his psychic nightclub act, he is no doubt glad he wasn't able to lose his strange affliction. So, probably, were the others who achieved instant ESP the hard way.

If you don't care to go through such trauma and yet have a desire to become proficient as a psychic, I'm afraid it is going to take some work. You wouldn't expect to become a piano virtuoso, a famous artist, or an author of note without undergoing years of practice, would you? Similarly there are definite techniques used by those who wish to acquire psychic ability, and they must be practiced over a period of time. Not to discourage the beginner, however, let me note that sitting for development of your psychic abilities will no doubt become one of your favorite pastimes, and you will probably look back on the hours you spent developing them as among the happiest of your life.

Reasons for development, the best techniques, and expected results will be the topics of this book. First, however, for those who do not have sufficient background, we will consider some of the basic fundamentals of psychical phenomena.

To be "psychic" means that you exhibit more ESP—extrasensory perception—than most people. Extrasensory perception is knowledge gained without using the normal means of reception—touching, tasting, hearing, smelling, and seeing. Kinds of ESP are classified as telepathy—awareness of something another person is thinking; clairvoyance—supernormal knowledge of a physical object or happening; and precognition—predicting a future event that cannot be inferred from present knowledge. Psychokinesis, or mind over matter, is also usually included with ESP.

Parapsychologists, or psychical researchers, are the scientists who study ESP and its related areas. Psychical (or "psi" as the parapsychologists call it) phenomena are those which have supernormal characteristics involving ESP. They include mediumistic utterances, faith or spirit healing, alleged communications from the dead, ghostly appearances, poltergeists and much else that today are considered supernormal because we don't know how to explain them. Someday, as more and more study is given to the subject, there is little doubt we will realize that all such conditions are perfectly normal; they just operate by laws as yet unknown to us. Saint Augustine said long ago, "Miracles are not contrary to nature but only contrary to what we know about nature."

For years laboratory experimentation has been used in an effort to prove the existence of ESP. Today much new research is being done through various mind control techniques. Spontaneous instances of ESP, where psychical phenomena may occur only once or twice, usually to those who least expect them, are not amenable to scientific observation or study because no repeatable experiment involving them can be devised; but they occur so frequently to such a great number of different people that they cannot be ignored. So in this chapter on instant ESP we will

13

use a few spontaneous cases to illustrate the types of extrasensory experience.

A simple instance of spontaneous telepathy was reported by British psychical researcher Rosalind Heywood in the *Journal* of the Society for Psychical Research (March, 1966). Mr. William Freed of New Zealand, who visited Mrs. Heywood in London, told her of an event which he had been tempted to think of as a lucky coincidence but which he submitted for her evaluation nonetheless. He said that about five or six years before, while working in his garden, he had felt a strong compulsion to drop his tool and go into the house to see his daughter Jane.

"I entered her room," he said, "just in time to grab her hand and to turn off the electric switch—she was holding live wiring, which she accidentally tore off while cleaning her lamp and was trying to squeeze back into the lamp holder! There was, and I remember the occasion well, absolutely no apparent reason for me to go into the room."

Mr. Freed may somehow have received the message from his daughter's subconscious mind that alerted him to the danger of her position, or some people would say he was warned by helpful spirits. Fortunately he had been receptive, whatever the source.

Clairvoyance is more difficult to distinguish, for it is hard to be sure that a fact that comes to one supernormally might not be known by someone else on earth and thus have been telepathically perceived. For this reason a heading of GESP, or general ESP, is often used for this classification.

An instance that could be called clairvoyance, even though it seems also to have elements of telepathy and precognition, comes from the *A.R.E. News* (October, 1971). Mrs. Mary D. Hickey wrote: "My son had been in a seminary studying for the priesthood for six years. In October of that sixth year I was talking on the phone with a friend who mentioned a priest she had met. As she described his habit, I said, 'He must have been a Franciscan (the order my son was with).' As I said that, I heard my own voice—within me—saying, 'I'll never see John in his brown robe,' and I started to weep. He had received it in a ceremony the previous July, which I was unable to attend."

Somehow Mrs. Hickey was able to continue talking, and her friend was unaware of what had happened to her; but because the experience was so vivid, it worried her. She tried to think of the many reasons why she would not be able to see her son in his priestly robes—she might go blind, she might die. She even spoke to a priest friend about it.

The outcome was much simpler than she anticipated. In January her son called and said he was leaving the order and coming home from the seminary. "So I never did see him in the brown habit, except in pictures," she says.

Precognition is easier to identify and harder to understand than any other psychic experience. When this is discussed, it is sometimes asked, "If such things are true, why don't people predict the outcome of horse races?"

That is just what Charlene R. Brody of Sun Valley, California, did. As she reported in *Fate* magazine (July, 1971), she dreamed one night about a *house* named Indian Gin. As she thought about it the next day and talked it over with two coworkers in a bank in Beverly Hills, she had a sudden thought that perhaps, with a dream's contrariness, the word "house" was really meant to be *"horse."* She asked her friend Ruth, a racing enthusiast, if there was a horse by that name.

Ruth nodded. "Sure is. Second race today at Del Mar. Interested?"

Was she? Indeed, yes, and right on the nose. She won $250.

When you begin to develop your ESP, you will find

15

that spontaneous incidents like these may occur more and more often in your life. In fact, there comes a time when you weigh each dream and each unusual idea that comes to you, just in case it will be discovered to have psychical significance.

2: PERSISTENT ESP

SOME people, as we have seen, achieve their psychic sensitivity accidentally or spontaneously, and it may not occur more than once or twice in their lives. Others, like lecturer-author David Hoy, have learned to use a talent that erupted spontaneously but has continued to exist ever since. He is a former Southern Baptist minister who lives in Paducah, Kentucky, with his wife, Shirley, and their three children, all of whom are restoring a two-hundred-year-old inn in their spare time. Hoy had a most dramatic experience when his ESP first became evident. He had been interested in extrasensory perception since his childhood but encountered it personally for the first time when he was a freshman at the University of South Carolina.

"This involvement," Hoy said, "started one morning when I got the impression that my father was soon going to die. He was only forty-seven and apparently in robust health, but the feeling was so strong that I mentioned it to several friends. That evening, when the phone rang, I said, 'That's it! That's the news of my father's death.' When I answered the phone, I was told that he had died of a heart attack that afternoon."

David's father was a minister, and his son thought this experience was a sign that he, too, should go into the ministry. So he chose the church as his career and had his first charge before he was graduated from the university. Later he found that his interest in psychical research conflicted

17

with Christian orthodoxy as it was understood by his church superiors, and he gradually withdrew from preaching. Now, besides collecting antiques and remodeling the famous old inn, he is a popular lecturer on ESP, frequently giving demonstrations of his abilities. He also presents what he calls an ESPosition at colleges throughout the country. A recent publication from Radio Station KMOX in St. Louis stated that as a special guest on a series of eleven one-hour programs in the fall of 1971, David Hoy received more than 140,000 phone calls from listeners.

His precognition has occasionally been startling in its accuracy. On October 31, 1967, he predicted on Radio Station KDKA in Pittsburgh that within sixty days a bridge spanning the Ohio River would collapse. Forty-five days later the 1,753-foot Silver Bridge at Point Pleasant, West Virginia, toppled into the river during evening rush hour, killing forty-six persons.

On Boston television and radio David correctly paired Jacqueline Kennedy and Aristotle Onassis two years before their marriage.

In a speech before an audience at Tusculum College in Greeneville, Tennessee, in May, 1968, two weeks before the assassination of Senator Robert F. Kennedy, Hoy predicted that Kennedy would win the California presidential primary but that the election would be marked by tragedy.

So far in 1972 he has made one prediction I know of that has come true, having said on New Year's Eve that a U.S.-registered ship would sink off the coast of South America within the first three months of 1972. One was found at the bottom of the Caribbean in February.

Not perhaps with such significant results but nonetheless consistently, ESP has figured in the life of June Lockhart, the well-known actress. She can recall instances of it from the age of six, when she began to have a vivid

18

dream many nights in a row. She saw the house across the street burning. From her window she watched the flames and the fire engines.

Her parents were away acting at the time, and she was staying with her grandparents. "At breakfast each morning I told my grandparents about the realistic dream," June told the *National Enquirer*, but they paid little attention to her chatter. "Then one Sunday morning I woke from my dream and found it was real—the neighbor's house was actually on fire."

ESP has been a valuable asset in the actress' life since then. "I put it to everyday use," she says. "With ESP I can find important lost papers and wallets, even parking places for my car on crowded streets. I just see these things in my mind."

Graham Greene, the famous author, admits in *A Sort of Life* that he has kept a dream diary for many years because he has been deeply influenced by his dreams. On several occasions in dreams he has witnessed events—including a specific ship sinking in the Irish Sea—which, he later learned, were occurring at the moment he was dreaming them.

You don't necessarily have to believe in psychic powers to have them. I know a woman named Lillian D. who looked up one evening from her sewing to see a ghost walking down her front stairway. It surprised Lillian very much. She was the wife of a professor at a large Midwestern university, and in her set nobody believed in ghosts. At first Lillian thought someone must have wandered in looking for the woman who rented a second floor room. She walked up to the foot of the steps and said to the little old lady she saw descending, "I don't believe Mrs. Jones is up there. She went to a meeting."

The little old lady didn't say anything, but she smiled sweetly at Lillian . . . then vanished right before her eyes!

All this caused my friend much mental agitation because, having refused ever to admit the reality of ghosts, she had obviously been confronted with one. To make it even more embarrassing, after hearing of the incident, Mrs. Jones, her upstairs roomer who always kept her domain tightly closed, finally relented and showed her a picture of her dead mother. It was the identical little old lady. The reason, Mrs. Jones said, that she kept her door shut all the time was that she and her deceased mother visited together every afternoon, and she wasn't quite sure how people would take that if they knew about it.

Being closely associated with the academically minded —Lillian's husband was later to become one of the most prominent educators in the country—she has never yet fully allowed herself to accept the term "spirit manifestation" as the reason for her apparition, although when she tries to make sense of any other explanation she finds herself no farther ahead.

Lillian even insists on arguing about another incident, which happened when she was in college in Illinois. One day she walked into a room in which several of her friends were playing with a Ouija board. They had been receiving nothing in the way of information, just the usual blitherings of the Ouija when no one particularly psychic has his fingers on the pointer. When the girls urged Lillian to sit down at the board, she did so reluctantly, for even then she had no belief in anything so "occult" or frivolous. However, the minute she put her hands on the pointer, it began to spell out a message for Lillian's roommate. It reported that her brother was at that moment undergoing emergency surgery for a ruptured appendix at a hospital in New Orleans.

"Why, what an awful thing to say," the girl cried. "Lillian, it didn't do anything like that before you sat down. You must have pushed it."

"Yes, how could you be so mean?" chimed in the others; but Lillian was as appalled as they at what had happened.

"You *know* I didn't do it," she said. "I don't even believe in this . . . this gadget."

Less than an hour later, her roommate received a telegram saying that her brother, who was in New Orleans, had just been rushed to the hospital for an emergency appendectomy.

These accounts reveal that many people are naturally psychic, even sometimes when they do not believe in such a possibility. As more and more are becoming acquainted with the existence of ESP, there is a tremendous burst of interest in it throughout the world. It will hopefully change conditions for the better, for, as we will see, those who have ESP and develop it can become forces for good in the world.

The late medium Arthur Ford wrote in *Unknown but Known,* "I encounter such cases so frequently as to be personally convinced that we are on the verge of so radical an overturn of materialistic values as to usher in an entirely new era of human experience. We are approaching a time when psychic ability will be found to be as common—and as varied in quality—as the ability to sing, or play the piano or guitar, or compose a poem or a picture. This awareness of an ultimate dimension of being may well be one of the great changes the twenty-first century will bring to man. The posture of the materialist is weakening. He is driven to more and more absurd 'explanations,' to more and more obvious evasions, as the psychic evidence mounts."

3: THE SCIENTISTS

PEOPLE who study psychic occurrences scientifically, or parapsychologists, research the faculties of man that appear to be of a nonphysical nature and hence inexplicable. Formerly such work was called psychical research, and many still prefer this name because they believe that parapsychology is not so much para- (past or beyond) psychology as it is paraphysics. When one considers all the eventualities that open up when psychical phenomena are really studied with an open mind, it is even probable that parapsychology, if and when it changes the tack on which it is now attempting to approach reality, will eventually be considered a philosophical or religious discipline.

Dr. Laurence LeShan of Rockland State Hospital, Orangeburg, New York, an enthusiastic student of the psychic, says, "Parapsychology is far more than it appears to be on first glance. In the most profound sense it is the study of the basic nature of man."

There are increasing numbers of academicians becoming active in this field today. Dealing scientifically with the unknown aspects of man becomes so fascinating that once one's interest is grabbed by it, he can't leave it alone. Professor Jack H. Holland, chairman of the Management Department at San Jose State College and a director of the Academy of Parapsychology and Medicine, discussed this problem in a paper titled "Let Us Look at Extrasensory

Perception," published by the *Parapsychology Periodical* of the California Parapsychology Foundation. From it we quote: "When one trained in the scientific pursuit of knowledge becomes interested in any phenemona that are not easily subject to scientific methods of investigation, the problem always arises as to the wisdom of developing and working with that interest.

"Certainly there are many academic fields which are not subject to great scientific investigation, particularly philosophy, religion and the fine arts. However, when one's whole academic orientation is toward the social sciences and/or natural and physical sciences even a cursory investigation of extrasensory perception and related phenomena is fraught with great personal disquietude."

This is probably because these subjects so thoroughly belonging in the realm of the unknown have in our culture been exploited by the charlatan, the quick-buck artist, and because they have attracted so many neurotic or disorganized individuals. It is an area that has, says Dr. Holland, "a very special aura of chicanery, fraud and deceit. How popular is this image of parapsychology! But how far it has come from this image!"

It is true that one can now feel academically acceptable even though he is exploring parapsychology. This is because so much is being published and researched in major laboratories across the world. It has not yet developed the respectability in America that it has in most other countries, but there is an increasing interest here by natural scientists, electronics engineers, philosophers, and physical scientists. And some large businesses are undertaking major studies in parapsychology along with many universities. American Telephone and Telegraph, through its Bell Laboratories, Sylvania, and IBM are just a few of the concerns doing major work in the area.

Buckminster Fuller, who designed the U.S. Pavilion at Montreal's Expo '67 and whom astronomer Harlow

Shapley calls "the brightest man alive," has not got around to considering any aspect of our study but telepathy yet, but on that he is emphatic. He told Walter McGraw, author of *The World of the Paranormal*: "I was only mildly surprised when someone discovered we have telepathic capability. I think it is something we really must start dealing with."

In addressing a meeting sponsored by the American Medical Association, Buckminster Fuller made the cold, blunt statement: "In a relatively short time, possibly ten years, we will have discovered that what we call telepathy is part of the electromagnetic spectrum."

Dr. Holland agrees with this, saying we have proof that man is an electrical machine capable of receiving electrical impulses. We have developed many electrical apparatuses that measure man's well-being by picking up electrical impulses—such as the electrocardiograph and the electroencephalograph, which has had a tremendous impact on the study of extrasensory perception. With this instrument, which was designed to measure brain waves, we can observe the thought process by recording graphically the vibrations given off by various thoughts.

"I have been fascinated by the proof this machine has provided of the importance of positive thinking," says Dr. Holland. "(I wish I could, in this short paper, give the theological and personal implications of this!) On the electroencephalogram positive, good thoughts fan out at a high rate; negative, poor thoughts go out almost on a straight line and some seem to go back into the individual. Worry, intolerance, hate, etc., have been given the 'credit' by medical men as a prime reason for ulcers and other digestive disorders—of course, biologically, we know that certain enzymes are active when we worry, etc., but here seems to be the catalyst—the electric vibration we are discharging. Think what happens to a battery when it 'turns in on itself'!"

The proof of the fact that thought—conscious or subconscious—involves electrical waves is certainly evidence of the possibility of extrasensory perception. Any time electrical waves are activated there is a perfectly good chance of those waves being received . . . isn't there?

We're hearing so much about work going on currently in Russia in various areas of psychical research. They have apparently found, too, that humans send out at a level which is above all those that can currently be tuned in by regular, existing conscious faculties, like the dog whistle which human ears cannot hear. And, Dr. Holland says, "I personally have seen experiments at the University of Utrecht, in Nepal, at Heidelberg, and at several Japanese universities which convince me that people with great determination and intellectual curiosity can become adept at communicating with certain others and learn to discipline themselves in order to become a better sender or receiver. According to Professors Bergier and Pauwels, the Russians are training some of their astronauts to do just that. I know for a fact that this very area is being investigated at the San Antonio Air Space Medical Center in this country."

This is exciting news because no avenue of learning should be neglected in our exploration of the universe. Nothing which man can conceive as being possible should be neglected, because all lines of exploration are valid. In fact, if any research today goes along lines counter to what is accepted by society, it is more likely to achieve success in the long run. Minds which are expanded by meditation, illumination, cosmic consciousness, psychic development, or enlightened mediumship may receive data that will astound us. It should be accepted and studied instead of being cursorily rejected because of its source. Those who close their minds to this possibility just because they think it is too naïve or old-fashioned are rejecting untried the most progressive new avenue to learning.

It is doubtless true that many scientists who are in the front ranks of their profession are even now receiving inspiration from supernormal sources. Some realize it but would never dream of confessing it to their fellow workers. Others, not aware of the source of their inspirations, nonetheless accept them with gratitude.

If anyone were to suggest to them, however, that they might attempt to prove scientifically the existence and the survival after death of the human soul, they would run shrieking. It is still only ESP research that has its foot in the door. The spooks and the spirits remain out in the cold.

Being careful not to commit themselves any further along philosophical and theological lines than would be strictly scientific, parapsychologists do not allow themselves to accept anything that has so far come through mediums as actual proof of the existence of the soul or its survival after death. Thus they feel it necessary to ignore a great deal of very good material that is at least "highly suggestive" of survival evidence.

In the main, they seem to be embarrassed by the amount of evidential information produced by mediums and home circles. They do not know what to do with it because it is so controversial, and they don't want controversy. Most parapsychologists want to protect the scientific acceptance of ESP that has been partially achieved by the affiliation of the Parapsychological Association with the American Association for the Advancement of Science. They know that their sponsoring of survival evidence would weaken their previous efforts instead of strengthening them. Therefore they attempt as much as possible to dissociate ESP from the ghosts and deathbed scenes and séances which inspired their predecessors in psychical research. The fact that several large sums have recently been willed to various parapsychological organizations

26

specifically to be used for *survival* research is no doubt quite disconcerting to them.

In so carefully approaching the aspects of the subject that deal with evidence of the human soul, parapsychologists are doing survival research a favor, however. If they went into it in a big way now, they would achieve only scorn for their efforts. But when scientific stature is definitely achieved by ESP, its related areas of psychical phenomena will then necessarily have to come under consideration. For this reason I do not decry, as some amateur workers in the field do, the reluctance of parapsychologists to become associated with survival research at the present time. Let us be grateful to them for their efforts to gain scientific acceptance for ESP. The rest will come soon enough.

When repeatable experiments in card guessing were devised—and indicated that ESP does occur more times than chance, scientists in other disciplines were very slow in acceptance, attempting in every possible way to discredit the experiments and to disavow the evidence. Because of this, parapsychologists are overly conscientious in all their efforts. We can only give them credit for what they have accomplished and all the assistance we can as they proceed with further experimentation. It takes a brave and original thinker even to enter the field of parapsychology at the present time.

The challenge of the unknown—the excitement of reaching out for new ideas and new experiences—does not have a great deal of appeal for most of earth's citizens. How many actually take up the gauntlet and run with it to anything out of the ordinary? How many are willing even to talk about ideas which are not familiar to their fellows?

Dr. Jack Holland is one of those forward-looking thinkers who is helping ESP to progress scientifically as fast as it is.

"Of course," he says, "the philosophical and theological

implications of this whole field are enormous. However, I personally believe that much of what all the great religious teachers of all religions taught, believed and practiced can now be given a scientific basis through some of the research findings in the field of parapsychology.... I believe most of the scientific work in the field will be centered on the fact that man is electrically charged. But I believe that the greatest gain for man in studying this field is a further and deeper understanding of himself and his interpersonal relationships."

Or as Albert Einstein put it, "Anyone who studies physics long enough is inevitably led to metaphysics."

4: PSYCHIC CHILDREN

MEDIUMS, of course, are the traditional subjects of study of those attempting to understand ESP. One who wishes to develop his extrasensory abilities will make an effort to become more psychic, or sensitive, and the most advanced form of this is mediumship.

Most of those who become professional mediums are born with natural psychic abilities and give evidence of them from their earliest days. It has been noted by some researchers that perhaps many more children are born psychic than is indicated by the number of adults who practice it professionally or even have frequent spontaneous psi experiences. In many children the stigma of being different or the fact that they are scolded for their "imaginings" are credited with causing the suppression of these unusual talents until they become submerged or atrophied.

Many persons who have natural psychic abilities have had mothers similarly endowed; so the capacities may safely be classed as hereditary. Chicago medium Ellen Cook says in her booklet *How I Discovered My Mediumship* that it had been perfectly natural for members of her mother's family to hear admonitory voices just as she did. She wrote that when as young as four years old she would frequently hear a voice say, "Don't do that!" when she could see no one anywhere in her vicinity.

"Be careful, Ellen," the voice would say. "Come this way—don't go around that way!" And it became natural

29

for her to do its bidding because she usually discovered there was a reason why she should obey.

She wrote: "Somehow, it seemed perfectly normal to have friends whom others could not see or hear. I marveled not at all at the voices. My astonishment was that my playmates did not have voices to guide them.

" 'Why did you stop playing over by that tree, and run away from it?' my mother would ask me.

" 'Somebody told me I must come away,' I would answer, and my mother would shake her head but make no reply.

"I did not know then that she had heard the voices, as had her mother before her—and others far back in my ancestry. The heritage was mine. It belonged in the family."

Various surveys of professional mediums reveal that at least half of them exhibited their psychic gifts before they were ten years old. Those who did not become aware of them until they were older then realized the significance of certain childhood experiences of a psychic nature which they had not understood at the time. None of them as children had known they were different from others until it was forcibly pointed out to them because of what was considered their peculiar behavior.

Jacqueline Eastlund of Los Angeles, probably the prettiest psychic in the business, told me she at first believed that everyone else saw and heard the same things she did, and she was surprised when others began to refer to her as strange.

"I knew I wasn't strange," she said. "They were strange."

Because she was considered different, however, she learned to "keep her mouth shut." She is reticent to this day when among strangers, even though she has forced herself to learn to stand on a platform and give readings before hundreds of people.

Children who are branded as liars and dreamers when they tell of their psi experiences often feel misjudged and misunderstood for the rest of their lives. No child wishes to be set apart; he wants to be just like everyone else. He naturally develops a feeling of inferiority and insecurity when unjustly criticized and reprimanded. To be scolded constantly for playing with spirit children who are as real to you as your other friends is disheartening as well as very confusing.

All parapsychologists are familiar with the story of the spirit playmates of the famous medium Eileen J. Garrett, who was the president of the Parapsychology Foundation in New York until her recent death. She first met "The Children," as she called them, when she was about four years old, and they came to see her daily until she was thirteen. They were as real to her as living children and as soft and warm to the touch, and they all talked and laughed and played happily together.

Eileen's aunt, with whom she lived, could not see the children, and to hear about them made her enormously unhappy. So the girl was often punished.

Well known also are the "Happy Valley" visions of Gladys Osborne Leonard, the great English medium. Gladys thought everyone else shared these with her until the morning when she said to her father, "Isn't that an especially beautiful scene they are showing us today?" His amazement, when she insisted that she was actually seeing on the wall pictures of beautiful people among enchanting scenery, quickly changed to misgiving, and he demanded that she immediately put all such fantasy out of her life.

Ellen Cook played with the spirit children as Eileen Garrett did, and she found them to be much kinder and gentler than her physical playmates. She listened to her admonitory voices and found that they protected her from danger, warning her, for instance, when she was about to step on a snake; but they never kept her from learning

31

lessons which were necessary for her personal development. And yet she would hear neighbors say to her mother, "The child is queer, very queer. I would correct her of these notions if I were you. They are harming her."

Mrs. Cook wrote, "What a thankless sort of life, I have often mused, for a little girl to live. A child with a gift such as mine cannot be said to have all the simple pleasures of childhood."

Jack Harrison Pollack in his book *Croiset the Clairvoyant* brought out just how much Dutch medium Gerard Croiset's unfortunate childhood affected his personality. Of course, negative factors other than his mediumship were in operation. Croiset's father, an actor, was a Socialist and an atheist who deserted his wife periodically. Eventually there was no homelife whatever, and Gerard was placed with a foster family when he was eight years old. During his youth he had six sets of foster parents, was sickly and undernourished, and had rickets. Is it any wonder, Pollack says, that he was childlike, theatrical, insecure, tense, talkative, and suffering from stomach disorder? Croiset also had great vanity, aggressiveness, strong craving for power, and lack of social propriety, which occasionally brought him into conflict with others. These Croiset faults may have stemmed from his father's anarchistic philosophy, his childhood insecurity, and his growing success in many well-publicized cases of psychic performance.

They undoubtedly came additionally from the fact that he was forever being unfairly punished when he spoke of playing with his unseen little friends or told of his paranormal impressions. At six he was already different and set apart from others.

There are two excellent professional mediums named Douglas Johnson. One lives in London and has achieved a good bit of fame throughout the world; the other has a devoted coterie of followers in Los Angeles. The California Doug Johnson, who came from Lutheran parents of Scandinavian descent in Minneapolis, started at the age of nine seeing spirit forms of people he knew. They came to give notice that they had just passed away.

"I would jump up and tell the family," Johnson informed me, "that so-and-so is standing here talking to me and telling me he has died." This, naturally, was greeted with scorn at first. But when, invariably within perhaps ten minutes or half an hour, word would be received confirming the death of the individual in question, Doug's relatives began to take his childish ramblings seriously.

This phenomenon, with ramifications, has lasted up to the present, Johnson says. And "if anyone in my family is going to die, I hear a voice telling me about a month beforehand." He has learned to accept these as predictions which invariably come true. Eventually people began to acknowledge that Doug could observe spirits. Their ultimate support went a long way toward convincing him that he was a natural medium, and his professional career has been the logical outcome.

Fortunate is the mediumistic child who is able to convince his parents that he is not daft. Rosemary Brown, the British psychic who is currently the object of much attention because she purports to receive musical compositions from great composers of the past, says in her book *Unfinished Symphonies* that ESP enabled her to see and hear a great many of her father's friends who had died, and they supplied details about themselves which she could not possibly have known normally. It was when she received a message for him from someone called Black Alec that he started to believe her.

"Apparently," she writes, "Black Alec had been something of a black sheep, which accounted for the nickname. He had been a friend of my father's when they were both in their twenties, but Black Alec had pulled some shady deal on my father and from then on the friendship had ended; and my father had completely put him out of mind.

"My father had his faults in his lifetime, but he was fantastically honest and could not bear any sort of behavior which he felt was not straight."

Black Alec died young, and much later he came through to Rosemary because he wanted to apologize to her father for the harm he had done him when on earth. She dutifully passed on the message.

"My father was astounded by this," she wrote. "The man had died before I was born; even my mother knew nothing of him; and when I gave my father a full description of the man and told him of the apology, this seemed to clinch the whole question of my ESP and life after death as far as he was concerned.

"After that he was convinced that my visions were not just childish fantasies and his whole attitude changed."

Leslie Flint, another British medium who has recently published his memoirs, had a poverty-stricken childhood, but his psychic experiences helped him endure it. The first event he recalls occurred when he was six years old, during World War I. His aunt Nell came into his grandmother's kitchen and flopped into a chair crying, having just learned that her husband had been killed in service in France.

Leslie saw a soldier following her, ". . . looking lost and sad, pulling at Aunt's sleeve. She took no notice and later he vanished."

When Flint told what he had seen, he was berated by both his aunt and his grandmother for telling lies. Yet years afterward, when he looked at a family photo, he recognized his uncle as the sad-looking soldier he had seen.

Today, unfortunately, professional mediums are often fraudulent or else just inept. Those such as we have discussed, who have grown up to realize their best potential, are in the minority. But when the time comes that psychic capabilities are recognized early, given long and thorough training, and treated with respect, there will be a whole new generation of responsible mediums who will respond accordingly.

Every home would be better off if it had its own psychic. I don't mean a professional medium, who must make a living at his trade and therefore may on occasion provide fraudulent evidence when he is unable to produce it genuinely. I mean nonprofessional sensitives—you and you—anyone who has psychic talents and learns to use them well.

It is not by any means recommended that people sit alone and attempt to develop their own mediumship. But home circles which sit regularly for meditation and development of the psychic abilities of their members should be started wherever possible. And children who exhibit psychic tendencies should be encouraged to develop them.

5: THE PSYCHODYNAMICS
OF MEDIUMSHIP

IT is hardly any wonder that with such complicated childhoods most professional mediums grow up to be rather complicated adults. A bit of analysis of their psychodynamics (motives or other causative factors in mental life) might therefore be in order. "Psycho" means life, soul, mind, mental processes and activities. "Dynamics" are defined as the moving moral and physical forces operating in any field or the laws relating to them. So here, then, we are dealing with the various factors which operate in the mind or soul of mediums in an attempt to understand the emotional differences between them and other people.

We can hardly hope to comprehend how some individuals are born with stronger capabilities for extrasensory perception than others, for at this stage of our knowledge we recognize little more about psi than that it is an unconscious mental process. We should expect that the lives of those who have it will develop in a way that will exhibit the value of these unusual abilities. This is not necessarily the case, usually because of the misapprehensions about mediums that are fairly consistent in the public mind. Living with such an image is undoubtedly a great chore.

Horace Leaf, a medium himself, understands their problems. He says in his book *Death Cannot Kill,* "It is rather exasperating for a medium to find himself rated as a schizophrenic, a psychopath, an obsessed hysteric, or a

36

self-deceiving fraud. . . . Mediumship definitely involves a change in the individual's psychophysical makeup, and is perhaps invariably accompanied sooner or later with psychological instability, but not of a harmful kind."

Mediums have an ambitious requirement to assert themselves, yet usually feel that what is expected of them is humiliating. They are seemingly tired of having continually to play a defensive role. For some persons the derision or hostility of playmates and older people may be the beginning of a reticence or distrust of almost everyone in later life.

Rosalind Heywood, a thoroughly objective Englishwoman who possesses psychic powers but who does not consider herself a medium, has expressed in her book *ESP: A Personal Memoir* the feeling of most who consistently have psi experiences.

She wrote: "I cannot be sure of the cause of my experiences, but I can be sure that they occurred. They could be more easily swept aside as pure imagination were they unique. But they are not. Thousands far more impressive have been reported throughout the ages and from every culture, and it is probably a safe bet that yet more are not mentioned for fear of 'what people would say.' Many, too, have been carefully checked by such bodies as the S.P.R. [Society for Psychical Research] and the American S.P.R., whereas mine rest on nothing but my own word. Even so, they may at least demonstrate the conflict which can be created when experience contradicts the official beliefs of the society in which one lives."

Although medium Arthur Ford later mellowed considerably, in his book *Nothing So Strange* he said that at one time "I resented the fact that nearly everyone I met looked upon me as a charlatan or a lunatic, or at best as a guinea pig to be used for interesting experiments."

Scientific investigators are hard to take, too. Dr. Ian Stevenson of the University of Virginia pointed out in

Gateway magazine, "To many sensitives, the interrogations and the controlled conditions of the parapsychologists are a terrible nuisance. I could not agree more heartily. It is a bore to have to put up with all sorts of seemingly irrelevant questions or requirements in order to convince someone else of what seems obvious to you. But if these questions and controls of scientists were only tedious I do not think many sensitives would object.

"What they really object to, I think, are doubts about their intelligence, memory, or honesty, which these questions and controls sometimes *seem* to suggest. But here I think sensitives often misjudge the investigators, at least those I know. Now it is true that scientific investigators of psychical phenomena usually do have *general* doubts, based on various experiences of earlier investigators or their own. But this is not to say that they approach a particular case with *specific* doubts about *its* informants. I think it fair to say that they do *not* have such doubts particularly about any person or experience they are at the moment studying. If a scientist had evidence leading him to doubt the intelligence, memory or honesty of a sensitive he is actually studying he probably would not take up the case at all. . . ."

Even with the unusually great insecurities which beset their lives, most mediums have made satisfactory adjustments, Stevenson thinks. ". . . by themselves and among their own trusted circle of friends, gifted sensitives usually come to accept their experiences more or less without question. They integrate their psychical experiences into their lives just as the rest of us accept our dreams as something which is a natural part, though imperfectly understood, of our inner life."

In 1962 Professor W. H. C. Tenhaeff, of the Parapsychological Institute of the State University of Utrecht, published a paper, "On the Personality Structure of Paragnosts," in which he announced the results of a psychodiagnostic investigation of forty mediums (called para-gnosts in Holland). In this he reports on testing with the following:

1) Rorschach Test
2) Thematic Apperception Test (Murray)
3) Color-Pyramid Test according to Pfister-Heiss
4) Szondi Test
5) Luscher Color-Selection Test

Professor Tenhaeff stated that the first characteristic revealed by his tests was the paragnosts' great "sensibility" for everything coming from the outside world. The word "sensibility" gives an excellent clue to understanding the makeup of a medium. The term "sensitive" is used interchangeably with the term "medium" because it is descriptive of a medium's most widely known attribute. One may wonder if persons who are especially receptive or reactive to external stimuli—or sensitive—are more likely to become mediums naturally or if the converse is true, as those who have sat for development know—that the progress of mediumship means an opening of the centers of awareness so that one becomes more sensitive to his environment.

It is fairly well accepted by researchers that primitives have more ESP than most civilized men. (Tenhaeff and Sigmund Freud and J. B. Rhine all have commented about the atavistic nature of psi). There is scientific evidence for it among the Australian aborigines, the most primitive of peoples, who live in Stone Age conditions. Centuries of struggle for existence have sharpened not only their physical faculties but their psychic powers which, according to Albert Abarbanel in "Are Aborigines Psychic?" "startle those who have given them controlled ESP tests." He also points out that the various methods of clairvoyance and divination of the Kaffir of South Africa has been investigated and confirmed by numerous author-

39

ities. One might additionally mention reports of the psychic evidence from numerous other primitive cultures, including the Maori of New Zealand and the shamans of the Mixtecan Indians, who become clairvoyant after chewing sacred mushrooms.

Perhaps it is both the primeval and the childish characteristics of mediums which account for the great personal charm many of them exhibit. The very childlike quality which makes them view the world magically also makes some of them radiate warmth and love of life. The hearty laughter of Lotte von Strahl of Los Angeles, the zest and enthusiasm of Charles Cassidy, the gentleness of Jackie Eastlund, the earthy humor of Sophie Busch of Miami would endear them to others even if they were not in the public eye.

The Polish medium Stefan Ossowiecki radiated cheerfulness and vitality, according to Andrzej Borzymowski in "Experiments with Ossowiecki." He possessed an inexhaustible supply of optimism and faith in people, and when he was carrying out an experiment of his psychic power, he became vigilant, alert, and intense. Yet he was often childishly lost in dealing with the details of everyday life.

Borzymowski wrote that once "Ossowiecki, who had been invited to lunch, absent-mindedly turned up at another home. He was cordially received, since he was generally well-liked, but his hosts were rather surprised by the unexpected visit. Before lunch was served, however, Ossowiecki realized his mistake, apologized with some embarrassment, made for the right address, and finally sat down with his friends at the right table. But the party was not undisturbed for long; soon the telephone rang. It appeared that Ossowiecki had invited guests to his own house for lunch that very day!"

On the opposite side of the coin, Dr. Tenhaeff's tests show that mediums have a desire for sensation, yet also feelings of fear and impotence. The fear is understandable when one realizes that, in keeping his centers of awareness open perhaps too much of the time, the medium may receive many impressions of a negative sort from which others are protected by their insensitivity. Ouvani, the trance control of Mrs. Garrett, once said, "Even when the instrument [Mrs. Garrett] is sleeping or walking or dreaming, do not forget that this polished bowl is very vulnerable." Mrs. Garrett had much illness during her life and numerous operations. It is noted that many other psychics seem to have more illnesses than normal.

Mediums make their living by an unconscious process which cannot invariably be relied on or always called into play on demand. Their reputations may depend on this elusive power of their subconscious minds. When a medium goes into trance, he does not know whether or not he will give information or produce phenomena that will satisfy his sitters. If he does, he and the sitters are happy; if he does not, there may be unpleasantness or he may be made to feel that he is taking money under false pretenses. Pollack said that Gerard Croiset's self-confidence was increasing because his paranormal capacities did not seem to ebb and flow like many more unstable mediums, and so he could depend on himself when he needed to.

It is known that some psychics' power may simply desert them for a period of time—days or even years. Then they either lose the reputations they have built up or, in some cases, resort to fraud to make their livelihoods. The ideal medium is one who does not have to take any money for his psychic efforts and thus does not feel compelled to produce on demand. Unfortunately, there are so far no funds provided to support mediums so that they won't have to perform under anything but the best conditions. It is little wonder that a feeling of fear may thus surround them.

41

Besides this, there are said to be actual physical dangers in the profession of trance mediumship. One who goes into deep trance may become deathly cold during the entrancement and appear as if dead. Recovery may be either slow or quick, returning time varying sometimes between fifteen minutes and several hours. Mediums who are not entranced often feel considerable pain or discomfort as they are impressed with the symptoms which caused the death of the entity they are attempting to describe.

Jacqueline Eastlund said of a girl who once came to her for a reading, "I told her her father was there. Then I suddenly felt as if I were choking. I began to cry and relayed the message that her father was saying, 'I'm sorry.' The sitter then told me that her father had hanged himself."

If entranced by a "malevolent entity," the medium may suffer bodily harm by getting into a fight or by undergoing the tortures of the entity's death.

Those who have carefully observed séances over a period of years insist that if someone unexpectedly comes too close to one who is in trance or if a light is flashed suddenly, the sensitive may be physically harmed or even killed. There have been several such instances of deaths during séances. Friends say it is a result of sudden light or noise causing shock. Skeptics have suggested that it was from heart attacks owing to being discovered in fraud. Some scientists who have studied psychics for a period of years have been inclined to go along with the point of view of the actual danger involved. Dr. W. J. Crawford, who investigated the Goligher phenomena in Ireland, wrote that the "power" he observed to be present at telekinetic séances was so great that, had it been misapplied, it could have destroyed everybody in the room in a second's time. Later we will discuss a medium's sudden loss of her abilities because of being in trance during the Long Beach earthquake.

42

Tenhaeff found in a few of his paragnosts the "scientifically unjustified tendency" to consider their gift an evolutionary phenomenon. He preferred to think of it as predominantly of an atavistic nature, which must therefore be regarded as a phenomenon of regression. This tendency, he says, to look upon their aptitude as a sign of evolutionary progress is linked with an inclination to regard paragnostic powers as "powers of a divinatory nature." From this follows the fact that some of his testees had a tendency to venerate themselves. Some felt they received their call from a higher power. He said, "In some of the testees examined by me in the course of many years I found a tendency to feel like a 'Magus' (and, as such, a 'Superman')."

As a discussion of this, it is interesting to contemplate an in-depth analysis of the psyche of Eileen J. Garrett, which actually seems to have produced magi of considerable interest. It was undertaken by Dr. Ira Progoff and the results published in his book *The Image of an Oracle*. He had been asked by Mrs. Garrett, for her own peace of mind and her desire for inward integrity, to search for an answer to a problem which had bothered her for years.

Mrs. Garrett's question was essentially this: Over a period of more than thirty years, she'd had a variety of experiences in trance during which numerous voices had spoken through her. These voices purported to belong to individuals or spirit entities and spoke with a knowledge and independent awareness over which Mrs. Garrett herself had no control. They seemed to have access to information with which Mrs. Garrett was not familiar, and they had clairvoyant perceptions which she did not have without their presence.

Said Progoff, "When we came to know one another, Mrs. Garrett explained to me that, as she had reflected upon the events and situations of her life, she had progressively realized that a great many people around the world were basing their beliefs about the nature of immortality and their personal expectations for life after death upon the descriptions of certain experiences that had happened to her. But so far as she herself was concerned, she could neither validate them nor disprove them. There was not much that she could know regarding the validity or the meaning of the voices that spoke through her, especially since she was neither conscious nor awake at the time. She was lost in hypnotic trance so that her conscious judgment was not accessible. She had no way of verifying personally the reality of the voices that spoke through her; nor did she feel that she was capable of interpreting or even guessing what their presence and their message might signify. Nonetheless she felt a definite responsibility to the people who had expressed so great a faith in the phenomena of her personality that they based their beliefs about their personal future existence upon the testimony of her experiences. . . . Mrs. Garrett came to the conclusion then that it was her personal responsibility to discover what the true meaning of her voices was so that people would not be drawn into false beliefs through misunderstanding her personal phenomena."

Her question to Progoff then was clear and direct: Could he, on the basis of his studies in the field of depth psychology, tell her what was the nature and meaning of the voices that spoke through her? Were they in truth discarnate entities in which spiritualists were entitled to believe? Or did they have some other significance?

The doctor knew that Mrs. Garrett was a woman with a strong dramatic flair, but he felt in her a definite sincerity, a genuine concern. And there seemed to be a strong personal need in the question she was posing to him.

Dr. Progoff then used the new procedures of holistic depth psychology to draw forth from the recesses of the personality of Eileen Garrett and from the personalities of the predominate voices who spoke through her some clues as to the nature and meaning of the phenomena of mediumship as exemplified in her experience.

Two figures had dominated Eileen Garrett's trance sessions over a period of many years. These were Ouvani, who described himself as a young Arab soldier of the thirteenth century who had died in battle; and Abdul Latif, who claimed to have been a Persian physician of the seventeenth century. There were also the various alleged spirit relatives and friends of her sitters, who had communicated material of an evidential nature through her over the years. And then there were the others, the ones Abdul Latif and Ouvani turned to for guidance and information—Tahoteh, whom Ouvani referred to as "the keeper of the word" and "the giver of the key of knowledge," and Ramah, "one who cares very much," who is the "great master of Abdul Latif."

The process Progoff used was to ask Mrs. Garrett to enter into the trance state in her accustomed manner, and then he would speak with whichever figures appeared and whichever ones wished to appear. Above all, he would treat the figures as persons, whether or not he really understood them to be spiritual entities. He would seek, in his conversations with them, to reach into their personalities, to draw forth their desires, and to discuss with them their goals and possibilities of their existence, just as he would in depth psychological work with any individual who came to talk to him.

Using this technique with Ouvani first, the doctor learned that Ouvani was appointed the "doorkeeper" by those who, Ouvani said, "for want of a better word you will call the masters of her evolution or her destiny." The psychologist concluded that Ouvani was the guardian of the doorway to the psyche of Eileen Garrett, a personification of the self-regulative capacity of the psyche.

Abdul Latif said about himself: "I am not an entity. There are entities however ... that the instrument sees.

45

Just as I have now said to you, 'It is not possible to believe that we come in from the womb of a mother and go out here by this door, and that is all.' "

Eventually the time came when Dr. Progoff was allowed to talk with the god figures of Tahoteh and Ramah and to attempt to learn who they actually might be. Tahoteh told him: "I am the image of her unconscious."

Progoff wrote: "It is clear at this early point that the figure of Tahoteh wishes to present himself as a god. We should realize, however, that this is in no sense comparable to the Western understanding of what God is. Tahoteh does not present himself as an omnipotent being, but rather as a principle of life, and as one principle among many. He is thus a member of a pantheon of gods as would be the case in Greece or in India. The sense that we get from this discourse is that the figure of Tahoteh is presenting himself as a personification of a basic principle of life, and thus as a godlike figure but not as an ultimate God."

The fourth entity, with whom Dr. Progoff spent a considerable amount of time, was spoken of as Ra, or Ramah, or Rahm. This personality said of itself, "That is Rahm. That is the personification of the creativity of life that has broken man away, that has made him seek, breathe, demand, desire, and finally, having desired, found ways and means to make signs and sounds that finally have come together to make the poetry of understanding possible for his problems."

Apparently, with Ramah, Progoff felt he had reached the God principle which is within us all. The entity stated in relation to this that other men who spent much time seeking one little answer suddenly found illumination and said, "Let us deify it, because we cannot tell men that this is a principle contained within themselves. We must make them seek for it."

Progoff concluded that he was speaking to the principle

46

of life energy in the cosmos embodied as a personality in the symbolic form of Ramah. He, himself, underwent a powerful experience of unity with an abiding principle of life presenting itself as a person, a principle of transpersonal strength and significance. And, indeed, Ramah spoke in powerful and enlightening ways that would hardly seem possible to have come from the mind of Mrs. Garrett herself. The doctor realized that he was having a meaningful and fulfilling dialogue with a symbolic dramatization of an eternal principle, the God figure himself. He wondered, "Or was it the oracle of the God who brought it about? Was it that the oracle, out of her tremendous need to fulfill the seed-image of her oracleship, had set up a situation in which the God and I would say 'I am you' to each other?"

He concluded: "If we would say that all the events we have been discussing here took place in the psyche of Eileen Garrett, that would be true, and it would also not be true at all. The psyche of Mrs. Garrett supplies the context, the 'place,' within which all the psychic phenomena, all the voices, words, and concepts appear. But the psyche of Eileen Garrett is also a vehicle of something much larger than the individual whose name it bears."

It becomes obvious that mediums in general have an inkling of all this greatness which is within them or for which they are channels. They are amazed and impressed when they are told the magnificent words which sometimes flow through them when they are in a trance or semitrance state—words which they are sure they personally do not have in their vocabularies, ideas and concepts far beyond their known capabilities. It is also highly significant that their sitters fawn over them and their congregations revere them and treat them as either the earthly embodiment or the mouthpiece of great leaders and teachers, masters and gods. When this is contrasted with the scorn with which the subject of mediumship is dismissed by the larger portion of the public and with the clinical scrutiny mediums receive from the majority of scientists who pay them any attention at all, it is little wonder that for the preservation of their egos they flee to the Superman posture.

6: PROS AND CONS

THOSE whose ESP powers are developed enough to be called psychics, sensitives or mediums have learned to expand their awareness to the point where they achieve information from what purport to be external forces. In most cases we will find that these apparently external forces, when we do begin to reach them and have communication by or from them, will claim to be the spirits of the dead.

This should not frighten us. There is no reason why the idea of the survival of the human soul should startle anyone . . . except that thoughts about death are anathema to our culture. Dr. Thelma Moss of U.C.L.A. said in an interview in *Psychic* (August, 1970) that people often come to her because of their fears.

"The only psychic experiences they have are related to deaths—and they want to be spared that knowledge. Unfortunately, we don't know of any way to control this faculty. We can't turn it on at will—nor can we turn it off," she said.

Since this situation does occur, why should we not attempt to understand it and use it to best advantage? Immortality was a common belief of all mankind throughout history until the past two centuries, when it has been relegated to fable and folklore—temporarily—while the world is going through its materialistic phase. Even men in the earliest civilizations knew they would survive death. Why

49

else did the Egyptians and others bury artifacts with the dead? So that they could use their cup and their comb and their weapon in their future existence. Spirit communication through mediums, ghosts, apparitions, voices from the dead, and many other manifestations have occurred since the dawn of man's existence.

Isolation from the rest of the world makes no difference. Even the newly discovered primitives, the lost Stone Age tribe who calls itself the Tasaday, discovered in 1971 in the remote mountain forests of the Philippine island of Mindanao, 650 miles south of Manila, know about life after death. *Time* magazine (October 18, 1971) says that several families "cooperate in food-foraging, making decisions together and depending for advice on the most experienced among them.

"That advice, the Tasaday believe, is based on knowledge that is transmitted by their ancestors. In their dreams, the tribesmen may see the *sugoy,* their deceased 'soul relatives,' who live in fine dwellings among the treetops, as well as *Salungal,* 'the owner of the mountains,' who tells them where to search for palm pith and game animals."

Anthropologists are wont to maintain that dreams can entirely account for the feeling of certainty about survival, because when a man dreams of someone who has died, he believes he has actually been with that person. Since however every man, no matter how unlettered he is, dreams from his earliest childhood and soon comes to realize that his dreams seldom represent reality, this is not really a very good explanation.

Primitives have learned the truth about life after death because they have had the good sense to elevate their psychics to the highest positions in their societies as shamans, witch doctors, or chiefs. When modern civilization becomes cognizant of the value of communication, we, too,

50

will give our mediums more responsibilities. We will train them arduously and then put them in positions of respect.

Most mediums feel that Spiritualism provides a favorable climate for a better understanding of their own talents and contributes in considerable measure to a more intelligent awareness of the phenomena they experience. Let Douglas Johnson be the spokesman for all such as these.

Johnson says that he knows his information comes to him from the spirit world because he can *see* the spirits. He believes he is somewhat critical in his evaluations, having read a good deal of psychical and parapsychological literature. "I am aware of the possibility of hallucinations, and I know that the mind can play tricks," he said. "But when you, personally, can see the spirits of deceased persons and have seen them from your early childhood, and they bring you information you couldn't normally know, you tend to believe in their existence." Johnson does not go into trance, he has no "guides" or "controls," who are believed to protect mediums from "intruding spirits"; but in other respects his experiences conform to those of most other professional mediums.

"As a child I used to pray that I would find the truth," he told me. "There is an answer to everything. It is up to us to find it. We can't close our minds just because the idea of Spiritualism does not appeal to us."

Johnson is sure that his information comes from a higher intelligence and not telepathically from the minds of his sitters. He points to the fact that many of his predictions come true as evidence of supernormal powers beyond anything his sitters could already know.

"Where does my original knowledge come from," he asks, "if not from the spirit world?"

Johanna Ruhnau of Santa Barbara, California, who came to the United States from Heidelberg, Germany, before World War I, gives readings which seem to be a combination of clairvoyance and astrology. Not as articulate as Johnson, she had difficulty expressing what she meant about the source of her powers.

"How do your psychic impressions reach you?" I asked her.

"I don't know. I always had them. I get into a vibration. I see visions. You just come into the current of a vibration—a beam of light."

"Where does that beam of light come from?"

"From around and about me and from the center of the All-Knowing that some people call God."

"You don't think, then, that your information comes from the spirit world?"

"Everything is from the spirit world. There is no other way about it. Everything has vibrations and a sensitive picks up those vibrations. Some people are more sensitive than others."

Jacqueline Eastlund expressed her conviction this way: "Whatever I have has been given to me by God, from the Holy Spirit." Having been reared a devout Roman Catholic, Jackie has always felt close to God. From the time she was three years old, she accompanied her mother to Mass every morning, and from the start of her psychic happenings she thought of them as God-given. Because of her natural reticence and shyness, as well as her Catholic upbringing, Jackie for years fought going into mediumship professionally until, she says, "I was actually suffering from not being able to get it out of my system." Finally she gave up and began to give readings without pay in the evenings while she worked during the day. Becoming so physically exhausted by this that she lost a good deal of weight, she finally capitulated and started making her living as a psychic.

It is interesting to question mediums about the conditions of their lives before and after they began to allow their mediumistic talents to play a significant role. It is commonly understood among those here interviewed that

52

nothing ever went satisfactorily for them until they finally "dedicated their powers and services to the good of mankind," as they believe. The life of Edgar Cayce, the famous Virginia Beach seer, illustrates this. Illness of self and family, business reversals, even to the extent that his photography studio burned down, dogged his footsteps constantly until he finally gave up and worked professionally at his natural calling of seership. From then on everything fell into place, and he was "taken care of" financially and in all other ways. Mediums who are spiritualistically inclined point to this sort of thing as evidence that good spirits will protect you if you will put yourself at their disposal and attempt to use your life to bear witness for them.

Jackie Eastlund is sure that she has help from another plane. She says, "Several entities of high spiritual nature, both while they were on earth and now, are with me to help in my work. I know also that I receive messages from the Holy Spirit." As to how she acquires the material which she gives to her sitters, she says, "I try to get identification which confirms who the spirit entity is. I receive it in various ways. I feel his presence, I see him clearly in my mind and can give a description of him. Although I don't see him externally, as I see you, I am completely aware of him and know he is smiling or frowning and can hear what he is saying. I experience the feelings that he is trying to impress on me."

Some mediums may acknowledge a belief in the existence of evidence for a life after death, and even of spirit communication, yet do not claim that their own talents lie in that direction. JoAnne Chase of New York City calls herself a sensitive and believes that her power comes directly from God; she gets her psychic inspiration completely through God, with no help from spirits.

"God is within my makeup," she says. "How he comes

53

to me I do not know; he just comes. From my spiritual being."

JoAnne Chase gave readings for the patrons of New York's Little Club for nine years, but after 1955 she began to work privately. She told me, "I was born with psychic talent." But she added that everyone else is, too. Her success, she says in her book *You Can Change Your Life Through Psychic Power,* is a matter of practice and experience and a sympathetic early environment. She declares that psi is definitely *not* supernatural, or ghostly, or mysterious, or even unusual, "as you'll see when you try using it."

Tenhaeff, in his discussion, is pleased that he has found some paragnosts who follow the scientific line. "As against the so-called 'revelation Spiritualists' there are those who adhere to a more scientifically defensible view of life. . . . I should here, however, emphatically point out that there are also a few among our Spiritualistically oriented testees who did their very best to repress any inclination to find a Spiritualist explanation for their phenomena."

Jimmie Gordon, a medium of La Jolla, California, declares emphatically, "I am not a Spiritualist." Gordon even warns people away from development classes and urges them not to attempt to try to learn for themselves how to communicate.

Ronald Edwin, who bills himself as Mr. ESP, is absolutely determined that no spirit shall get the credit for what he believes he accomplishes entirely by himself. At one time Edwin practiced mediumship in England with all the phenomena that trickery could produce. After several arrests he claimed to have seen the error of his ways and reformed. He wrote a book, *Clock Without Hands,* telling of his fraudulent practices, and thus cleansed his conscience.

Ronald Edwin now performs only as an exponent of extrasensory perception, and he does seem to evidence it to some degree. He told this writer about ten years ago that she would be getting married in less than a year to a soft-spoken Virginian with graying temples. But no such interesting Southern gentleman ever appeared. However at the same time he also told me I had a cousin Alice. I at first denied this until recalling that a first cousin of my mother's had married an Alice. They resided in a small West Virginia town a long way from New York, where I was living at the time of my interview with Edwin. He added that Alice had had a daughter, Blanche, who had recently died. And this also was true. He then said that Alice needed a hysterectomy. When I checked this a few days later, I learned that Alice had within the previous month undergone such an operation. It is just such inexplicable hits as this that keep researchers forever intrigued by mediums, psychics, or whatever they want to call themselves.

Edwin maintains that the paranormal knowledge he manifests comes from within himself, and himself alone. He even believes, from his past experience, that all those who claim to have the help of spirits in their manifestations are frauds.

"My powers are all mine," he insists, "coming from within my own physical body and mind. Nobody outside of me has anything to do with it."

Tenhaeff noted a different point of view. He says: "I am quite aware that the tendency which I observed in a few of our Spiritualistically oriented testees, to avoid the corresponding explanation of their phenomena—without, for that matter, denying their faith in Spiritualism—is linked, at any rate in a number of them, with a certain abundance of inner contradictions, which is peculiar to many testees. This form of split personality may be observed in several psychoscopists, when we have an opportunity to watch their behavior in different milieus, and notice how perfectly well they often manage to adapt themselves to the atmosphere that prevails there. Thus, in the case of . . . Mrs. Platt-Mahlstedt, I observed more than once that, in Spiritualist circles, she would be tempted by her desire to please to pretend that she attributed some of her phenomena to the influence of spirits; in contrast to her behavior in scientifically oriented milieus, where she readily seemed inclined to seek a predominant connection between her accomplishments and certain unconscious and involuntary influences emanating from the experimenters."

Mrs. Platt-Mahlstedt now lives in Los Angeles and is known as Lotte von Strahl, having married Baron Otto von Strahl in 1933 and since been widowed. I had independently noted the tendency mentioned above before ever reading Dr. Tenhaeff's statement about this psychic. She at first declared herself to me to be a sensitive and not a medium. When questioned about this, she was quite emphatic, and the distinction she was making seemed to be based on the fact that mediums dealt with spirits and she was "above" such superstitions. However, when I made it clear to her that she could admit to me communication with spirits without being considered either naïve or unsophisticated, she then confessed that she did believe she received spirit help.

"I am actually a medium," she said, "but I won't call myself that in the Los Angeles area because of the poor quality and character of other local mediums. That word has a bad name around here. I don't wish to be associated in anybody's mind with mediums here."

Sophia Williams, the late medium who was written about extensively by American author Hamlin Garland, said that she tuned in on "the overmind or stream of intelligence." She rather summed things up for us in her little book, *You Are Psychic*: "My own experience leads me to believe that there are two ways of 'receiving.' One seems to come by way of intermediaries or disembodied personalities. When I receive information through such sources I am able to name the personalities, describe them and give other positive proof and identification. The second method of contact is a direct one. In employing it I tune directly in on the overmind or stream of intelligence. This contact is far more difficult to make than one made through intermediaries. Sometimes I tune directly into the stream of intelligence with no difficulty. There are other times when I am unable to do so. I am still exerting every effort to overcome my inability to make such contacts at will, and am carefully studying how to do so."

This illustrates another point that might be well to comment on: We so frequently tend to expect that there has to be *one* explanation for extrasensory situations, *one* answer to the problem of communication. Yet perhaps we will discover that in many instances several different laws are in operation. Nothing in life is simple. There is never any one explanation for anything. Why should there be for ESP?

7: WHO SHOULD DEVELOP?

SHOULD everyone attempt to expand his awareness in an effort to become psychically developed? Definitely not. Under many conditions it would be playing with dynamite. The would-be adventurer into spirit realms should fit himself for it spiritually and mentally, just as if he were attempting to qualify for some specialized physical work. He must safeguard himself in his daily life by keeping sane and cheerful in every sense of the word and thinking positively all the time. If he isn't prepared to make the effort to do this, he should stay away from anything psychic.

Arthur Ford in *Unknown but Known* says, "People who want to develop their latent psychic abilities generally fall into one of three classes. In the first class I would include all those who seek a closer relationship with the Ultimate Power from whom all things emanate. The second category of potential psychic devotees is made up of those who have no spiritual aspirations, but who are curious in a casual or even scientific way about their abilities in this fascinating field. These people are herewith warned that, unless they remain open-minded about the possibility of being led into deeper waters and are receptive to such leading, their experience will almost certainly turn out to be a blind alley.

"The third category consists of people who covet psychic potency out of a lust for personal power, prestige, profit or sensual gratification. To these last my advice is unequivocal: either develop higher motivation or drop the whole business at once. The consequence of deliberate misuse of these abilities can be disastrous."

Ford and I agree that an objective scientific evaluation of all supernormal phenomena is the best. Those who go at everything without any critical appraisal will be handicapped in their ultimate achievements. Usually they find only one or two ideas that suit them philosophically and stay with them, so their development is stunted; and their naïveté is usually appalling.

Yet we find that psychical development is unrewarding to the person who goes into it *only* with scientific detachment in an effort to be totally objective at all times, for he is likely to make participation no more than an intellectual game. His approach must be seasoned with a willingness to accept enlightening spiritual adventures as they come, for that is the only way he will be successful. When sitting with development groups, I have learned that it is never wise to put them under such rigid scientific control that spiritual elements cannot enter. If a meeting is not begun with prayers, for instance, it is not as likely to be successful. It doesn't matter to what specific God or what interpretation of God one appeals. In the mere fact of appealing, a certain openness to receptivity is achieved by the group that cannot be acquired otherwise.

Those of us who have sat for development for many years know that there is nothing more disconcerting than to have an individual in the class who has no belief of any kind in anything outside man and is determined to maintain his "intellectual standards." I was an agnostic when I began my psychical research, and I must admit that I added nothing whatever to the groups I attended until my thinking changed. One can be an opinionated atheist and nonetheless be so receptive to new ideas that he doesn't disturb the group. Others may express their personal convictions so belligerently that they influence the rest in a negative way.

There was a young man who eagerly attended a development circle I held regularly in Miami. He considered himself scientifically interested in ESP, yet he had no belief in any spiritual approach to the subject. He particularly could not abide the saying of the Lord's Prayer. It, he said, made his "stomach squirm." He would always walk outside the room while the members of the class recited the prayer, but his influence was felt just as chillingly as if he had been right there mentally agonizing over every phrase of it. Needless to say, he didn't last long with us.

Another whom it is difficult to have in a development class is the one so self-satisfied with his present stage of development that he can learn nothing new. No one can tell him anything because he already knows it all, and he's likely to state that "when you are ready," you'll see things his way. He might have had a few personal psychic experiences, or he might have read a few books and latched onto certain philosophical concepts. These have elevated him so high in his own estimation that he has become an authority. Unfortunately, this type of person loves to come to newly organized development groups, to give them the benefit of his presence and his great experience. He will superciliously observe what is going on, but he actually contributes nothing but discomfort to his classmates.

Today when many young people are on drugs, it is likely that some habitual trippers will attend development groups. Unfortunately, their influence is very bad. Although telepathy and clairvoyance are frequently experienced by drug takers, seldom does anything of an enlightening nature occur to them. They may soar into highly mystical realms on occasion, it is true; but nothing of evidential value is ever produced, and if they should become mediumistic, they will undoubtedly attract only the lowest element of spiritual helpers into their presence. This is definitely to be guarded against.

In *Your Mysterious Powers of ESP* Harold Sherman discussed this problem: "Men and women tend to follow the path of least resistance. Instead of making a sustained conscious effort for self-development to activate the higher powers of the mind, they are seeking mind expansion and greater sensual pleasures by the shortcut methods of hypnotic, electrical and chemical devices." There are many detours, pitfalls, and hazards this way, as all of us who have worked long at it have come to realize.

Sherman continued, "It is often mentally and emotionally unstable people who venture into these areas, because they have had fragmentary experiences with hallucinations, fantasies, distorted visions, and dreams that have aroused curiosity and caused them to believe that if these illusory sensations could be explored, perhaps more could be learned about the mystery of life, including the mystery of their own selves. Young people, new to the field of sensation, willing to try anything once—and more often than that if they discover that there are thrills and kicks in it—are more prone to these mental and emotional adventures that give promise of greater sexual at-one-ness as well as spiritual illumination.

"Unhappily, what has resulted thus far has been, in the main, more confusion, bewilderment, demoralization, frustration, fears, insecurity, and despair of finding the ultimate reality or any dependable reality at all.

"There are, of course, the staunch supporters of the intelligent use of drugs under proper guidance as a means of releasing one's hidden potentials and liberating the 'sleeping genius' within. Opposed are those who just as strongly declare that these methods for expanding one's consciousness and inducing greater creativity are extremely dangerous and self-defeating."

Canon William V. Rauscher, pastor of Christ Episcopal

61

Church, Woodbury, New Jersey, and one of the pillars of Spiritual Frontiers Fellowship, has written in a paper titled "The Mystical and the Psychical": "We can be psychic but not necessarily spiritual. Many wish to be psychic but do not wish to be concerned with the ethics and spiritual disciplines which ought to accompany it. When someone wishes to be psychic, we ask, 'Why do you wish this? What are your motives? What is your aim?'"

Unless your aim is definite self-improvement, don't bother to read the rest of this book. This is not a text which will give hocus-pocus tricks to make you psychic. I have been asked by a publisher to write "how-to" books with such chapters as: "How to Get Rich with ESP," "How to Acquire a Lover with ESP," "How to Keep Healthy with ESP." I have refused. In the first place, it isn't all that easy. In the second place, no one who would read such a book would be willing to undergo the self-discipline necessary to achieve genuine psychic abilities. It is to those who *will* that this book is addressed.

8: GOD AND PRAYER

BEFORE we start our ESP development, we really should discuss prayer. But then the question is immediately raised: To whom does one pray? God, you say, but to what concept of God? Each person undoubtedly has his own, and yet there are certain overall characteristics of Godness that we must understand in order to pray successfully.

Few of us believe today in an avengeful, anthropomorphic God sitting on a throne behind the pearly gates passing out justice and injustice, evaluating lives as good or bad, or in any other way using personal emotionalism on mankind. God, instead, is now more often thought of among Christians as a loving Father or else as the Christ. To others He is known as the Prime Mover, the Cosmic Mind, the Atman—the Godhead within man. Paramahansa Yogananda, the Hindu yogi master who became well known to us in the West because he lived here thirty years, preferred to give God the name Bliss because, he said in *Science of Religion*, an analysis of the motives and ends of men's actions in the world shows that the ultimate end, which all other ends merely subserve, "is the avoidance of pain and want, and the attainment of permanent Bliss. And so "it is in Him as Bliss that our spiritual hopes and aspirations find fulfillment—our devotion and love find an object."

I like that. I also like the definitions of God that I have

received over the years by automatic writing: He is the State of Highest Awareness, Power Most Superlative, Illimitable Love, Infinite Consciousness. The entity called James, who purports to correspond with me, uses as the terms for God: Ultimate Perfection, Divine Consciousness, Supreme Intelligence. He says God is the sum total of everything in the universe, from which all life begins, in which all life exists, and to which all life returns. James describes what might be called a great mosaic in the universal plan into which each perfected individual consciousness of every human being born on this earth or any other inhabited planet must eventually fit in order to complete the pattern and to find his particular area of eternal usefulness . . . and, yes, Bliss.

Since the consciousness of each man came originally from the Divine, there should never be a feeling of separation between us and God. Because, however, each consciousness is associated while on earth with an individual physical body in which it lives in order to function in the material world, we come to have a feeling of apartness from other men and from God. Yet ". . . the proof of the existence of God lies in ourselves," Yogananda says.

"Our ordinary conception of God is that He is Superhuman, Infinite, Omnipresent, Omniscient and the like. Some call God Personal, some see Him as Impersonal. The point emphasized . . . is that whatever conception we have of God, if it does not influence our daily conduct, if everyday life does not find an inspiration from it, and if it is not found universally necessary, then that conception is useless.

"If God is not conceived in such a way that we cannot do without Him in the satisfaction of a want, in our dealings with people, in earning money, in reading a book, in passing an examination, in the doing of the most trifling or the highest duties, then it is plain that we have not felt any connection between God and life."

While agreeing that we must know God in all things, great and small, I feel I must add some superlatives to Yogananda's list: in looking at a flaming sunset or a magnificent scenic view or a newborn baby, or listening to great music. It is times like these when I feel the strongest need to thank God and share His wonders with Him.

Really to pray and meditate properly, we must begin to be aware that we are one with the Divine. We then also become conscious of our unity with all other men. We could reach this state earlier and maintain it more successfully if children were reared with this knowledge so firmly in their minds that they hardly question it. Then it would be almost natural for them to have a feeling of love for everyone.

Men differ, and some are not very lovable. It helps when you realize that one day, by his own conscious efforts to improve himself in the afterlife, your present enemy will become the personification of perfection; you can achieve a kindly feeling toward his potentialities even if you cannot presently see anything attractive in him. You may then feel sorry for him because he does not realize the great future ahead of him and is wasting his time on earth being unpleasant . . . and miserable. By the time you have rationalized your compassion for him you are not really too far from a spiritual kind of love for your antagonist. It takes effort, but somehow, when you persevere, you are usually able to work it out.

It is unfortunate that man's unconscious yearnings to return to his origins and to be aware of his unity with God and man have recently been so ignored philosophically. It has put us all in a position of having to deny our instinctive drives. Even when Carl Jung found himself able to admit that some religious instincts are an innate characteristic of man, others argue just as vehemently that a human being is nothing but a machine. At the present time some of the profoundest-sounding arguments are coming from our most honored religious thinkers and teachers as they attempt to debunk all the psychical experiences recorded in the Bible. Demythologizers dominate much current thinking, and the "Is God dead?" question has actually been taken seriously. In an effort to prove whether or not Christ's Resurrection is a fact worthy of acceptance, these sophisticated seekers-after-truth would not dream of looking at anything so lowly (to them) as the beliefs of the Spiritualists or the evidence of psychical research. And so the controversy goes on at what purports to be an academic level. Can theirs truly be an intellectual approach when material tending to prove the argument, such as certain spirit communications, is completely overlooked because of disbelief in its true source?

Is the Biblical God dead? Hardly, but He has taken on new dimensions. No longer the patriarch with a long white beard who reacts to man's misbehavior with hellfire and eternal damnation, the Jehovah of the Israelites must now be recognized for what He was—a reflection of the insecurities of the ancients. Biblical prophets and Jesus Himself attempted to depict for man his true and magnificent destiny, but our limited concepts have always kept us from adequately accepting it. Now, with union with Ultimate Perfection as our personal goal, we will no longer be able to limit God to the bounds of our own comprehension. To try to expel Him altogether, however, is only to follow the old atheistic pattern, which leads to emotional bankruptcy.

Are the Biblical tales of miracles merely legend? No, indeed. Many similar phenomena have been produced by great physical mediums. By attempting to explain them all as misapprehension or fraud or to ignore them, along with spiritual healing and the evidence for precognition and other forms of extrasensory perception, as well as the unusual activities of the saints, modern man has endeavored

66

to eliminate entirely all phenomenal wonders from his life. In so doing he has also raised the suicide rate and the instances of insanity to an all-time high in the history of the world. Trying to live without rational understanding of himself or anything else, and denying the evidence of history and of his own experience have made man so confused that he often cannot cope with his existence. When he accepts once again the testimony of his psychic experiences, admits the reality of spirit communication and survival, and adapts to it intelligently, he will become better adjusted to every phase of life.

When man learns to know himself as a true son of God, with the importance he actually has as an integral aspect of Divine Consciousness, he will have more respect for himself and his fellows. When he accepts the truth about survival, he will also understand the necessity to live wisely on earth. It is not just an hypothesized ideal for which he should strive but an actual physical reality, which should be such a part of his life that no other possibility exists for him but to think positively and constructively and to have compassion for all others. "Life on earth will alter abruptly for the better when this is understood," says James.

We are told by him and other communicants that we start learning these lessons on earth and continue them after death. Those individuals who have advanced by their own efforts to higher spheres of existence are so purified and beautiful of soul and glowing with happiness that there is a great shining light surrounding them. Although humans can seldom actually see them, psychics are sometimes aware of their presence because they see the light in which they appear. These souls are so perfected that they can be called angels. They return to earth constantly to assist men. No human life is ever left completely on its own. No individual comes into the world without an advanced spirit who is personally interested in his growth and de-

67

velopment. Everyone, then, has a guardian angel as well as spirit friends and relatives available to help him. When you pray, reaching out to the highest forces in a receptive effort to know your unity with them, an answer is always available. It may be a feeling of warmth and peace, an assurance that someone is with you and cognizant of your needs, an awareness of the presence of spirits whom you know and love, or the actual conscious feeling of the presence of God within you.

Actually, in this chapter I am leading up to this one thing: your efforts to achieve awareness of Ultimate Perfection within and all about you. True prayer and true meditation are this, above all. It doesn't matter if you address the Divine Presence as God, Father, Christ, the Blessed Mother, Supreme Consciousness, Ultimate Perfection, or in any other way which may appeal to you. You need not specifically address anyone or anything. All that is important is to reach out, open your consciousness to an inflow of the spirit of the universe, knowing that it is in you and you are in it. To attempt to communicate verbally with a prayer may make you more content, but it is not necessary. It is the reaching out, the expanding of your conscious awareness, the knowing, that counts.

As far as a specific answer if you have prayed about a specific need, that depends on your own belief and your receptivity. All the prayers in the world asking for help cannot bring it if you don't truly expect it. In fact, for most successful results, you must *know* it. What you truly know must come into being. Knowing is more than idealizing, more than wishful thinking, more than petitioning. True knowing is being in that creative mental condition where things move, molecules regroup, creation operates, and the thing is done.

Opening yourself to acceptance of the spirit of love and peace which constantly radiates throughout the universe will bring you happiness and serenity. When you pray,

68

then, your prayers are answered through God's love and with the goodness and love of angels and spirits at differing levels of advancement. Their thoughts in your behalf will give you the assistance you need. A concentration of powerful mental activity on the part of a group of advanced spirits can cause things to happen, just as your own achieving a state of complete knowing can accomplish it.

If you have prayed urgently for handy transportation, for instance, it is hardly possible for your spirit associates, because they work within natural laws, to materialize a new car on your doorstep. Yet you may find that a day or two after your prayer your eyes seem to be directed to an advertisement in a newspaper where you had not consciously intended to look, and if you go to see the automobile listed, you will probably find that it is just what you wanted at a price you can afford. Efforts from the spirit world are responsible for much that works out smoothly and successfully in your life—which you usually attribute to chance. If you are trying to develop your psychic powers and to live a positive and constructive life, you will find that your footsteps are constantly guided.

James says, "Believe me when I say that anything necessary for your well-being and your efforts in behalf of others can be accomplished by an individual who lives to love his fellow men, who keeps a positive outlook, who does not allow negative thoughts to dwell in his mind, who firmly knows he will have success, who protects himself constantly from dissident forces, and who maintains receptivity to thoughts and assistance from his spirit associates. It will seem to you uncanny how his life will change for the better. I am sure that some of you must know persons who have begun to use this approach, and you must have seen many curious and advantageous changes begin to take place in their lives. Much that is considered to be lucky breaks or happy coincidences may begin

69

to happen to one who opens himself to being receptive. If he needs something, it is frequently provided in the simplest possible manner, as illustrated in the case of the car. Be grateful for all the kindnesses you receive this way, and allow your life to be directed for the better wherever possible."

One who learned constantly to live with the knowledge of the God presence within him was Walter Russell, a great artist and sculptor who never asked God to give him the power to do anything, for he knew that he already had that power. What he asked for in his wordless, inspirational communion was to keep forever aware of that universal Omnipotence within him.

"Inspiration," he said, "comes only to those who seek it with humility toward their own achievements and reverence toward the achievements of God. With love of your work, love of life and reverence for the universal force which gives you unlimited power for the asking, you may sit on the top of the world if you desire to sit there."

When you are alone, in your room or out in the woods, said Russell, as quoted by Glenn Clark in *The Man Who Tapped the Secrets of the Universe,* "the universe talks to you in flashes of inspiration. You will find that you suddenly know things you never knew before."

Yet Russell doesn't mean just sitting silently in a prayerful attitude, as though separate and apart from God when you pray, but actually becoming one with Him, desiring with Him as co-Creator of all things, desiring without words, desiring dynamically with knowledge.

"Not with blind faith and belief," he said, "but with knowledge that fruition will ... surely follow that desire. . . ."

9: THE JOURNEY INWARD

IN many ways meditation is much like prayer—a tuning in to the God within and without. Yet after we learn the techniques, meditation is to be applied in a manner differing from prayer as we use it to sit properly for our development of ESP.

Harold Sherman gives us a generalized concept of how to go about meditating in "Pastoral Uses of ESP": "In meditation, as in the practice of ESP, you have to get the Self out of the way. If you wish to make attunement with the mind of God and develop a 'knowing awareness' of the God Presence within, you must learn how to relax your physical body, how to make your conscious mind passive, how to turn the attention of your conscious mind inward, and how to fix your attention upon what you visualize as the God Center of your being."

Making your conscious mind passive, or getting your sassy little ego out of the way, is the hardest part. At first everyone who attempts to meditate has a million thoughts running around in his mind. Eventually (hopefully) it is possible so to concentrate on the mental picture you are looking at that you can think of nothing else . . . and this removes your ever-active "I" from the picture. You don't go into trance, however. What you are aspiring for still involves your mental appreciation of your situation, an attempt to be in conscious attunement with cosmic forces, or an awareness of God Consciousness. This is definitely

71

not easy. It takes a lot of work. Yet many people find it so rewarding that they look forward to their daily meditation period more eagerly than to their dinner.

What surprises me is that so few are zealous to undertake this; so few seem to experience that "divine discontent" with their way of life or have a desire to change their character and personality if it takes work and self-discipline. Our mental habits are usually lazy and we find ourselves in intellectual ruts, but we seldom want to do anything about it.

Many people who diet constantly, stuff themselves with vitamins, jog religiously, or exercise before an open window every morning so that their physical condition will be excellent don't pay a moment's attention to their mental state. If their negative attitudes, their racial prejudices, their harsh judgments of others are brought to their attention, they say, "That's just the way I am. I know it's wrong, but there's nothing I can do about it."

Why should they hold this viewpoint? There *is* much that can be done about it. *One should be just as aware of his spiritual condition—his mental attitude about life—as he is aware of the need to care for his body.* The higher qualities of the mind and heart must receive some of his attention. Patanjali, the most quoted ancient yoga philosopher, who compiled the yoga sutras (or aphorisms) to restate yoga philosophy and practice for the men of his own period, affirmed at the outset that human unhappiness results from man's acceptance of a state of servitude to the low conditions of his own mind.

One way to improve such conditions is by meditation. It is important that this not be done for selfish or egotistical reasons, however. You don't meditate to make yourself feel big and important or to show how much you can surpass your fellow men. This is a purely subjective thing between you and the God presence within you, and its end results should be to make you a better person in all ways.

72

As Arthur Ford, the old master of techniques for psychical development, once warned us in a series of classes I attended, "Get yourself straightened out before you begin to experience phenomena, or there is danger. When you open up psychically, whatever you have within you will become worse or better."

Ford also said, "As practical people we must not be disappointed if the gates of heaven do not swing open at the first discordant blast of our new bugle. Many people quite unrealistically believe that meditation is going to result at once in marvelous paranormal or occult experiences. It may do exactly that, but also it may not. We must be prepared, as all the great ones have been, for the long haul."

At the opposite extreme, some believe that they must discipline their bodies until they are under complete and perfect control before meditation can be successful. We hear a great deal these days about transcendental meditation and other yoga techniques, and indeed the supreme forms that meditation can take are undoubtedly achieved by yogis. This is all likely to be far beyond our humble efforts. If you wish to spend a lot of time in the hope of eventually gaining the serenity, ability and strength of some of India's great sages, saints and heroes, meditation is one of the ways to do it. Few of us today have either the time or the inclination to make this our life's goal, however.

In a very brief and superficial review of yoga ideals, we must realize that it takes a fantastic amount of effort (possibly, they believe, through many lifetimes) to reach the high state of ultimate absorption of the soul into the Supreme Spirit. The eight limbs (or tools or aids) to achieving the realization of the Atman or the Godhead within man are: abstention, observance, posture, breath control, sense withdrawal, concentration, meditation, and contemplation. The last three involve the training and the use of

73

the mind. The state of samadhi (contemplation) arises only when the process of meditation on any subject reaches its end, having completely coordinated all the contents of the mind which have relation to that subject. An important part of meditation consists of the recital of mantras, words of power and influential chants, which must be repeated with concentration on their meaning. Om is the greatest of all mantras, for it is the word that expresses Him—the Atman or God.

Of mantras, Ernest Wood says in *Yoga*, "Certain statements beautifully and aptly expressed are regarded as very influential, and are repeated not only for the purpose of keeping a thought before the mind, but also with the idea that the words themselves, as sounds, produce effects in line or in tune with the thoughts which are being concentrated upon."

Unfortunately, because there is so much glamor attached to yoga today in the Western world, many attempt to use bits and pieces of the principles without being aware of what they are doing or why. I know home circles, and, for that matter, circles which have grown up around mediums, that try to apply a certain few yoga techniques spottily. In some groups many of us have sat self-consciously reciting Om . . . or Om Mani Padmi Hum . . . only because we were told to, and this completely defeats the purpose. If you are going in for yoga, do it right. Take a course in it.

If it is ESP development you want, yoga is not the place to search for it anyway. Patanjali didn't think too highly of it, even though he suggested that we try to develop some "extraordinary perceptions" for ourselves. In *How to Know God: The Yoga Aphorisms of Patanjali,* "We are told that if a man concentrates on the tip of his nose he will smell wonderful perfumes. If concentration is fixed on the tip of the tongue, a supernormal sense of taste will result; if on the palate, a supernormal sense of color;

74

if on the middle of the tongue, a supernormal sense of touch; if on the root of the tongue, a supernormal sense of hearing. Such powers are of no value in themselves, but they at least serve to prove what can be done with the mind, just as acrobatic tricks in a gymnasium prove how powerful and flexible a trained human body can become."

Wood says in *Yoga*: "In the very extensive and varied yoga literature of India, both classical and modern, there is frequent reference to psychic powers, but not usually—somewhat to the surprise of the Western enquirer—enthusiasm about them. They are regarded as coming by the way, and are not treated as something to be sought for or especially prized. Indeed, the highest authority of all. Patanjali, speaks of the arising of higher senses of hearing, touch, sight, taste, and smell but immediately adds: 'These powers of the spreading (or outgoing) mind are injurious to contemplation.' " No objection to them is indicated otherwise than as temptations to linger by the wayside with these new enjoyments.

After all, the dedicated yogi is aiming at the experience of inward illumination beyond all sensation. He is hoping not to be governed by any impulses from outside, however relatively superior they may be. He aims at the mountaintop, not to rest on any object along the way.

Perhaps unfortunately, perhaps not, we moderns do not have the leisure or even the will to engage in prolonged periods of meditation or to submit to the rigid yoga disciplines. For us it must suffice to use in the best way possible what time is available.

As far as the actual steps you should take when you meditate, Arthur Ford suggests these: "Each beginner should find a place where it is as quiet as it is possible to be in this noisy world. He should shut out as much light as possible and sit in the most restful position he can." If the yoga postures are comfortable for you and you have learned to use them, by all means do so. Get your body as relaxed as possible.

Many mediums insist that the feet should not be crossed while meditating. Ford said it didn't make any difference. But he was strict about the spine. You may sit upright or lie supine, but you must keep your spine perfectly straight, he says. This is best managed for many by simply lying flat on the floor, and that's all right with Arthur. You want to become unaware of your body, so get yourself in the best position to keep it from demanding your attention.

Until one joins a class and begins to sit for development, all experienced authorities agree that meditation begins by being alone and being quiet, really alone and really quiet . . . deep in the body, deep in the mind, a very deep, still "soul quiet."

Light, as well as sound, is distracting, so sit in the dark, a dim light, or close your eyes. If you must be in a lighted room, tie a handkerchief over your eyes.

After seeing that his environment and positions are satisfactory, the meditator must first do a series of deep-breathing exercises. These are very important, for learning to breathe properly is helpful to both physical and psychical well-being. Two deep-breathing exercises are recommended, both techniques learned from the yogis. In the first and simpler one, you close the right nostril by holding it shut with your right thumb, while inhaling quietly through the left nostril. Then place your little finger of the same hand over the left nostril and breathe out through the right. Breathe in through the right, put the thumb over the right nostril and breathe out through the left. Continue doing this several times at first, building up gradually until you are doing it ten times before each meditation period.

The second breathing technique is the one I prefer, although some like the other better. It should also be started gradually. One should breathe in long, slow breaths through the nose, expanding the stomach as you do so. Then pull in the stomach gradually as you exhale the air forcibly from your mouth. Pulling in the stomach as you exhale causes your muscles to tighten up and push, thus expelling all the air that had gone deep down into your lungs.

It is always good if you do what is called characterized breathing, meaning that when you breathe in you are consciously aware of absorbing the good qualities to enrich your bodily systems and replenish your reservoir of inner strength. Think as you breathe, "I am inhaling peace, love, perfection." "I am exhaling hurts, anger, unhappiness." Whatever particular areas of your character you feel need working on can be cited from time to time.

Max Freedom Long, who studied the magical secrets of the Hawaiian kahunas, or priests, had a great deal to say about proper breathing in *Growing into Light*. It all sounds highly sensible and practical.

"Research in physiology has disclosed the extent to which oxygen is necessary for the health of the cells," he says. "We know that oxygen burns the sugar in the blood and creates energy. Physical activity takes care of the deep breathing needed to acquire more oxygen than our regular quiet breathing gives us. The trouble is that in this modern age of the automobile we take too little exercise to cause us to breathe deeply."

Long learned from the kahunas that mana is the invisible force which can be directed to any part of the body, outward to other people, and upward as the supreme gift to the High Self. He says, "Those who know that they are accumulating an excess of mana when breathing deeply approach the exercise with interest and clear purpose. They know that the breath is the 'spirit of life.' Something far more vital than just energy for physical effort is being generated."

He recommends that we visualize the body filling with

vital force as the breath is slowly drawn in. "Then, as it is very slowly blown out under pressure through the pursed lips, visualize the excess of new mana gathering in and around any part of the body which needs healing or correction."

Never do deep-breathing exercises right after meals, Long says, and I agree with him from personal experience. I tried it that way the first time and made myself sick. "Oxygen dizziness," Long calls it. You should never meditate right after meals anyway, or after drinking alcoholic beverages or taking drugs of any kind, or when you are either stimulated or depressed. Sit at a time when there is nothing bothering you or demanding your attention. Pick a quiet period of the day, early morning if you are an early riser, before bedtime if that is your quietest time. Start your meditating by sitting approximately five minutes. You may build up to a longer period, fifteen minutes being the preferred length of time for an experienced sitter at home alone. With a development group you may sit a half-hour or possibly longer but never when alone. Even a virtue, when carried to extremes, becomes a vice. Prolonged meditation can be mentally disturbing if you aren't careful. So don't go overboard with it any more than you would constantly overeat or do anything else to excess.

After you have done your deep-breathing exercises and found a comfortable position, it is time to begin to meditate. Concentration is the first lesson, and it is usually difficult initially. Nonetheless, it is essential for further progress. To concentrate means to bring the mind to "one-pointed condition," as Ford calls it, and then to be able to hold it there for a time. This requires an object of concentration. Some people find it impossible in the beginning to use any abstract concept as their object of concentration, so they should think about some simple physical

78

object: a ring, a pencil, a rose, a tree, or perhaps a beautiful scene of a placid lake or rippling brook.

If you picture an object, say a rose, to meditate on, don't just look at it in your mind's eye. Try to identify with it. Touch it mentally, feel the velvety softness. Be aware of its gentle configurations, its scent, the shaft of its stem. Does it have thorns? Turn it and observe it, admire it, prolonging the time in which you engage in a very satisfying experience. As you do this, you are shutting out discord or other routine thoughts.

Another type of mind may prefer to concentrate on aphorisms, such as: "I am free from all thoughts of worry or anxiety, for I place myself and all my affairs in God's keeping" or "The love of God manifests through me and I am filled with light, wisdom and peace" or even "Love God with all your heart, mind, strength and soul."

Whatever way you've chosen, stay with it until you are deeply, perhaps totally, in empathy with it. When this happens, the workaday mind and body are at rest and out of the way, and the subliminal consciousness can come into play.

"Meditation is not *emptying the mind*." This is stated emphatically by Charles C. Wise, Jr. in "A Meditation on Meditation" in *Spiritual Frontiers* (Autumn, 1971). "In this connection," he says, "Jesus' cryptic Parable of the Displaced Demon (Matt. 12:43-45; Luke 11:24-26) speaks its warning. After the evil spirit was cast out, it found no new home. So it returned to the mind it had left. Finding it empty, it moved back with seven other devils more evil than it, and the man was worse off than in the beginning. Certainly this parable means that you cannot break an evil habit merely by getting rid of it; you must fill its place with the wholesome and constructive or there will be a relapse. But it also means that, if you just sit passively with your bare mind hanging out, you are inviting possession by any peripatetic evil spirit which happens

79

to be around. This is the great danger of the Ouija board and of automatic writing, and is why a successful trance medium always has a strong control standing guard. Meditation must be centered on *something*. And it is well to begin with a prayer invoking divine protection."

Wise has a story to illustrate his definition of meditation. "A good short course in its essentials was given the author many years ago. Age and arthritis then kept Uncle Henry out of the fields, but he still occupied his cottage and shared in the produce of the farm. All summer long, on every sunny day, he could be seen rocking on his porch. Once I asked him, 'Uncle Henry, what do you do in that chair all day?' Thoughtfully he replied, 'Mist' Charles, sometimes I sits and thinks, an' sometimes I jes' sits.' Exactly! And in that order! That's meditation! Work hard; relax, and think to the limits of thought; then relax unthinking, and allow the Infinite to lift your understanding toward His."

Meditation is a growth process. It is not a specific technique producing guaranteed results, according to Wise. "It is acquired slowly and haltingly, and then only where there is a persistent search motivated by disciplined desire. How any individual can best progress in it is not a matter of dogmatic rule, and varies widely from person to person. The best that can be done is to indicate in the most general terms the elements involved and to let each individual find his own way by trial and error. No guru should be trusted utterly; let God be your guru."

It isn't easy. Although one may and must seek with all application and diligence, the answer does not yield automatically to effort. "Desire for gain is not the key," says Wise; "one must give one's self utterly in love to the area of knowledge, interest, or art—or to God—in order to receive. We lose by grasping, and gain by letting go." But don't let go to the point of going to sleep. "St. Morpheus is no more the patron saint of meditation than is St. Vitus.

Prayer before meditation is good preparation. Ask God to 'quicken' you. Realize his power to activate as he fills your life. And be *interested* in what Infinite Mind is going to reveal."

After a time you will find it is not so difficult to concentrate, and then perhaps you will be able to hold your mind on the indwelling Christ, the sense of contact with God, or the great and the good. A few brief moments of this are so overpoweringly inspiring that you come out of your meditation period sailing, able to live with yourself in peace and serenity.

As Simons Roof, student of the occult and lecturer, says, "Meditation is only a technique—not a philosophy of life. The real work (and the real worth) comes when the knowledge gained through meditation is applied to study and service."

Just the very act of meditation changes your attitude entirely for the better. Roof expresses it this way: "When you get a taste of divine honey at the superconscious level, nothing else satisfies you for the rest of your life."

10: THE DEVELOPMENT CLASS

THIS chapter will give the techniques for sitting for development of .your psychic abilities as I learned them from personal experience with Arthur Ford, Douglas Johnson of England, Gladys Osborne Leonard, and a number of other prominent mediums, plus the accounts of several of the best writers on the subject.

A group of not more than fifteen but as small as four to six, who have like interests in psychically improving themselves, should begin to meet regularly once a week, always on the same night and at the same time and place. They should sit in a circle, with the men and women alternating sexwise if possible. (Why are there so seldom enough men to go around?) They should come in quietly and settle down without much talk at first. There must be no smoking or drinking before the meeting starts and no frivolity because if you get too excited, it will be difficult to sit quietly during meditation. The time for fun and games is after the serious portion of the meeting, when you are comparing notes on your mental adventures and discussing mutual interests.

When a new group begins, it is always good to have an experienced hand present at first. If you know a professional medium you can employ for a few meetings, it might be wise to do so. Or you should attempt to get someone who has sat in development circles before. If these individuals who start you off make suggestions about procedure that differ from mine, go along with them while they are there. Then when you are on your own, if you wish, you can change back to the methods described here. It should be possible in most communities to find a medium who will come for a contribution of $1 from each member of the group.

Strangers should not be encouraged to drop in from time to time. It is better for the same people to meet regularly, and after the second meeting the membership should be closed. However, after you have become thoroughly established, some of your members may start other groups for newcomers. Make sure they are definitely interested, however, and intend to come regularly once they have started. It isn't good to have a crowd that changes from week to week. Of course, if an occasional member is sick or out of town, that is different; but attempt to establish a night on which everyone will be able to come regularly, barring unforeseen obstacles.

As soon as all have arrived and settled down comfortably in their chairs, start the meditation period. You will use the techniques for this that we have already discussed or perhaps one of those for developing the alpha state, which we will review later. Be sure everyone is seated comfortably, with shoes off and girdles or bras loosened, if they prefer, in a straight-backed chair or else lying flat on the floor. The greatest mediums insist the spine should be straight and who's to dispute them?

As the quiet period starts, a prayer will be said: a few words from your leader directed to God, Ultimate Perfection, Supreme Intelligence, or whatever you care to call the Divine Presence you desire to be aware of as participating in your meeting. Then an affirmation such as one of the following may be read:

> The light of God surrounds us,
> The love of God fills us,

83

The power of God protects us,
The presence of God watches over us,
And wherever we are, God is.
No harm can come to us.

I prefer a somewhat longer reading that is (to me) anonymous. It says what I particularly like to hear:

Meditation

Deep within the inner recesses of my being,
In the creative silence of this moment,
I hear God speaking.
I feel the rhythm of infinite harmony flowing through
me.
I become aware of the Divine Presence and the Living
Law of the Universe.
I am one with it.
All people everywhere are one with it, and one with the
spirit of Love
And Peace.

The inspiration of this radiant moment illumines me,
Even unto the darkest corners of my thought.
I am uplifted in the consciousness of unity and light,
And all thought of tumult or despair is stilled.
I am now aware of abounding health, abundant supply,
deep joy and perfect peace.
I speak and know the word of Truth,
And I rest in the consciousness of Infinite Love
Enfolding me, now and always.

After this ask the entire group to say the Lord's Prayer aloud, or you may sing a song if you prefer—any song which you feel is appropriate. In these ways you are reaching out to the highest powers for assistance and participation in your efforts and for protection of your circle from any unpleasant influences. After the prayer and affirmation, each member of the group should privately establish his awareness of protection. Spirit intruders may attempt to enter your circle at first, and you must be sure to exclude them. The leader can say something about this if he wishes, stating that no entities may participate in your meeting except those who come from God in love and peace. If nothing else, this frequent mentioning of God and the higher forces will tend to discourage those who have come just for thrills, and they will probably go away. Still, it is wise for each person also to guard himself mentally. Then you can be sure you are safe.

The following means of protection, which should be used at all group meetings, is also important to employ at all other times. Especially, never sit down *alone* to meditate or to try to communicate with spirits—which I do not recommend at any time until you are thoroughly developed in your psychic abilities—without using this method of protection. In your mind's eye take long strands of white light and wrap yourself in it, or picture your force field like a shell around you, closing out all but good. It is your consciousness of the protection this can give which causes it to be successful. The power of your thoughts completely walls out any harm, any intruders from your vicinity. This is a mental process which safeguards you by the strength of your thought. It doesn't matter how you describe this protection to yourself, except that you have to believe in it. Some persons use different terms for the substance with which they protect themselves, those of more orthodox Christian bent calling it the White Christ Light.

Even if you just envision yourself encased in a cocoon of protection, it will work if you believe it thoroughly. This is not just an idea of mine. All development groups throughout the world provide protection for themselves in some similar way. Each member should use it at other times as well. When traveling in an automobile, airplane or train, you will arrive at your destination safely if you surround the entire vehicle in which you are traveling with protection. If each of you does this before your meeting begins, the spirits who are unwelcome—the earthbound malevolent spirits, the tedious, the compulsive talkers, any whom you do not want—will see the white light surrounding you and know that they cannot enter.

Even if you take these statements very lightly, try using the system of safeguarding I advocate. Envision yourself constantly wrapped in protection and observe how much more secure you continue to be from then on. This is one of the truths of life which has only to be tried to be proved. Many of the people you think of as oddballs have been doing this for years, and they have gone unscathed through situations which would have massacred the unprotected.

Now your quiet session will begin. The lights are lowered or extinguished, whichever the majority of your group prefers, and you will probably want to close your eyes also. Then everyone should breathe deeply for at least five or more inhales and exhales—use what I referred to in the meditation chapter as characterized breathing.

After this perfect stillness should prevail for at least a half-hour. When you have sat together regularly for a time, you can extend this time if you wish. It is very important that you have quiet so that anyone who is capable of developing trance may do so. Also those who have visions or other mental experiences need quiet. Under no circumstances should the medium speak at any length during this period. Many professional mediums who conduct classes of their own seem to feel the necessity of pointing out everything they see or hear, and this is wrong for your development. What he or she has seen can be discussed later. This is a class to improve the powers of the pupils, not the medium.

If anyone sees or hears something which he is positive is external to himself, such as what appears to be a three-dimensional figure in the room, he may mention it quietly to attract the attention of those whose eyes are closed. Then this may be discussed briefly as one or another speaks of what he sees. Usually a group will not have much of this nature to report for a long time. Yet again, if you have one or two especially "strong" people in your group, phenomena may begin early. By strong I mean that certain individuals seem to have more psychic force or power than others, and it seems to rub off on the rest, helping them develop faster. On many occasions everyone in the room may feel so much of this power that he almost seems to tingle with it.

Each person sitting in the darkened room should make a special point not to make any abrupt loud noises or touch his neighbors during the meditation. One who may be going into a very relaxed state or a trance might be startled by a nudge, a gesture, or a sudden sound. (This does not apply to the character who goes to sleep and snores so loudly that it disturbs others. He should be awakened by a shake, if necessary, from his nearest neighbor, no matter how much he complains about the indignity.)

As you start your meditation, reach out mentally. Open your centers of awareness as much as possible, yearning for contact with God, with good, and with whatever forces will help you develop. This reaching out, as you also attempt to achieve complete relaxation, is about all you can expect to accomplish at first. You will find that it is complicated by your attempts to still your thoughts. Don't be discouraged. This has to be learned and it takes a while. If you have been meditating at home and have begun to learn, you will go into the same routines, whatever they are, that have been successful for you.

Many people achieve the best results in stilling their minds by attempting to visualize a blank screen or a blackboard in front of their eyes. If you concentrate on this and not on the events of the day or what you are going to wear tomorrow or the latest gossip, you may soon begin to see pictures or words written on this blank space. You won't know whether or not they have significance until the meditation period is over and you discuss them, but no matter how trivial or insignificant they seem, make a mental note of them so that you can recall them later.

Some persons prefer to try to visualize a color or a picture of a calm scene like a lake surrounded by trees—rather than a blank screen. To learn to visualize, if you don't naturally have that ability, you may practice by trying to reproduce a flower or a bird or any other object in front of your closed eyes. Once when trying to achieve something of psychical interest for a friend, I saw a tiny picture, in startling detail, of a brilliantly colored peacock. As it turned out, this did have significance for my friend because she had just visited her boyfriend in the hospital and found that he had peacock feathers instead of flowers in his room. His brother, it turned out, ran a rare bird farm.

After this, my peacock was for a long time the first thing I would see when I began to meditate. Perhaps only a few of its feathers would appear, or its head, and occasionally its whole figure. I called it my test pattern. After seeing it, then perhaps I could visualize other objects of significance.

As time goes on, you may sometimes see a variety of pictures which seem symbolic and which must be interpreted. Most psychics learn to have their own interpretations for these, for there are few standards that can be depended on. Try to learn for yourself what certain symbols portend for you and your group.

After a while you will doubtless find that you are experiencing so many things during the quiet period that you can't remember them all, so be sure to bring a notebook and pencil with you every time and make brief notes of your impressions. You may be lucky enough to be able to decipher the scratchings when the light is turned on. Not only does having a written record give verification later if two or more people have visualized or heard the same thing, but it helps you remember all those fleeting bits of information which come to you.

Beginners often ask me how you can tell the evanescent thoughts that fly through your mind from genuine psychical impressions. There is a definite chance that most of them are actually subjective. Yet again some of them may be significant. It has always been my experience that the psychic views are in brilliant technicolor, and they remain for a few moments so that they can be carefully observed. They may be extremely minute, but somehow they can be seen in every detail. However it is also true that some fairly good bits of evidence can be seen as a mere flash, not concretely defined. That is why it is better to comment on everything that comes to you that you are able to remember. Something that seems to be just a passing image may be of significance to someone.

One of the rather odd things that may start to happen to you, especially if you find yourself being developed as a trance medium, is what your guides call "changing your chemicals." You will begin to have strange happenings while you are meditating. They will be gentle but so definite that you cannot escape noticing them. You may feel for some time as if there were a wafting of feathers all over your face, as once I did. Another experience I had for some two or three weeks was that of having a spot on the center of the top of my head feeling as if it were opening and closing. After a time it stopped, and I never found out for sure what had been going on. But I learned that similar oddities occur to others who have been told their chemicals are being changed. Some people find that their appetite for various foods and their tolerance for drink alter during this period. Don't be disturbed if it happens to you. It is just one more of the peculiar situations in which you may find yourself, but it is in no way harmful.

There will be some in your meeting who never have much that is unusual happen to them. They may not be strongly psychic themselves or have much potential for development, but they perform a useful function by lending their power to the combined group power for the use of others. They may find that spending their time each week meditating with a group, even without much to show for it in the way of psychic development, gives them rewarding relaxation. So don't feel discriminated against if others report seeing lights and figures and colors you cannot see. Above all, don't scoff at them. Someday you may see something far more sensational, and then you will want others to believe when you tell of it. Remember that *patience* is the most important necessity for anyone who desires to undertake meditation or development. Usually you will be rewarded by a wonderful feeling of peace, if nothing else, after the session is over, so your time will never be spent uselessly when you meditate.

Helen MacGregor and Margaret V. Underhill, two of the best development leaders ever to write on the subject, say in their booklet *The Psychic Faculties and Their Development:* "That mysterious, but very real essence which we call psychic power does not always affect people in the same way. Those who are insensitive may sit in circles year after year and never develop their powers. Others have gifts which lie dormant and their development appears to be slow, but eventually these gifts will unfold and they may prove very fine."

There was a man known as Farmer Riley who sat with a group regularly for many months with nothing ever happening to him personally. At the end of this time, suddenly trumpets began to sail around the room in his presence, loud rappings were heard, and other physical phenomena began to be exhibited, for he had become a strong physical medium. So you never know. Patience is the hardest part of development.

Yet when the psychic power lies near the surface—or in other words, when the individual is ready to bring forth his gifts into the light—the effect of development will be marked and speedy. Then it is necessary to proceed with caution and, above all, never to force any growth or manifestation before the psychic has acquired mental poise and has lost all feeling of apprehension.

"When a new and desirable power begins to manifest, whether mental or physical, it is best to take it as a matter of course," say MacGregor and Underhill. "Think about it as little as possible and do not talk about it, for the progress of the psychic may be greatly retarded by paying too much attention to his budding powers. It is as though concentration of attention had a shattering effect upon them.

"The habit of comparing oneself with others also retards psychic growth. No two persons work in the same way; a slow, or an apparently slow, growth may be manifested by an individual, and yet the actual unfoldment of psychic power, character and personality be far greater than is visible on the surface, for the most important part of psychic growth takes place in the soul. When psychic powers are suddenly manifested they are either the result of a soul-growth which has been going on for years, or are due to great emotional disturbances—shocks—which, as one may say, precipitate the individual into a higher state of consciousness. In the latter case the essential foundations may be lacking which are truly laid by the individual who has reached the higher consciousness through soul-growth. Psychic awakening which is due to shock is apt to be of a transitory nature and is occasionally accompanied by symptoms of abnormality."

Whoever has a watch with a lighted dial should be designated timekeeper, and at the end of a half-hour he will quietly state that the time is up. Then the lights are turned on, low at first so that eyes grown used to the dark won't be shocked. As the meditation concludes, it is usually the custom for everyone to stand in a circle and hold hands. Then the leader or someone delegated by him says a prayer for healing. After that, while still in prayerful attitude, various persons in turn voice the names of friends to whom they wish to send healing. When this is concluded, after a few stretches everyone returns to his seat. Then in his turn he tells of his experiences during meditation. Usually, even if he has nothing psychic to offer, he expresses the great feeling of peace and relaxation he has had.

Don't be discouraged if others have more personal experiences to relate than you do for some time. The slowest starters may become the strongest psychics in the long run. Remember Farmer Riley! When you make your report of all the things you have seen, heard, pictured or otherwise become cognizant of during the quiet period, do not hold anything back. Something which seems to you so insignificant or trivial as to be unworthy of mention may have significance for another. If you have thought of each person in turn around the circle during your meditation and attempted to tune in to him with as much empathy as possible, there is the chance you might arrive at a fact about him that you had no normal way of knowing.

Then again two or three of you may have experienced telepathic rapport and all have seen visions or received impressions of the same thing. Often those who sit opposite each other become batteries, have great mutual harmony, and sense the same things during meditation. When notes are compared afterward, it is frequently exhilarating to realize that something very definitely supernormal has occurred, even if only to a few of the group.

As a rule you all become very friendly as time goes on. If it should occur that you don't, if there should be any friction of a sustained nature, it might be wise for the leader to ask the one on whom it centers to leave the group. This can possibly be done tactfully enough to keep from hurting feelings. When an entire meditation period is spoiled by a conflict of personalities, it is best to remove the chief offender to keep from disturbing the morale of the rest. Peace is your goal, and it should be achieved without conflict of any kind.

If an individual feels uneasy or strange in the company of certain people, it is best to accept it as a warning and withdraw. The circle itself may or may not be all that it should be, but one particular budding sensitive may be out of harmony with some of its members, in which case he would make better progress in other surroundings. It is never wise for anyone to force himself to stay in uncongenial conditions.

Open circles, that is, circles to which people are admitted regardless of their fitness for development, are not wise. Proper conditions cannot be obtained and maintained unless the circle is carefully chosen and only healthy-minded people who can get along together admitted.

When the recital of experiences is finished, refreshments may or may not be served, according to the preference of the hostess. After that, if there is time, psychic games may be played, and then the meeting is adjourned. Usually a few will be so full of their mutual interests that they will stay and stay, talking animatedly. All will almost invariably agree that the evening has been *most* rewarding, one way or another.

11: PSYCHIC GAMES

PSYCHOMETRY can hardly be called a game because it is a serious means of producing evidence for psi. But for a development group, it is always an entertaining addition to the meditation, done after the group is relaxed and enjoying itself.

The premise behind psychometry is that each person and object has a force field around it. In humans and animals this is known as the aura, of which more later. Or it could be considered the evidence for those electrical impulses we have already discussed. Whatever it is, the force field surrounding an object is said to retain a saturation of impressions about its present and previous owners. Psychic persons, then, are often able to learn a great deal about an individual by holding an object that has belonged to him. It may be a ring, a bracelet, a billfold, a photograph, or anything else. Peter Hurkos has said he can get the best information when holding someone's shoe. San Diego's well-known psychometrist Kay Sterner prefers to hold your watch when reading for you.

A developing psychic can hardly hope for anything even remotely as successful as the pros achieve, but if he practices psychometry often he may someday become proficient.

It is a good idea to ask someone in your class each week to bring an object next time to be psychometrized. After the meditation period, pass it around, asking that no one look at it but only hold it and try to get impressions from it. Then let each person say what occurs to him while he is holding it. At first there may be only a few hits, yet again there may soon be many.

I remember that once when we were trying psychometry in a development class in New York City, a tiny roundish object was passed around. When it came to me, I held it for a few moments, and during that time it seemed to jump in my hand. I naturally suspected it must be a Mexican jumping bean. But the only feeling I had about it was one of deep sorrow. I mentioned this, and others had similar responses to mine. None of us had much to say about it, but we all felt that tears and unhappiness went with it. Later we learned that the object was a small pebble a man in the class had picked up in the Garden of Gethsemane on a visit to Israel.

Another "game" that may be played is one I learned from the sensitive Maile Krush in Seattle. In her circles one person is chosen at a time about whom the others will attempt to receive psi impressions. This one who is "it" will be seated in the center of the circle, always facing south. Everyone then spends five minutes trying to receive information about him. Maile says that what you see to his left represents a future happening, to the right is something from his past, and straight ahead represents the present. For some unknown reason, having everyone at once concentrating on one individual in this manner sometimes brings specific results of considerable interest.

Some people try to develop or play psychic games by looking at a lighted candle which is placed in the center of the circle and concentrated on for not more than twenty minutes at a time. Look at it without blinking for as long as you can and then close your eyes. The candle will continue to appear in your mind's eye and will be seen to move. Don't follow it with your eyes, but think it back into its central spot. If you lose the image, open your eyes

95

again and repeat the process. After you learn to control this technique, you may see a door open in your mind's eye and inside will be all kinds of psychic goodies. I have never attempted this, but I'm told that a white candle will appear lavender with your eyes closed, and that as you concentrate on different emotions, the candle changes color.

The game of trying to see auras is much fun, and it soon turns out to be no game at all but the way to acquire a new talent. Auras are variously reported as being the external radiation of the force field which interpenetrates and surrounds every living being, or it may be the glowing externalized portion of an inner body, the spirit or astral or etheric body as it is variously called. It may be a combination of both of these explanations, for what is to keep a spirit body from being composed of force or energy which radiates outward? Whatever the explanation, there is little doubt that many persons can naturally see auras.

Sometimes the aura appears to be just a clear light. Others see it in any of a variety of colors. If the hues are pale and clear, they usually indicate good health, and if dark and muddy, bad health or violent disposition. The person who has done the most research on auras is Dr. Walter J. Kilner of St. Thomas' Hospital, London. In the early 1900's he discovered that by looking through glass stained with dicyanine he could see auras around human bodies. They looked to him like clouds of radiation extending out from six to eight inches and showing distinct colors. Fatigue, moods, and disease could alter their size and color. From this observation he developed a system of diagnosing illness from the aura.

Scientists in Russia today are doing interesting research involving the spirit body (although they wouldn't dream of calling it that) and auras. Semyon Davidovich Kirlian, an engineer of the city of Krasnodar, and his wife, Valentina, invented an entirely new method of photography that allows them to film what appears to be not only the external luminescence around a person, plant or animal but also the life force within them. Their work is exciting the interest of many scientists of various persuasions.

The philosophical implications are even more extraordinary, according to Sheila Ostrander and Lynn Schroeder in *Psychic Discoveries Behind the Iron Curtain*. This photography seems to suggest that living things have two bodies, they say, "the physical body everyone can see and a secondary 'energy-body' the Kirlians saw in their high-frequency photos."

The aura is more easily distinguished by the naked eye when the subject is in front of a pale-colored blank wall. Most groups attempting to see it find it simpler to stand one member at a time on a chair in the center of the room, if the ceiling is painted a light color. Then his head will stand out clearly as observed against the ceiling.

Some persons can immediately see the aura. Others must squinch up their eyes and get them slightly out of focus to do so. Don't try to look at the outside of the head, where you expect the aura to appear. Instead, look at the spot on the forehead just between the eyes. Then a pale glow may be seen around the head.

If you then turn your eyes ever so slightly toward the aura, it will disappear. Some who have learned to see auras this way have become able to see them at any time they wish and to distinguish a variety of colors, shapes, and conditions from them.

Being ever critical, when I first sat with a group who said they were seeing auras in this manner, I thought they were "seeing things" instead, for I could not. Then gradually, as the ability came to me, I thought I was merely seeing reflected light. However I persevered and began to distinguish somewhat between the pale colors I could see. Some were almost clear white, some light blue, and some faintly green. Once I saw the aura as a darker green in a big bulge behind a man's head, unlike anything I'd seen before. Instead of speaking up about what I saw, I waited to learn if it was my imagination or if others observed it too. In fact, several people mentioned the more unusual dark-green color and commented on how it bulged out at the back of his head. So I decided I must actually be seeing auras after all.

Another game that is exciting to play is lifting someone into the air. One individual lies on the floor, and six others kneel around him, two on each side, and one at his head and one at his feet. They place the index finger of each hand under his body. Then he is put into what might be called a mild form of hypnotic trance as each person around him repeats slowly and quietly in turn the following ritual:

> You are tired.
> You are very tired.
> You are very very tired.
> You are growing limp.
> You are limp.
> You are light.
> You are very light.
> You are very very light.
> You are as light as a feather.
> You are floating like a feather.
> You are floating.
> We shall lift you!

As the last word is spoken each person raises his index fingers into the air, the body rising so lightly that it is held up without any feeling of weight. It will be possible for the supporters to get to their feet and continue raising the subject sometimes as high into the air as they can reach. This can also be done if he is sitting on a chair, with the chair, body and all being lifted after the proper words are said.

I think it probably takes a person who is easily hypnotized to be the subject. Or at least someone who firmly believes it can be done. I've seen it tried with a nonbeliever, namely me, and it didn't work, even though I had seen it work at previous times with others.

Incidentally, one of the games you must not attempt to play is the "game" of hypnosis. This is very risky for amateurs and is not to be tried except by those who have had a great deal of experience at it.

Neither do I recommend Ouija boards or automatic writing for beginners. And you will find that professionals abjure them entirely, unless one happens to be a trained automatist. I have rarely known mediums who would touch a Ouija board. They know the dangers, which are, pure and simply, that intruding spirit entities invariably feel welcome to come and write on the Ouija with you. They don't care who they pretend to be, just so they get the chance to write, and will claim to be any relative you seek or even a famous person. After all, they are invisible, so who can be sure they aren't the individual they claim to be ... until they lead you down false trails? But enough of that here, we'll talk more about it in the chapter on "Pitfalls."

Table rapping or tipping seems to be somewhat safer and can be one of your games. Several people sit around a small table. Large, heavy tables have been known to move or even to lift up into the air; but you might as well make it easy for the invisible tipper, so begin with a table that is small and light. Even a sturdy card table can be used. Each person places his hands lightly on it, and then everyone sits quietly waiting for it to make some response. Actually, there are two schools of thought about this. Some people prefer to sing or to chatter innocently rather than to sit quietly. It seems to work either way if it is going to work at all. If the combination of persons doesn't cause the table to begin moving, change one or two for someone else. A different combination of sitters might be more successful.

Eventually small raps may be heard in the table, or it may rise up on two legs. If it does this, give it a code by which it may rap answers. Tell it one rap alone will mean "Yes," two "No," and three "I don't know." Then tell it that it can spell out words for you by rapping at the letter it wants as you repeat the alphabet. It raps by dropping to the floor at the desired letter, then rearing back up ready for the next letter.

People will tell you, of course, that this is done purposefully by one member of your group who moves the table by conscious pressure of his hands. Others say the activity comes from his subconscious mind, which moves his hands without his conscious knowledge. It has never been conclusively shown just how it really works, but the fact remains that sometimes evidential information can be received from a tipping table. I don't know why there are few reports of its being as chancy as the Ouija board, but perhaps it is because it is so difficult to do that not too many people try it when alone.

I know a group of attractive young matrons in Bal Harbour, Florida, an exclusive suburb of Miami, who believe one of their member's uncle communicates with them via a tipping card table. They meet regularly for meditation, luncheon, and then a table session. This alleged uncle has accurately predicted, among other things that have come true, most of the successful candidates in a forthcoming election.

12: FROM A CLAIRVOYANT'S
VIEWPOINT

A PERSONAL account of how she developed her psychic abilities has been given us by Mary Tallmadge of Verona, New Jersey. Mary sat for years with Miss Gertrude Tubby, one of this century's most competent developers of mediums. Now Mary holds her own classes in various cities in northern New Jersey. She has written for us a personal account of how she sees psychic pictures and what they mean to her.

"The world the subjective clairvoyant sees in his mind," Mary says, "is a new world and yet a familiar one because he sees recognizable forms such as people, material objects, animals, scenery. But through the cultivation of this faculty there is a greater range of vision than is possible with the use of the physical eyes. He is able to see scenes of the past, present and even the future, as well as to penetrate matter—by looking into the internal structure of the human body.

"When he peers inwardly with his eyes closed, he may first see on the inner screen of his mind nothing but a reddish, bluish or blackish haze, but as his consciousness becomes absorbed with looking, the haze will fade, and in its place may appear a letter, a shape or a human figure in faint light; and as his concentration becomes deeper, he will begin to see single images or scenes in color.

"In learning to open this faculty he may not be sure that he is not imagining what he is seeing, as the images

101

will come and go very fast until he has learned through practice to hold the images in order to study them for their content and meaning." When he reports what he has seen to his classmates and discovers that it may have some significance for one of them, he then begins to realize that what he has seen has not been subjective, but psychic instead.

"Usually the clairvoyant images I see appear small in size as if I were viewing them through the wrong end of a telescope," Mary says. This is apparently the usual experience. My tiny peacock test pattern is an example of this, and most of my other strongly relevant pictures have been seen the same way. Mary goes on, "Normally these visions appear true in perspective, but occasionally due to some fault, I believe, in my reception I have seen them upside down, sideways or partially materialized, such as seeing only the lower half of a person's body or just the head with no body.

"My clairvoyant imagery at its best manifests in bright light and vivid coloring, similar to technicolor movies. But many times the figures appear on the inner screen of the mind silhouetted in dim light, with no color at all, against a dark field. Or sometimes their composition is in reddish, grayish or bluish tones. I can only liken this type of reception to the reproduction of photographic prints on red, blue or black-and-white paper.

"Usually when I open my clairvoyant faculty, I find that I follow a pattern in my reception. First I will see images in dim light, and as my concentration becomes deeper, the colored images start to come. If I am very tired, or the atmosphere is heavy, I find it difficult to get my clairvoyant faculty to function fully. I may see only images in dim or black-and-white light. If the atmosphere is clear and I am rested, and especially if I am near a body of water, I find that my reception is much sharper, and it is invariably in color.

"There is a faculty of expansion in relation to the reception of the images. The image will widen, not unlike the enlarging of a movie on a cineramic screen, so that my whole inner screen is completely covered with a picture. At other times I see only the diminutive pictures. They are in full color and detail but appear to be way off, and they take up only part of the inner screen, thus leaving the rest in darkness.

"Objects are at times magnified on the screen, such as a diamond ring which appears before my inner sight so enlarged that its facets show the intricate cutting of the stone. Or a single pink rose may be shown, looking fresh and dewy. Or a book bound in leather with its title tooled in gold letters, the details standing out clearly as if the object were mounted against a black velvet drop.

"It is not uncommon to see movement in visions such as people walking and talking. Since the clairvoyant's vision is not limited by time and space, it is possible to see action taking place in other parts of the country or the world or in previous periods of history. Or even in the future.

"The clairvoyant can also have the feeling of mentally moving above the ground and surveying a landscape below as if he were a bird in flight. Or he may find himself viewing a scene from a different angle than the angle he would normally find himself if he was standing or sitting observing the scene taking place in front of him. Once, for example, I saw a scene involving an American Indian sitting on the floor of a room surrounded by Indian bowls, rugs and other wares. In front of him stood a woman who was obviously interested in purchasing something. I found myself observing this scene from a point in space slightly behind and above the woman.

"Another time I found myself traveling mentally at a very fast speed through darkness. Upon arriving at my destination, I saw shadowy outlines which changed into a bright and colorful scene of American Indians riding horses and engaging in combat with each other on a grassless plain. I could also see two Indians crouched behind some low-lying bushes in the foreground of my vision, getting ready to spring into the fray. I did not hear any sound this time; but while observing his visions, a subjective clairvoyant will often be aware of hearing sound such as music or talking.

"Many of the clairvoyant's visions will be in a symbolic form. The makeup is such that the sensitive usually recognizes it as being of that nature. Many symbols are of religious origin, as well as universal, and many times will necessitate research to arrive at their meaning.

"The psychic will also have his own personal symbolism which will appear pictorially on his inner screen. For instance, if I see a fleur-de-lis, I immediately think of France. If I get a mental impression of the name Cooperstown, I think of baseball because that is the place where the game originated.

"Many messages received clairvoyantly are enacted in a symbolic form. For example, in reading for a friend and answering a question about her business, I closed my eyes and concentrated for a short time. I saw a vision in color of a loaf of bread poised on the gangplank of a boat similar to the *Mayflower*. Its cellophane wrapper was open so that pieces of bread fell one at a time into the green sea below. The thought immediately came to me that this meant she was casting her bread upon the waters. This apparently satisfied her as an adequate answer to her question.

"Many visions of this type are obscure when one attempts to reason out an interpretation consciously. The clairvoyant should let the real meaning come through his intuition rather than jumping to a conclusion through conscious reasoning. Sometimes future events will be enacted symbolically such as in the following instance. I saw a friend standing in a room by a very large gambling wheel and got the impression that she was going to take a very big chance. After my seeing this vision, she later became involved in a situation in which she was taking a big risk.

"Some symbolic visions pertaining to future events and situations are so complex in their structure that they take much thought and meditation to arrive at their meaning, if, indeed, it is possible to do so at all. Yet when the preshadowed events occur, the clairvoyant will then realize what the visions had been trying to convey.

"A psychic's desire to gain certain information will direct the area of his concentrations. In other words, although he can sit and meditate and open up his clairvoyant faculty and let whatever he can pick up come to him, he can also direct his concentration so as to receive specific information. In my own case, if I want to see scenes of a person's childhood or home or gain information about his personal problems, I begin my psychic reading with this thought in mind. It is sometimes difficult for me to pick up specific information at the start of a reading, but as I get further into a psychic state, I find that I have begun to get on the right wave length and correct information will start to come through pictures, mental impressions, etc.

"It is important to have your mind in a positive state, with your desire for the knowledge you are seeking uppermost in your mind.

"Reading or attempting to get information for oneself is more difficult. It is probably the emotional aspect of what one wants to know about oneself that blocks the knowledge from coming. When reading for another person, there is usually an impersonal approach that does not hinder the flow of correct impressions.

"In seeking knowledge through reading for another, it is quite important that harmony be built up between the psychic and the sitter. Some people consciously or uncon-

105

sciously put up a barrier; the psychic cannot reach the mind of the other person until this barrier has been removed. This may necessitate reading more than once for the person until a good rapport can be established."

The "I don't believe a word of it, you've gotta show me" attitude of some sitters is definitely the reason why they have such poor results; but you'll never be able to convince them of it. They are the ones who are sure the entire subject of psychical phenomena is all malarkey, but their attitude puts up such a barrier that very few sensitives can get through it to achieve rapport with them.

"Once I tried to read for a man who boasted he could not be read for," says Mary. "I could sense an invisible wall being built between us. I found myself floundering and getting only incorrect impressions. I was getting nowhere, so I stopped the reading."

A clairvoyant is always learning something new about his abilities, according to Mary Tallmadge. Once when doing a psychometric reading for a friend, she found herself describing a Nativity scene on a stage which was pictorially presented in color on her inner screen.

"Then this scene passed," she says, "and I saw bolts of beautiful silk material in different patterns. What I was seeing did not seem relevant to the object I was holding, and I was having difficulty getting impressions that I thought should relate to it. My sister-in-law, who was sitting near me, knew what was happening, however. I was reading *her* mind instead. She had been sitting there thinking of how she was going to present a Christmas pageant at her church and what materials she was going to use for the Wise Men's robes. I had apparently picked up her creative imaginings, and they were presented on my inner screen in picture form while I was in a receptive and clairvoyant state. They completely blocked out what I was trying to accomplish psychometrically."

Mary feels that clairvoyance could be very helpful if

106

the medium were to practice and concentrate so that he could develop his ability along specific lines. For instance, if he were to study anatomy, he could become very useful in the field of medicine by seeing into the physical body and locating unhealthy conditions. Or he could go back in history and concentrate on a specific era to learn more about the people and their way of life, thus being of aid to historians.

13: THE TRANCE

IN your development class you may begin to realize that one or more of your members are becoming trance mediums, for they will start to go into a withdrawn state in which their conscious minds become inactive and their voices will speak words which purport to come from spirits.

Sometimes the first to use the sensitive's voice to communicate may be a guide. This is said to be an entity who comes to all newly developing mediums in order to protect them. Until the guides or teachers (sometimes called masters) arrive, there may be no restraint over who talks through the potential medium, and any spirits who wish to do so crowd in and try to make themselves known. The guides will attempt to protect their medium from such intrusions, and so their advent is always looked for eagerly.

The "control" is the entity who will be the main spirit contact. When he, or she, arrives, he begins to screen all those who wish to communicate, and in this way he protects the medium from intruders. Usually the guides, teachers, and control will identify themselves and explain how they expect to work with the medium. The control will act as master of ceremonies, introducing the entities who will attempt to speak through the medium when his trance is well established. One medium may have several guides, and sometimes several teachers or doctors, especially if his development tends toward healing.

108

Those who know little or nothing about mediumship find the idea of Indian guides highly amusing. Instead, they are so helpful and protective that all mediums who have Indians are eternally grateful to them. It is possible to have guides of any nationality, of course, but American Indians, who were closer to nature during their lives on earth, for some reason like to become the protectors of those who are developing mediumship. It is said to be easier for them because they are so strong and capable. Whatever the reason, when an Indian "gatekeeper" flexes his mental muscles and says "Go away!" to an intruding entity who wishes to speak through the entranced medium without legitimate right to do so, the entity leaves pronto. Part of the value of sitting for development is to acquire guides and controls for members of the group and to learn to let them work with you. After you have them, you are much safer when you attempt communication.

On many occasions, however, a newly developing sensitive who does not yet have his guides may be host to earth-bound spirits who are not harmful but merely wish to make their presence known. It is wise, therefore, for the leader of the group to speak to each entity who attempts to talk through the entranced one and to ask for identification. When someone comes for a specific member of the circle, he will quickly designate himself as "Uncle Oscar" or "Cousin Emma" or whoever, and make an effort to give evidence as to his identity. If the voice instead does nothing to specify who he is, merely blathering about how glad he is to be there and muttering inanities, the leader of the circle should be pleasant but firm and ask him to leave. It isn't necessary to allow a spirit any length of time unless he is saying something worthwhile. Those who merely wish to intrude because it is an opportunity to make their presence known to someone on earth, even though it is someone they don't know, will take up as much time as you will allow them. Don't let them start a practice of doing this.

One of my first trance experiences occurred before my guides arrived, when someone who had an excellent reason for wishing to speak pushed himself in and took me over in an attempt to bring evidence of his identity. Under the circumstances, this was really legitimate. And it helped me realize that a person in trance can be awake and alert and still have supernormal information spoken through his mouth . . . information that he didn't consciously instigate.

In Daytona Beach, Florida, in 1957, I had begun the second phase of development of my psychic capacities. The first was automatic writing, the many aggravations and complications of which I have detailed in *Confessions of a Psychic*. Then entities began to talk to me and through me. I didn't go into trance, however. I was fully conscious as the words were spoken by my mouth . . . words I did not expect until they were voiced. Naturally I was critical of this, wishing some way could be found to supply evidence so that I could be sure it was not my own subconscious mind producing the words. Then I had several experiences which tended to indicate that the information came from external sources. The following is one of those:

One day my friend Irene Kellogg phoned to say she was dropping by to visit me. I hadn't told Irene or anyone else of this new phase of my development. People then looked even more askance than they do now at any evidence of unusual psi experience. So when Irene came in, I was prepared to talk to her about the weather or anything else that had nothing to do with my current psychic activities. However, almost the moment Irene sat down, words began to gush from my mouth that I was not personally saying at all.

"Irene, this is your father speaking," I said. "Listen

carefully because I may never have the opportunity to talk to you again."

I knew my friend's father was dead, but his intrusion at that point surprised me no end. I interrupted him to tell Irene that I had become mediumistic enough that entities were able to speak through me sometimes and that perhaps her father really was there and wanted to let her know.

"Do you want to talk to him?" I asked.

Irene was definitely eager to hear from him, although she was too stunned at the idea to say anything. She nodded her head. Her father had died several years before after having been in a coma for a long time. Once or twice he had roused from it and had been his rational self for brief moments; after that he became once again a pathetic lump on the bed, unable to communicate in any way.

When I let him resume talking through me, he rattled on as fast as possible so that he could say all he wanted to before my own mind got in the way and took over. He told his daughter she must realize that he was always with her and that he loved her and would help her whenever he could.

"Your mother won't be there with you much longer, and I want you to know that when she dies, she and I will stay with you and aid you all we can," he said. Then he got onto her with a lecture about smoking too much. Talk about embarrassment! I could have crawled under the refrigerator with chagrin. I wouldn't have dreamed of speaking to my friend that way.

Irene didn't object to the lecture at all, apparently. She just sat there with a dazed expression. Finally she rallied enough to ask, "Would you like me to give him a test question mentally?"

I thought this was a fine idea because, while I knew I wasn't consciously saying those things to her, I nonetheless questioned their actual source. In order to get an answer to Irene's question, I concentrated even harder than

111

ever to make my mind a blank so that I wouldn't intrude into her father's conversation. But he didn't seem to be answering her. He just rambled on about things in general.

Then he said, "You know, my dear, when I died I was exactly the same person I had ever been." He went on to tell how he just seemed to wake up from a long rest, and finally he realized that he had passed through the experience called death sometime while he had been asleep. Then after a few more loving and encouraging words to his daughter, he left us.

I was disappointed, feeling sure he hadn't been able to answer Irene's mental question, whatever it was. But she told me he had answered it beautifully. Her question had been, "How long after your death did it take for you to get back to your normal self?" And he had assured her he was his normal self when he passed over. He hadn't needed to change back, for he had never lost himself during that long period when he was in the coma.

Irene's mother died about a year later. She'd had chronic asthma but had not been particularly ill at the time of my sudden séance.

The need for evidence is so very important, and all those who are training should be conscious of it at all times. So many inept mediums are unaware of this. They give you initials and vague generalities but very little of substance to help with identification. They may also fish for information from you. This is deplorable, and it is part of what gives the field a bad name.

As you are developing, you should be conscious of trying to receive evidence. If you begin to go into trance, even the modified form of it that is the current trend, your teacher or the leader of your group should talk to your control and your guides and tell them you want the spirits who speak through you always to attempt to give data that will help identify them. Wouldn't it be exciting if through you, personally, should eventually come some kind of evidence so conclusive that it would confirm spirit communication and reveal to the world the definite information that there is no death? Don't count on this. It isn't that easy; but you can always keep hoping.

Occasionally strangers (communicants unknown to sitters or medium) give dramatic survival proof at home circles. Called drop-in cases by parapsychologists, they sometimes bring strong evidence—even though no evidence has ever been accepted by the scientific researchers as being *entirely* conclusive. When a professional medium gives information unknown to others, it may always be suspected, whether rightly or not, that he has acquired the information in some normal way and is giving it as proof of his supernormal capabilities. But when a number of people are sitting in a home circle, each as interested as the rest in learning proper techniques and growing in ability, there would be no point whatever for the medium of the group to attempt to falsify evidence. For this reason, more attention is usually paid to data received by the nonprofessionals.

Maurice Johnson, a reporter for the *Psychic News,* London, wrote in the November 13, 1971, issue, "I was present at a home circle last week when a 'dead' girl, a complete stranger to all the sitters, gave her name and address and details of her passing, which I have verified." The circle meets at the home of Sam and Hilda Patterson in Sunderland, and its medium is a natural psychic, Marion Jamieson, of Mill Lane, Whitburn.

During the meeting Mrs. Jamieson, in trance, said: "There is a young girl here giving her name as Ruth Heslop. She lives in Stoddard Street, South Shields, and was killed by a bomb in 1941 as she was crossing the marketplace to go to the air raid shelter after having been to the cinema. She says, 'You don't believe me, do you? My grave is in Harton Cemetery. It is beside the soldiers' graves.' "

113

Members of the circle investigated and found the girl's grave. Then the reporter took over the investigation. He learned the address from the caretaker and went to call on the girl's sister, Mrs. Grace Deakin. She confirmed that she'd had a sister named Ruth Heslop who had lived in Stoddard Street, that the girl had been killed by a bomb while crossing the marketplace. She also supplied the information that Ruth was with a friend named Gladys Stewart, who had been killed at the same time.

The reporter made it a special point not to mention what he had been told so that the medium would not know if information she later obtained had already been confirmed. Ruth came again at another home circle meeting, and among other information, she reported that a friend had been with her and also killed at the same time and that her body was buried near her.

Receiving such evidential information is one of the main goals of sittings, but we usually have to be satisfied with much less. However, if messages begin to come through for some specific individual in the group, it can be very encouraging, especially if they are from someone beloved. Questions may be asked of this person, in an effort to extract as exact an identification as possible. Sitters should be aware that they must never ask a communicating spirit for tips on the stock market or horse races or in other ways attempt to use him for their own material benefit. If they truly need help in some life situation they don't know how to control, they may ask for advice because there is an advantage to suggestions from those who have a wider perspective than they. It is not good to form the habit of turning development classes into séances for the purpose of trying to reach spirits for help, however. Evidence of identity of communicating spirits is the most important thing such groups can produce, in addition, of course, to the psychic improvement of the members and their growth in spiritual understanding.

14: CELEBRITY SÉANCES

AUTHOR Hamlin Garland was the instigator of a home circle formed in Hollywood in about 1927 which involved several popular movie stars. It doesn't take glamorous personages to make successful séances, but a few beautiful actresses don't harm any gathering—and something obviously made these extra special. The medium was a nonprofessional named Dora Drane, who had been a lifelong friend of one of the sitters, Ann Radford Johnston. Ann's daughter Julanne, a friend of mine, gave me this account of their fascinating experiences.

Julanne Johnston, who had been thrust into immediate fame in her first acting role with Douglas Fairbanks, Sr., in *The Thief of Baghdad,* tells me that she first learned of the circle when she returned to California after making a picture in Puerto Rico. Her mother's sister greeted Julanne with a phoned lament.

"I'm worried," she cried. "Ann has become involved with some strange cult." And sure enough, Julanne discovered that her mother had a roll of wrapping paper beside her bed at night to use for automatic writing.

When the lovely young actress inquired about this new activity of her mother's, she found nothing after all to make her suspicious. She learned instead that interesting activity was going on that she too wanted to share. Her mother had joined the group which had been started by Hamlin Garland to study psychic phenomena. Although he never attended personally, his daughter Isabel did and took careful notes for him on everything that occurred.

At the time Julanne began to go, the sessions were attended by the medium Dora Drane; Ann Radford Johnston; Isabel Garland and her husband, Hardesty Johnson, a professional singer with, Julanne says, "a heavenly voice"; the stunning brunette actress Virginia Valli; and Julanne. Later actor Walter Pidgeon and his wife, Ruth, attended, the star's beautiful baritone adding greatly to the power of the singing.

Plump little Dora was deeply religious, so the meetings began with singing the doxology. Then a prayer was said and a hymn was sung. Then all sat quietly in the semi-dark room and waited for the medium to settle back and go into trance. They all had made it a point never to eat dinner before their sitting, and this may somehow have contributed to the effectiveness, for unusual things soon began to occur. Afterward they would sit around and have a bite to eat while discussing the surprising events they had witnessed.

Because the meetings were always held in the living rooms of the participants, there would have been no possible way for the medium to have prepared any kind of trickery in advance, had she been so inclined; but there was never any question of her honesty. Still, when Julanne would observe manifestations and be completely convinced during a meeting that she was receiving communication from her father, at home later she always argued with herself that perhaps Dora's subconscious mind might be picking up information from her own mind and then somehow reproducing it through the trumpet. As previously noted, it is always well to be critical, especially when one is observing inexplicable manifestations.

For, yes, the group did experience phenomena that were supernormal one way or another. From the beginning Ann Johnston was able to see lights, but no one else

116

was. (She was probably strongly psychic, as later events would tend to indicate.) Actually, it was the great sense of peace and tranquility experienced by everyone that was most notable at first. Then Julanne began to feel pats on her face and hair and shoulders. Something was touching her gently. Was it her father, who had died when she was twelve, now somewhere on the "other side" giving her love pats? She also began to feel a lovely cool breeze, even though the rooms were invariably completely closed.

Two trumpets made of parchment paper were used in these séances. Luminous bands had been placed around their larger ends so that their positions could be tracked in the dark. Gradually, after weeks of sittings, the trumpets began to move, at first only three or four inches. Soon they were whizzing around all over the room, banging into the ceiling and walls, their luminescent bands clearly visible high in the air.

Then, at Christmas, came the most exciting event of all. Out of the trumpets flying in the air came the soft, sweet singing of Christmas carols.

After the trumpets found their voices or, rather, after the voices found the trumpets, lots of talking went on, purporting to come from spirits. From time to time an instrument would go up close to the face of one of the sitters, and a soft whisper would come from it. The other members of the group could hardly hear what was said, but it usually brought a message from some deceased relative.

The first time it happened to Julanne, the trumpet came up in front of her face and a low masculine voice was heard from it.

"The voice was speaking to me about my sense of values being wrong," Julanne says. "I went completely dead. I was so surprised I couldn't say a word in response."

So, not receiving an answer, the trumpet went away from her, down toward the floor. Then her vocal cords be-

117

gan to function and she cried, "Wait a minute! Explain to me what you mean!" So it came back up again and continued the discussion. Julanne felt sure it must be her father talking to her, although the voice was not necessarily identifiable. Her mother shared her conviction, for she also received messages from the same voice, which made the appropriate statements her husband would have made to her.

"Being quite young—in my early twenties—I was very impressed by it all," says Julanne. "Every time we went to the sessions after that there were messages supposed to be from my father, coming from the trumpet while the medium was in trance across the room. Yet when I returned home, I usually argued with the evidence. It took even more than that before I was thoroughly convinced."

Isabel Garland gave me her personal sanction of Julanne's story. She added an account of some of the private séances her father held with, as she calls her, Aunt Dora. Isabel said Dora Drane was a lifelong friend of her mother's, and while her father did not attend the sittings away from his home, "we had many, many sittings in Daddy's study on De Mille Drive. It was my husband who made the stiff paper cones that we used for the voices in our sitting, and painted the ends with luminous paint so that we could watch their progress around the room. In the semidark the five of us, Mother, Daddy, Aunt Dora, Hardesty and I, were all quite visible to each other. Those were amazing evenings. As Julie tells in her account, I remember one night the cone came to me and, after some quite clear conversation, came slowly up to me and I felt somebody looking at me very intently. Then the cone moved up to my face and pressed the small end against my cheek. As I said, it was made of stiff drawing paper, but it felt like a soft mouth against my skin. It was all most moving and exciting. Since it took place under test conditions in Daddy's study, there was no possibility of trickery and the question was never asked."

Isabel added that Hamlin Garland had many interesting conversations with various friends and relations who had "crossed over" but he never became convinced of the explanation. The phenomena existed, he affirmed, but he could not accept the spirit hypothesis. "Unexplored biology" he called it and was endlessly fascinated by it right up until his death.

Later Dora moved to Long Beach, and for years occasional meetings were held there in her apartment. Julanne didn't like to make the trip, and so she seldom went when the sessions were there. Once when the meeting was in Long Beach and Julanne did not attend, the great earthquake of 1933 almost decimated the city. Ann Johnston was there, and her daughter was desperate for hours until she learned that her mother was safe. Fortunately, the earthquake had zigzagged away from the apartment building in which the séance was being held, while completely shattering the ones on each side of it.

Dora was in trance at the time, and the shock brought her out of it so traumatically that her psychic powers left her in that moment. She was never able to go into trance again, and no supernormal events ever occurred around her after that.

Had there ever been any question in Julanne's mind of the honesty of the medium, it was completely allayed after Dora lost her powers by what happened in her own home one night. Ann was visiting her daughter and so was Virginia Valli when they decided to try to hold a private séance, just the three of them. They selected Julanne's large walk-in closet as a dark and secluded spot in which to have the cozy session. The radio, broadcasting a program of music live from the Hollywood Bowl, was their accompaniment. Even so, they started with the doxology and

119

said a prayer, as they had been conditioned to do. Then they sat quietly listening to the music.

Suddenly the trumpets went into abandoned activity, bumping into the hat shelf on one side, the clothes hanging on the other, down to the floor and up to the ceiling. Then a trumpet came up to their faces, and they heard voices speaking from it. Virginia was particularly impressed by words which she thought were from her mother.

"Mother, is that you?" she cried. Then she decided to test her.

"Please sing for me the favorite song of ours that we used to sing together," she asked. And from the trumpet came the faint tune of an old familiar hymn. As Virginia mistily joined in and sang with her mother, the other two sat with tears in their eyes and confidence in their hearts that the barrier between the planes of existence had indeed been broken.

15: THE PROFESSIONALS

THE ultimate goal of psychical development is progression toward successful mediumship, although most people who sit for development don't desire to get that far. Incidental to psychic advancement, however, should be spiritual growth. This does not necessarily follow, but it should.

My friend Clarissa Plantamura of La Cañada, California, is a past president of the Southern California Society for Psychical Research and an active worker in the field. Although she is extremely interested in psychical phenomena of all kinds, she is not a Spiritualist. Her late husband's grandfather, though, founded the Spiritualist community of Summerland, California, and he entertained all the leading mediums of his day on his nearby ranch.

Clarissa well remembers "Aunt Nona," his daughter, who had met all those who visited her father, saying what a shock it was to her as a young girl to realize that there was no necessary connection between being psychic and being spiritual. Nona discovered, she said, that some of the greatest mediums were some of the greatest rascals, drunks or liars. She well remembered one whose control was a pirate who would not hesitate to beat up or rob the sitters. Frequently after his séances, when the lights went on, some of the men had black eyes, and their wallets and watches were missing.

It is indeed possible to develop ESP without putting

121

God into it; but the converse—psychics of the type who consort with invisible pirates or black witches or spirits of any negative turn of mind—is to be deplored. As long as there are any dishonest mediums, those who are genuine, sincere, and hardworking are usually tarred with the brush of fakery in the eyes of the public. For this reason the Spiritualist movement itself should clean out all undesirables and set high standards of mediumship.

Another unfortunate disadvantage of mediocre mediumship is that the sensitive is not likely to attract a high type of spirit to be his guide. If he is not willing to work long and hard at his development, he will interest only spirits whose level of achievement is similar to his own. No matter how great a "master" or "teacher" those who speak through many mediums claim to be, they will usually be found to mouth only platitudes. Nothing really worthwhile comes through a sensitive who is at any time guilty of fraud. Neither will much of value come through those who, even though not actually deliberate fakes, are consistently giving less than adequate performances.

Perhaps as much as anything, because of the Superman concept, the example set the world by many mediums today is not necessarily a good one. Some are wise and peaceful souls, but more of them are not. Because they have been satisfied with a little talent, they have often gone into their occupation only half-trained. It is the custom for one who has had frequent spontaneous psi experiences in his youth or who begins in maturity to show psychic potentialities to sit for development for a brief while and then go out on his own professionally. There is no real improvement of his highest capabilities but only his clairvoyance and possibly his ability to go into trance and allow spirits of any old kind to speak through him. Many ministers who have their own churches, who revel in the adulation they receive from their congregations, give less than half of what they are capable of giving. Content if they can transmit a few brief messages identifiable by their sitters, they brag about having made any hits at all instead of trying for 80 or 90 percent accuracy. It is just a matter of having given up too soon in their training and being satisfied with less than their best.

Most mediums, no matter how naturally talented, should sit for development for a long time if they wish to become professionals. Through development, those who were merely routinely psychic to begin with have turned into genuine sensitives. And those born with a quantity of talent have become great. The fact is that no matter how good a medium one is naturally, in order to attain professional caliber he must work hard and long.

Gladys Osborne Leonard was a natural-born medium who had psi experiences from her childhood. It was not until she was a young woman, however, that she discovered her potential and decided to try to become a trance medium. She didn't anticipate how much effort it would entail before she was ready to go professional; but her guides made her practice for seven years before they would admit she was competent. At the end of that time she could go into so deep a trance that she could be controlled by successions of spirits who were able to bring striking evidence of their own personalities.

Once, for instance, the spirit of an elderly Scottish gentleman maintained unusually strong control of Gladys for forty minutes. He spoke throughout in robust and fully audible tones of a surprisingly masculine quality, interrupted at intervals by paroxysms of coughing and wheezing characteristic of the bronchial asthma which had afflicted him during his lifetime. The entire effect was unquestionably that of a masculine sufferer. Except for the wheezing, the voice didn't seem strained or forced, and Mrs. Leonard awoke with no signs of exhaustion. She entered immediately into conversation without a trace of hoarseness and appeared as devoid of all cough or chest obstruction as before the sitting. Naturally, no entity could keep such a control unless the medium was highly trained.

Many people who visit professional mediums have to be satisfied with poor performances, because the sensitive gave up before he was truly ready and started trying to make money out of a very meager talent.

Arthur Ford said about this, "Halting, broken messages, clumsily phrased, wooden, without the flair of the personality of the source communicator—these things are the mark of the tyro, but they are almost inevitable while the new medium is learning his trade. Imagine, if you can, moving into an entirely strange body (as control) and trying, even in a limited way to operate it. Wouldn't it take you a while to learn where the gadgets were? Or, on the earth side, imagine vacating your own body and turning it over to be inhabited for a time by somebody else. A certain amount of mutual accommodation is involved, a certain protocol. This has to be learned."

No matter what form of mediumship is considered, in most cases we can presume that some spirit entity is trying to communicate his thoughts through a human mind. And the statements made are invariably qualified and the ideas colored by the mentality and personal convictions of the medium. The ability to receive and transmit the precise meaning intended depends on the degree of rapport with which hearts, souls and minds contact each other. Thus a medium who is spiritually advanced is more receptive to the higher philosophy which comes through from advanced spirits; a mediocre medium with only mundane thoughts hampers such reception, and usually only uninspired concepts can be transmitted through him.

As Harry Edwards, the great British healer, says in *The Hands of a Healer,* "If a violin is of poor quality a master musician can only obtain from it the best it can give."

The deeper the trance, of course, the less the medium intrudes into the messages. Mediums today do not always

124

go into trance, even light ones. It used to be thought necessary to acquire a deep sleep state in order for control to occur and good evidence to be produced. It is true that the deeper the sleep, the less coloring occurs. But mediums don't like to go into deep trance and the present trend is away from it. In fact, Mrs. Leonard told me that if she had it all to do over, she would never have become a trance medium. She said she had missed too much of the fun that way. Being always asleep while working, she never knew what was going on until after the sitting was over, and then only if the sitter chose to tell her. The only way she even held conversations with her control, Feda, was through an intermediary who told her whatever messages Feda had sent to her while she was in trance.

An amusing instance of this sort of thing occurred to Arthur Ford shortly before he died. He said he was asked by three astronauts from a moon flight, I believe it was Apollo 11, to hold a séance for them at his home in Miami. Ford went into trance, and his control, Fletcher, talked to the men for a long time, presumably explaining to them certain phenomena they had witnessed on their space trip.

When the interview was over and Arthur came out of his trance, he asked, "Well, what did Fletcher say?"

"Sorry, that's classified information," he was told, as the astronauts snatched their tape from the recorder and hurried out.

Most mediums of the present era can learn to go into a trancelike state in which their conscious minds are withdrawn enough that they don't get too much in the way of the communications; and yet they are still awake, so much so that they are aware of what is being said through them. They also often relay messages while they are completely conscious, the words or pictures coming into their minds clairvoyantly and then being repeated orally. The way this may occur is described for us by professional clairvoyant

Mary Tallmadge: "At times, but not very often, I will be controlled by the communicating intelligence, although I am awake and aware of what is going on. This usually occurs without any conscious knowledge on my part that it is about to happen. I am then in very close harmony with the communicator, so that he can take over my vocal cords and physical actions as I am controlled."

During the time Mary sat for trance development many entities attempted to control her. Among them were a Southern woman named Julie, a New England farmer, a black man, a Scotsman, an Englishman, and others with accents peculiar to their countries or areas of the United States.

"My voice took on their tone and accent when they spoke through me," Miss Tallmadge says. "As the Scotsman became more proficient, his brogue became thicker. Once I was controlled by a man who felt my upper lip and wanted to know where his mustache was. Another time I shook unmercifully as if I had some kind of palsy. My voice took on various ranges from very high female to very deep male.

"I found all this very tiring and would wish they would go. I found myself mentally trying to eject them; but they would try to hold on, even when I wished them out. I don't like trance. I feel less confident when being controlled by an unseen entity than I do when I am giving readings and feel more the master of the situation.

"When I first began doing trance work, I thought I must be a very good actress because I could assume so many roles. It seemed that some trick of my mind must be creating these characters. But when the people for whom I was sitting recognized them as someone they knew, I began to feel differently about it.

"I found that I was having a battle of minds with these entities, my mind interfering with their minds so that any messages given when I was conscious of what was being

126

said must have been a blending of two minds. Of course, the deeper I was in trance, the more my own conscious mind would abate and I would have very little recollection of what had been said. This is a far better state, I believe, for trance work."

Two splendid and charming people who have developed their psychic sensitivity almost to the point where they could be professional mediums if they wished are David and Rosalind McKnight, who live on a hilltop in the Shenandoah Valley of Virginia. David teaches English and an adult education course in ESP at a nearby community college. They met in 1964 at Union Theological Seminary in New York City, where they were both working for Bachelor of Divinity degrees. They dated during their last year at Union, were graduated in the same ceremony in 1967, and were married two years later. Becoming interested in spirit communication through attending ARE and Spiritual Frontiers Fellowship meetings, they began to attend development classes led by British medium Katie King after she moved to New York. (This is not the original famous Katie King, who was an apparition, but a prominent sensitive with the same name.)

In these classes, David told me, "We soon both began to experience trance condition, or overshadowing, and learned the way in which entities from other realms can influence one's gestures, thoughts and words. Rosie was the first to experience this phenomenon and was being influenced by personalities clearly of a high origin." Then one evening they were amazed to "meet" a person who has become a source of wonder and warmth to them. Rosie was in a light trance state when a young man with strong musical interests came through. He spoke with Rosie's vocal cords in a very low bass voice. "This amazing and amusing voice," David says, "is easily recognizable to all of our friends now as 'Ralfonzo,' as we inaccurately came to call him. He said, actually, that his name

127

was Alfonso Vicinilli, that he had been something of a musical child prodigy in Italy early in the last century, especially playing and composing for the pianolike instrument of the day. He stated that he died in his late teens in a carriage accident on his way to a musical festival in Rome, but has since been composing and playing, sometimes with other like-minded musicians, in a much more expressive and fulfilling world. He further explained that he desired, always with Rosie's permission, to play the piano 'through her' for the benefit of others. Since then, Rosie has allowed 'Ralph' to play on a number of occasions to interested groups. There are sometimes mistakes, particularly since Rosie always has her eyes closed when she is in the trance state in which Ralfonzo communicates through her. Rosie had several years of piano lessons as a girl, but she is in no sense of the word an accomplished pianist and has been unable to duplicate Ralfonzo's playing in a normal state."

I personally heard Ralfonzo play, and his music is fascinating. It is almost modern, rather wild and far-out, and yet at the same time melodious and most pleasing.

David went on, "We are anxious to confirm Ralph's historical existence and began our search two summers ago when we were in Italy for several days. Though we have not met with success yet, we have been cautioned that such investigative work is sometimes difficult and long-drawn-out, and we don't plan to give up. Interestingly, Rosie was one day doing some automatic writing—in which she has become quite proficient—and the communicator instructed us that he desired to put on paper some of Ralph's music! He then proceeded to draw strange triangular and squarish notes. A little research soon after at the Juilliard School of Music library revealed that such notes were characteristic of the period when Ralph stated that he had lived in Italy.

"Many sensitives have since spoken of and said they

could see Ralfonzo, describing him with striking agreement. This has encouraged us to believe in his reality—although I'm afraid we have come to do so anyway! In the meantime, Rosie hopes to let Ralph practice playing through her much more in the future than she has had time to do in the past. And Ralph continues to delight nearly all who hear him play—and listen to him speak, often with a wonderful sense of humor, of the serious purpose of his music, and of all life."

16: SUCCESSFUL
PARAPSYCHOLOGICAL
WITNESS

IT is possible for an individual to be a medium and still consider himself a parapsychologist. A natural-born psychic who is keenly aware of the need for scientific research and evidence is Kay Sterner of San Diego, California.

I had several "now it can be told" interviews with Kay in the spring of 1971. On other occasions when I have been with her she has always been reluctant to talk about herself, her California Parapsychology Foundation being the principal subject of her thoughts and her conversation. Now, however, she is ready to admit that her own psychic sensitivity for physical phenomena is of imminent concern to her.

"Long ago I realized," Kay told me, "that, with my background in education and psychology, there would be no possible way for me to go into parapsychology unless it was strictly scientific. However, I have seen apparitions and materializations all my life. I come from a family who had this ability, and my daughter and her little son also have it. Yet who would have believed me initially if I had spent my time developing the *physical* aspects of my mediumship? All the same arguments would have been heard against my honesty and dependability that are heard about most other mediums. No, I had to establish my reputation as an objective researcher first."

This she has done. Because of her determined perseverance and unrelenting faith, her California Parapsychology Foundation has gained a worldwide reputation sponsoring experimentation in ESP and related phenomena, and she has been acclaimed as a psychometrist who has willingly given her time unstintingly to research. Now she feels she can spend her efforts on her own development of physical mediumship so that she will be able to lend her talents to research in this direction as well. Actually, Kay says she is not so much "developing" her psi capabilities in a new direction as allowing them to "surface," for they have always been there. Hopefully she will be able to produce under controlled conditions the same type of manifestations that have always occurred to her spontaneously. This, she believes, would produce evidence for survival, which is her main interest.

The first specific memory Mrs. Sterner had of seeing an apparition (or materialization, as she prefers to call it) occurred in Akron, Ohio, when she was eight years old. Although she may have seen many of them before that, she was unaware that they were not ordinary sights that everyone saw. But when she was eight, she remembers waking in the middle of the night and seeing a figure all in gossamer white leaning over her. She presumed it was her mother, although her mother's homemade, heavy, striped flannelette nightgowns could in no way be mistaken for the glowing whiteness that surrounded this entity. She spoke to it, but it did not respond, turning away and retreating through the door instead.

"I thought this was strange, so I asked Mother about it the next morning," says Kay. "She had not been in my room; but she didn't want to encourage my seeing apparitions because her own similar talent had given her such a bad time. She was a Catholic, and as she later told me when I was grown and she and I compared notes on our experiences, when she had asked a priest about these manifestations of hers, he replied they were evil spirits

131

and that she was obsessed by the devil. It was horrible what she went through! When I told her similar things then and played with my dolls as if there were someone else there with us, she realized I had the same sensitivity. She didn't want me to go through what she had, so whenever I would tell her about anything I'd experienced, she would remain silent or else shoo me out of the house."

Yet as a child and later as a teen-ager, Kay could envision things that had an uncanny way of coming true. And she continued to see the materializations. Even after she was grown, she saw entities, wearing garments of their era and country and always in full color, who were so real she could even see their facial pores; but for a long time she didn't know what they were.

"One thing must always be borne in mind," Kay told me. "I saw apparitions before I knew anything about such things."

It might have been the same gossamer-white figure she saw as a child who appeared to her one night after she was grown. She awoke and thought she saw a big sheet floating up toward the ceiling. Then the sheet divided, and she saw a fully garbed nun, as if suspended from the ceiling, her coif and robes gleaming. The white sheet that she saw, she now believes, was ectoplasm drawn from her own body.

Another night Kay woke up about 3:00 A.M. and saw something in front of her. She had the feeling it might be a man, but it was not completely formed and could also have been an animal, it looked so weird. She was frightened, then prayerfully asked whatever it was to show itself properly to her. It filled in and began to speak, revealing itself to be a flyer who had been killed in the Korean War. He had on his goggles and oxygen mask—no wonder he looked so outlandish!

Mrs. Sterner has also had experiences with the ghosts of animals. When her Doberman pinscher, Lady, had to be put to sleep because of a malignancy in her mammary glands, Kay and her husband grieved. Two days later, while hanging clothes out to dry, she looked behind her and to her great surprise saw Lady, as if in life, with her nose buried in the trash can. Her coat appeared to be glossy and sleek, and her mammary glands were no longer swollen and distended. In a moment she disappeared without having even glanced in her owner's direction. Kay almost felt hurt at her pet's seeming unconcern, until her husband told her that on the dog's death he had put her feeding dish into the trash. So Kay believes that Lady, not understanding that she had died, was looking for food.

The cat they called Boy was particularly enjoyable to them because of his purr, which they maintained was the loudest in town. He was injured so badly that he, too, had to be put to sleep, and Kay hoped he would be able to show himself to her as Lady had. One night she was lying face-down on the bed when she felt something jump up beside her, just as her cat so often did. It walked across the bed and snuggled beside her on the pillow, sticking its nose near her ear and purring just as noisily as Boy had always done. Kay felt the animal in all respects, but because of her position she couldn't see him. She attempted to move, but this evidently disturbed the cat so that it couldn't hold its manifestation, and it disappeared.

Kay was born in Steelton, Pennsylvania, of immigrant parents, Henry and Katie Schmidt. The family soon moved to Akron, Ohio, where she and her sister grew up. She attended Akron University and then Columbia in New York. She also studied music at Juilliard. She then returned and taught in the public schools in Akron, at which time she became particularly interested in clinical psychology. As a psychologist analyzing her own unusual experiences, she decided she was dreaming or hallucinating. And yet she knew it was neither. Eventually she said to herself, "Dear God, what I'm seeing could be what they

133

call spirits!" This was so unthinkable to a psychologist that she totally rejected it.

A long time later, about fifteen years ago, at a Unitarian Church in San Diego, California, Kay met Paul Harris and his wife. Harris, an English author of books on Spiritualism under the nom de plume of Paul Miller, recognized her at once as what she was, a psychic.

"He said the strangest things to me," she says. "He told me that he could tell by my eyes that I was psychic and could hear voices and know the future. 'How does he know such things?' I wondered. He reassured me that I had nothing to be afraid of and said to still my mind and ask for guidance. He later gave me some books to read that I was embarrassed to open because of my strongly critical bent."

But she did read them, and she tried to still her mind to learn what was happening to her. During this she began to feel as if she didn't have a body. Then she saw a white form that emerged into a man who stood before her, short in stature, dark-brown eyes, strong features. She was to learn that he was from India, and she saw him often, for he was a spirit collaborator of hers. Her room lighted up with the glory of the moment, and a transcendental love flooded her entire being. Later, trying to rationalize what had happened, she realized that she might never understand it, but she could no longer *deny* it.

"I had no answer for it," she says, "but that was the turning point."

As Kay Sterner began to study in this field, a group of like-minded people assembled around her, and they formed an organization called the San Diego Parapsychology Study Group, which met Sunday afternoons at Balboa Park and talked about psychical phenomena. As the group grew, it began to include ministers and professors from the numerous local colleges, as well as many intensely dedicated laymen. Two years later, in August, 1957, they incorporated into the California Parapsychology Foundation, a nonprofit, educational and research organization with offices and lecture rooms at 3580 Adams Avenue. It was formed to afford a broader scope and a wider range of activities and to encourage research in ESP and psychical phenomena; its growth was encouraged by such leaders as Dr. J. B. Rhine and Eileen J. Garrett.

In the years since then the CPF has sponsored many research projects, and there is hardly a prominent person lecturing in the field who has not spoken to its San Diego membership at least once. It has become so well known that in the southern part of California the word "parapsychology" is thought by the public to mean Kay's group. Most people, even those in the know, refer to her organization as Parapsychology and nothing more.

As Kay began to receive impressions or advice from those she believed to be unseen intelligences assisting in her work, she asked them if she should not develop her own potential mediumship. She was told that she could not further the work of the foundation and her own unusual abilities as well. It was suggested that for her to establish the foundation solidly as a genuinely scientifically oriented organization would give her more of a background for later work she could do with her own psychic abilities. However a number of scientists and professors at various universities pushed her into their research work, as a guinea pig in psychometry.

During the years she has been tested for psychometry by various researchers and professors, she has had some exceptional results. She usually holds an object belonging to a member of the audience. It must be something that has been touched by his skin, often a wristwatch. The vibrations from this seem to tell her facts about him.

In February and March, 1969, Kay met with forty-six members of the Psi Study Group in a series of controlled experiments at the foundation headquarters. Each person was to take part in two sessions, two weeks apart. During the meetings, Mrs. Sterner touched an object belonging to each person, one at a time. While handling it, she gave impressions of present or past events relating to the owner, as well as events that might be precognitive. Members of the groups were asked to take notes, in duplicate, of all these statements, leaving the original with the foundation for purposes of evaluation. On these notes, they were to table all items relating to the past or present as true or false and identify precognitive items with the letter *k*. Approximately eight months later Mrs. Victoria Baker made follow-ups to determine what precognition had occurred by then. Since this was an empirical study, the results cannot be considered scientifically precise; however, in spite of many factors that could not be exactly controlled, the results are interesting.

Kay Sterner sensed a total of 178 past or present occurrences to 33 of the 37 percipients, ranging from none for three people to a high of 17 for one person. In all but seven cases she scored 100 percent accuracy; only with one person was she 50 percent inaccurate. The overall percentages were 95.5 percent correct, only 4.5 percent wrong. Summarizing the precognitive items, we find a total of 170 statements made to 35 of the 37 people. Of these, 80, or 47.3 percent, had come to pass by the time the check was made. Seventy-seven, or 45.2 percent, were still future possibilities. This left only 13 items, or 7.5 percent, which should have occurred by the date of the replies but had not.

It was due to the CPF that Dr. Milan Ryzl, biochemist, physicist, and internationally noted Czech parapsychologist, taught a three-unit accredited course, "An Introduction to Parapsychology," in the fall semester of 1969 at San Diego State College, Extension Division. This was, according to Kay, the first three-unit accredited course in parapsychology in this country. As early as 1964, James

T. Mullin, pioneer member of the research committee, included a study of parapsychology in his various philosophy classes at City College, Mesa College, San Diego State College Experimental Department, and accredited night classes for adult education at Hoover High School. He also conducted a three-unit accredited course in parapsychology at the University of California in San Diego, Extension Division, in the spring quarter, 1970.

On April 6, 1970, Instructor Mullin supervised an experiment in psychometry under test conditions at his UCSD extention class. Token objects worn by participants were placed in unmarked sealed envelopes. The results showed that Kay made a total of 43 past and present statements to eleven women. Of these, 37, or 86 percent, were true; 6, or fourteen percent, were marked false.

At Redlands University, near Riverside, California, Kay Sterner had two particularly interesting occurrences. There she spoke to nearly four hundred people, including students, faculty, and the public. She discussed primarily her recent year-long around-the-world tour when she had lectured for and been interviewed and tested by numerous university groups and psychical researchers. Then she gave a demonstration in psychometry.

Holding an envelope in which an object had been placed, she said, "I have something here belonging to a student with dark hair. But although he is young, in his early twenties, he has the beginning of a receding forehead. I see him smoking an unusual type of pipe." She described it. Then she stopped. She always makes a point to reassure her audiences that she won't say anything that will embarrass them, so she decided not to pursue the pipe bit any further for fear the youth had been smoking pot. He gave her no chance to continue, however. Running down the aisle, he was holding out the very pipe she had just described.

"You were a hundred percent correct," he said, "and I

137

don't mind for you to see that I'm dark-haired and have a receding hairline." Then he rushed out of the hall, accompanied by a roar of amusement from the audience.

On another occasion during this demonstration Kay revealed the quirk psychometrists sometimes run into of reading information from the mind of one person that belongs to another. She described a lady whose watch she had been given and said she was a professor. The woman acknowledged the identification. Then Kay spoke of a red Volkswagen and said that her mother was ill and would be going to the hospital.

"Do you want me to continue?" Kay asked, and the lady professor agreed, although she did not identify the car and said that her mother wasn't sick. Kay felt that the mother would die, and she told this, even though the woman claimed none of it. Kay wondered if it might be thought transference and asked if someone seated next to her accepted the information, but no one did.

The next day, however, the professor wrote to Kay and told her that after she thought about it, it occurred to her that her hairdresser drove a red bug and that she had just been to the beauty shop before coming to the meeting. She recalled also that her hairdresser had mentioned that her mother was sick. Following this up, Kay learned that the mother had gone to the hospital, where she later died.

Perhaps the most exciting of all Kay's research has been done with hauntings, San Diego's Whaley House being the best example. The oldest brick house in southern California, it was constructed in May, 1857, by Thomas Whaley, merchant prince and very solid citizen. At one time in its varied career since then, it was the San Diego Courthouse, at another time the jail. In its heyday, many visitors enjoyed the hospitality of the Whaley House, including Presidents Ulysses S. Grant and William Henry Harrison. Kay Sterner picked this up psychically on her second visit, saying that people of state had at one time been visitors there. Located in what is known as Old Town, the Whaley House is now a museum.

In recent years neighbors have been busy calling the police because the burglar alarm keeps ringing at night. The fact that the windows, which automatically trigger the alarm when they fly open, have always been bolted every night with three four-inch bolts on each side apparently does nothing to keep the spooks who allegedly continue to inhabit the house from opening them frequently. Screams, footsteps, and other noises have been heard upstairs when no physical being was up there, and various other signs of infestation have continued over the years.

Prior to Kay's initial visit to the Whaley House, accompanied by her secretary, who took notes of everything she said, she knew practically nothing about the place. The first time she went there it was sunset and the museum was already closed. She walked around the south side of the building and immediately saw an objective picture of a primitive, spectral scaffold with a man hanging from it. Her impression was later corroborated by Mrs. June Reading, the director of the museum, who informed her that nearly ten years before the house was built, a sailor called Yankee Jim Robinson jumped ship, helped himself to the pilot boat for a ride around the bay, and was captured. Because the pilot boat was valued at $6,500, he was charged with grand larceny and summarily sentenced and hanged. There has been controversy since then about the fairness of this, and Yankee Jim seems to be one of the main contenders. He was quite justifiably the first of the midnight stalkers Kay saw.

Continuing around to the rear of the house on that first visit, the sensitive happened to glance up just in time to see a gaudily dressed woman with a garishly painted face leaning out a second-story window. It was later revealed that in November, 1868, the second floor of the house had been leased to a theatrical organization known as The Tanner Troupe.

Almost immediately, however, another vision blotted out the painted actress. A woman in a mauve gown was peering far out the window, staring down at Kay. On her second visit, when she spent some time inside, Kay identified the same gown on a mannequin in one of the bedrooms. It had been made by one of the Whaley daughters for her sister. This person, then, could be identified as either of the Whaley girls, Lillian or Violet. It is significant to Kay that, of all the apparitions she saw there, this lavender lady was one of only two who appeared actually to be cognizant individuals, aware of her presence. All the others were those typical haunting ghosts who seem to be more like picturizations than real surviving entities. "Memory images in the atmosphere," or "psychological marionettes," or "veridical afterimages," they have been called by psychical researchers trying to find the answer for this type of ghost, which seems to be nothing more than a moving picture of the past somehow continuing to be shown in the atmosphere for psychic people to observe.

Among this latter type of haunt, Kay clearly saw on subsequent visits to the Whaley House rowdy, rough seafaring men, gaudy women, a tall, rugged man wearing dark clothing, vest and dusty boots, and an attractive young woman wearing a well-made gown and carrying an old-fashioned open razor with a whalebone handle, who she later learned had actually killed herself.

She also observed a grisly murder as it was given an instant replay for her. The event started with the reenactment of a violent quarrel between a Mexican man and a dark-haired young woman wearing a colorful blouse and long, ruffled skirt, whom he appeared to be accusing of unfaithfulness. Then Kay experienced the horror of seeing him slash the woman with a knife, practically disemboweling her. Mrs. Reading later revealed that at one time a

140

Mexican couple were tenants and that the husband had murdered his wife after a bitter quarrel.

On another occasion a stocky man wearing boots and limping from what must have been a leg injury came toward Kay carrying a logbook in his hand. He appeared to be disturbed, and Kay picked up the fact that he was upset about a case he had adjudicated; also she felt that he was a very scrupulous man.

June Reading told her that her description matched that of Squire A. R. Ensworth, who had been Mr. Whaley's lawyer and business manager, also a magistrate. He was the type to be gravely concerned over his cases. June also revealed that Squire Ensworth had fallen into a hole on the property and broken his leg. It had never been properly set. Sometime later he went to Los Angeles for treatment but died of gangrene. There are, incidentally, more than twenty thousand documents on file pertaining to the Whaley House. Kay wonders if some of her psychic information came from them.

She saw numerous other ghosts on her visits, all seemingly oblivious to her presence except the lavender-decked Whaley daughter previously mentioned and one unidentified gentleman, wearing a black suit and a stiff, very high white collar, who bowed to her and smiled.

Kay had another interesting experience with a ghost (or materialization) when she first arrived in Egypt on her around-the-world tour. Having decided to do a bit of sight-seeing before she announced herself to the psychical researchers with whom she was to work for three months, she felt psychically led to Tent City, where the tourist stays overnight in excellent accommodations inside a tent.

"It was impossible for anybody to come into my tent unless he was permitted to," Kay says, "but about 3:00 A.M. I awoke and found a man looking into my face. He was obviously a Pharaonic king, for he wore a high-crowned headdress of gold, brilliant white robes with

141

elaborate ornaments, and much jewelry. He held a scepter in his hand and looked kindly. He was young, of the Mediterranean type, short, with brown eyes and dark skin." She held the picture of this apparition in her mind and told her parapsychological associates about him later. They readily accepted his advent and assured her that because of his youth they suspected it was King Tut-ankh-amen.

"Why should a king come to me?" Kay asked. She always asks questions and prays continuously to understand what is going on with her and with others who have her unusual potential.

"How can you study the nature of man and exclude materializations?" she asked. "In fact, no student of this field should exclude from his research any of what we call mediumistic phenomena. We must examine all of it."

An experience that occurs spontaneously to children is bound to be perfectly normal and natural, even if it is rare, and it should be investigated thoroughly, Kay believes. When her daughter Alma's husband died as a young man, Mark, his five-year-old son, was not informed. Yet the child noticed the excitement and explained it to his mother. "I know," he said. "My daddy died." From time to time ever since he has said, "I saw my daddy. He came and covered me up in the night." Nobody has ever mentioned in his presence or told him personally the possibility that the dead might continue to live and reappear. The child knew nothing about it. And yet he admitted to Kay experiences the same as those she has had all her life. Just recently he said to her, "My daddy and grandpa were in the room and my daddy covered me up."

Kay asked him, "Which grandpa?"

"Grandpa Sterner," he replied.

Shortly after that at about dusk the boy was out on the sidewalk playing a game with a ball and a paddle. When

142

he came in, he said to his grandmother, "My daddy was there and he held his hand out to me."

Kay said, "Mark, did you see him like in life?" He looked puzzled. "Did you see him like you're seeing me?"

"Of course!" answered the child.

Despite such incidents as this, even the most active researchers find that they cannot entirely accept apparitions and materializations, and so they play them down all the time. That's why Kay Sterner is hoping to develop physical phenomena so that she will at least be able to produce a few good forms that can be examined under test conditions.

"I'm a very practical person," she says, "a realist as well as an idealist. I hope these qualities can help me produce phenomena that will be of value to research."

Kay sits regularly with a group of six or seven persons who have some ability at physical manifestations. This will help all of them build up their powers.

"I predict," she says, "that we're going to develop some fine physical mediums, and we will do it under such controlled conditions that people will have to take us seriously when we produce phenomena."

17: PHYSICAL PHENOMENA

IT is safe to say that most of what passes for professional physical mediumship today is fraudulent. I don't doubt that occasional genuine phenomena can be provided by some physical mediums, but I'm sure it would cost a lot to get them to do it. To go into deep trance is just too much trouble for those who can receive ample funds from sufficient numbers of people who are satisfied by phony acts.

In home circles and development classes physical phenomena are often produced, however. If you should be informed by his guides that one of your circle members is being developed for physical mediumship, by all means encourage him, seek advice from the guides as to the procedures that will help his progress, and attempt to carry out any suggestions received.

In home circles I have seen, among other things, trumpets move about without any obvious means of support. I have felt cool breezes in a completely closed room. I have also heard loud and rhythmic banging on a coffee table in accompaniment to the crowd's brisk singing. With this much personal experience to go on, I am willing to accept the reports of friends like Julanne Johnston and the historical testimony of the many competent researchers who claimed to have seen and heard exciting manifestations.

An excellent example of the kinds of carefully observed

144

and evaluated phenomena that may be produced in home circles was published in the *Parapsychology Review,* November-December, 1971. Titled "Séances with Dr. R. G. Medhurst" by Benson Herbert, the article gave details of sittings at the homes of the late Dr. Medhurst and Mr. Herbert over a period of years. Because they revealed phenomena similar to the type any development class may be lucky enough to experience if physical mediums are being developed, I will report the case in some detail.

From the start, Medhurst and Herbert decided not to use professional mediums but to invite as sitters only their personal friends. During the evenings they played records of atmospheric music by Moeran, Stravinsky, Holst, and similar composers; they found it helpful to maintain a relaxed party atmosphere.

Herbert writes: "We used total blackout, with a red light of controllable intensity available as required, and sat regularly each Thursday evening, for a session of two hours during which our target was physical phenomena, followed by a coffee break of half an hour, and ending with another two-hour session in which we concentrated upon trance phenomena (with us, the two types did not seem to occur simultaneously, it was usually either one or the other). The sitters, usually four, were varied from time to time in the hope of finding the optimum grouping."

For the first six months nothing happened and after that there were only slight movements of the table on which their hands rested lightly. See what I told you about patience! Theirs was rewarded when finally the table began to tilt and spell out messages. Entities then introduced themselves and took charge of the séances, telling them what experiments to carry out.

"Once physical phenomena had commenced in total darkness, they would continue with only slight diminution in good red light, and would also continue if each sitter left the room in turn. It was as if some influence had attached itself to the room, independently of any particular sitter. In between sittings, movements of objects occasionally took place, sometimes in broad daylight," Herbert said.

On one occasion the sitters sat around a table in one corner of the room, in red light, and both saw and heard a second table, in the opposite corner, over fifteen feet away, tilt by itself and deliver intelligible messages. On another occasion, four of them, including George Medhurst and his wife, Sylvia, were sitting around a table in darkness and discovered that instead of eight hands on the table, there were apparently nine hands. The extra hand was located between Herbert and Sylvia. Sylvia volunteered to pass her fingers along the extra hand to determine if it were attached to anyone. She gave a running commentary as she did so, stating that the hand felt cold and clammy. She felt as far as the wrist, then screamed, exclaiming that the hand ended at that point and was not attached to anything—there was no arm. The scream alarmed the fourth sitter, who turned away from the table to switch on the light behind him; at the same time they heard a curious slithering sound, suggestive of rubber, and they thought the hand was being drawn away from the table. As the light came on, they could see nothing unusual. A search revealed no rubber glove or apparatus, nor would there have been time for anyone to conceal such because no one knew the lights would be turned on.

A substantial rectangular table about four feet by two feet was involved in some levitations. It would remain a few inches above the floor, undulating slightly, while each of the sitters in turn crawled under the table with a flashlight and passed their fingers below the four legs to satisfy themselves that all the legs were off the ground at the same time, and that no one had his thumbs hooked beneath the edge of the table or was supporting it with one knee under the table or one foot under a leg of the table.

One night they had a newcomer, a girl of unusually stout proportions, known to all as "the fattest girl in Chelsea"; her weight was indeed prodigious. They laid her flat on the table and asked two of the men to try to lift her. They were barely able to raise her the slightest bit and had to stand up to do that. Yet after they had turned off the main light and left only a dim red lamp glowing, the table, with her on it, eventually rose as usual about four inches from the floor, while all sitters remained seated, for as long as two minutes.

Herbert went on: "Other physical phenomena included a sound as of birds winging their way over our heads. On turning on the light, we found that an entire ream of paper, originally on a shelf, had fluttered over our heads sheet by sheet, dispersing themselves over the floor in the opposite corner. Cushions would occasionally fly in circular motion around the table, behind our backs, as discovered when one of us groped behind his chair on hearing a swishing noise, and the cushions touched his hand as they passed by. On some occasions, the flights of furniture became so violent that we were obliged to take shelter behind a sofa. I did not dodge quickly enough, and a chair struck my head, breaking a tooth, this being the only case of personal injury."

Another evening Benson Herbert bumped into someone (in red light). He said, "Oops—sorry!" Then he realized that everyone else in the room was some distance from him. He turned around quickly to see whom he had collided with, and no one was there.

"During this period," he says, "it was not surprising that the table suffered bad damage; and it was our habit, at the end of each sitting, to stand around the battered remains of the table, without touching it, and watch it slowly and spectacularly break itself up completely, so that finally all the legs were wrenched off and the table split. Each week the table had to be rebuilt. This period was at the peak of activity and lasted about six weeks."

Eerie sounds of different sorts were commonplace, as well as raps on the table and from parts of the room beyond their reach.

There were other phenomena too numerous to mention, but after a long time the principal control stated that he had to leave them and said good-bye. From that moment no further manifestations of any note took place.

18: SLATE WRITING BY SLADE

MANY interesting phenomena occurred in the past century that are almost unheard of today. We're too sophisticated for them. Even the words "slate writing" cause scorn because we know it is so easy to fake that we presume it is *always* faked.

In the past, the small school slates children used were found to be very successful items for spirits purportedly to use to give written evidence of their presence. The slates were usually held under a table, with a piece of chalk on top of them. The sound of writing would be heard, and then the slate would be drawn out with a message on it. It is so easy to substitute another slate with a previously written message on it for the blank one under the table that slate writing is almost never taken seriously today. Even the great Henry Slade, an American medium who made a sensation in Europe in the 1870's, was accused of slate fakery and brought to trial.

Professor Johann C. F. Zollner's report in *Transcendental Physics* reveals, however, that Slade was later able to produce fantastic manifestations in the light under controlled conditions. And he was honest enough to say that he was too tired to work when he felt unable to. It hardly seems likely that such a man would try to fake his fantastic feats at other times. Just the fact that he was tried in court has ruined his reputation historically, though, as it did the reputations of various other mediums.

149

Perhaps this is part of the reason so few people attempt to develop physical mediumship today. They suspect from the beginning that no one is ever going to believe them. I hope this condition will change, but it will improve only when such strong mediumship is developed that tests can be made in the light, with the medium's hands and feet either tied or held tightly. After all, whether or not any genuine phenomena of this kind will ever prove survival, as Kay Sterner hopes, they definitely prove that some supernormal activity is occurring. It is activity that does not follow the natural laws we know. What laws does it follow? It will take many more physical mediums than we now have to help us learn this.

A recent editorial in the bulletin of the Southern California Society for Psychical Research points out the trouble so many researchers have had because they have staunchly stood up for certain mediums and their manifestations. The editorial starts: "At a recent gathering of the Society, one member, on mention of Sir William Crookes, remarked, 'But you really have to discount his investigations. After all, Katie King [the alleged materialization he spent some time investigating] was found to be an imposter.' So much for Sir William Crookes! Actually, any such statement rests on a firm foundation of quicksand."

Such implications can ruin a researcher's reputation, even if they are false accusations. The editorial goes on: "But the whole affair only proves that untrue, or even partially untrue, charges against a medium are almost universally believed, while the retraction of the charges or the disproving of them goes unnoticed. Like gossip, people are quick to believe the worst and are very reluctant to listen to the explanations. Perhaps it has something to do with wish fulfillment."

It also seems true that most people are afraid of the unknown. They will jump at any straws to try to prove the

150

unreality of supernormal phenomena. On top of this is the fact that many physical manifestations are definitely spurious. Even those mediums who are able to produce apports, for instance, or other curiosities are likely to put on fraudulent acts if they think their audiences are the types who can be duped. Eusapia Palladino was famous for that. Probably the greatest physical medium who ever lived, she nonetheless would invariably try to use her feet or hands to fake phenomena, if she thought she could get away with it. Yet when she was under such control that her hands and feet were bound or held by competent researchers and in the light, she could produce completely inexplicable oddities.

The best way to discount manifestations produced by famous mediums is to try to discredit their investigators. They are called either too young to observe carefully or so old that senility makes them unable to comprehend what they are seeing. Zollner, the man who was chief deponent in favor of Henry Slade, was forty-four when the investigation occurred, in the mature vigor of his intellectual life. He was professor of physics and astronomy at the University of Leipzig and was in the front ranks of the scientific men of Europe. He included among the friends invited to many of his Slade séances several other professors of like repute. It was not surprising that the testimony of these men, publicly given to such feats as I will describe, caused much excitement and controversy in Germany.

To satisfy others who had not personally taken part in sittings with Slade, Zollner hit upon the idea of buying a number of book slates with hinges. You could hardly suggest a man was sticking a piece of slate pencil under his fingernail and writing on a slate if the slates were inside a fold. The edges of these wooden frames shut together tightly. The hinges were of solid brass. On the outside the slates were cased with brown lacquered wood.

Zollner took one slate to the home of his colleague

Wach, professor of criminal law. He wrote, "Professor Wach was entirely of my opinion that such a slate, if firmly sealed after insertion of a small piece of pencil, and then written upon inside in the presence of Slade, would afford convincing proof, even for persons who had not themselves taken part in such a sitting, of the reality of one of the most remarkable phenomena occurring in Slade's presence."

So after a small splinter of pencil was laid on one of the slates, the slate was shut and then fastened by gluing two strips of paper around the outside. Over the edges of the glued strips Professor Wach also placed two seals, on each side, impressed with his own signet. With the slate thus fastened, Zollner repaired to the home of his friend Oscar von Hoffmann and showed it to him and to others there. They all agreed that it was securely sealed.

The next evening, May 6, 1878, at about 8:45, Zollner held a sitting with Slade. By shaking the slate, they were satisfied that the small piece of pencil was between the surfaces of the two slates. Then the slate was laid with other objects on a card table, on which there was also a brightly burning candle. Slade picked it up and asked Zollner whether he wouldn't like to affix his own seals on it. Since a stick of sealing wax was lying on the table among other writing utensils and Zollner had his own signet in his pocket, he at once complied. When the wax had become cold, the two wooden edges of the closed slates were so tightly connected that it was impossible to push even a sheet of paper through those parts which were not stuck with paper and seals. Then he laid the slate on the table at least a foot and a half from Slade, and he held the medium's hands to have control of them.

Talking to Slade while awaiting the start of the phenomena, Zollner asked whether he had ever tried to obtain writing with lead pencil and paper as a variation of the slate writing. Slade replied that he had not; but he was at once ready to make the attempt. They unlinked their hands, and the professor took from the writing utensils lying ready on the table a half sheet of common letter paper. He folded it in the middle and laid a piece of graphite between the two halves. Slade then suggested that he tear off two bits from the corner of the folded paper and keep them by him. Zollner at once recognized the importance of this precaution—to establish the identity of the piece of paper in case it disappeared and reappeared after some time. Two pieces were torn off at the same time from one corner of the folded half-sheet, and these he forthwith put into his coin purse. Then the sheet of paper was pushed under the two sealed slates so that it was completely covered. After that the men laid their hands on the table as before, Slade's hands firmly covered by the professor's and thus prevented from moving.

Nothing occurred for about five minutes, except that Slade often shuddered, as if a spasm passed through him. They then became impatient, and Slade asked if he should resort to his usual expedient of begging information from his spirits, by help of a slate held half under the table. They unjoined their hands for this purpose. Slade took another slate, laid a splinter from a slate pencil on it, and held the slate with his left hand half under the table, while he placed his right hand again under both of Zollner's. They forthwith distinctly heard writing and very soon afterward the three ticktacks that announced its finish. When the slate was drawn out and eagerly examined, the following words were written on it, "Look for your paper."

Zollner immediately raised the sealed slates. But the folded sheet of letter paper with the bit of graphite inside had disappeared. They couldn't find it, so finally they importuned the spirits again with the other slate. When it was withdrawn, written on it was, "The paper is between the slates, and it is written on it" *(sic)*. Zollner grabbed the sealed slates, shook them violently, and heard the shifting movement of paper inside.

He said, "Notwithstanding the lateness of the hour (it was about half-past ten) I repaired at once to the residence of my colleague Wach, in order that the double slate, sealed by him in the morning, might be opened in his presence. . . ."

Not finding Professor Wach at home, Zollner left word that he would return in the morning; and he didn't let the slate out of his custody overnight. The next morning at breakfast Slade fell suddenly into one of his trances and, with eyes closed, stated, among other things, what would be written on the paper when the slates were opened. He said: "As regards the manifestation of yesterday evening, you will find upon the paper sentences in three different languages; there were some faults in the German and English. At the lower end you will find circles, by which we will denote the different dimensions of space."

When, a little later, the slates were unsealed and opened in the sight of Wach and von Hoffmann, the piece of folded paper was there with the stick of graphite, completely smooth, without showing any folding which could denote a forcible insertion through any clefts in the sealed slates. After the opening of the slate, Zollner took from his purse the two bits of paper torn off the evening before, and all the little irregularities of the edges fitted into each other exactly.

Most of the writing on the paper was in German and a strange language which Zollner thought might be Javanese. There was also a sentence in English reading, "Now is the fourth dimension proved? We are not working with the slate pencil or on the slate, as our powers are now in other directions."

On another occasion Slade placed some coins into two small cardboard boxes, which he sealed on the outside with strips of paper. He had these in his possession for some time, and then, having forgotten what coins were in the boxes, he laid them on the card table during a sitting. All present shook the boxes and confirmed that the coins were indeed inside. Then while sitting holding his slate under the table, Slade in a trancelike state said, "I see *funf* and eighteen hundred seventy-six." *Funf* was five, and they were trying to think what this number meant when they heard a hard object fall on the slate under the table. When they drew the slate out, on it was a five-mark piece, with the date 1876. Zollner snatched up the pasteboard box on the table, and it was silent, having been robbed of its contents.

Soon the same thing happened to the coins in the other box, but there was a further complication. When the box was shaken afterward, there was obviously something rattling in it, though not in the same way the coins had rattled. They wondered what it was but didn't want to open the box to find out until they tried to get more information. They asked Slade to put his slate under the table, and he received the message, "The two slate pencils are in the box." And, sure enough, they were!

Zollner wrote: "The foregoing facts are of great value in a three-fold aspect. First, there is proved the occurrence of writing under the influence of Slade, the purport of which was necessarily unknown to him before. It is consequently impossible that these writings occur under the influence of the conscious will of Slade, whatever *modus operandi* is presupposed.

"Secondly, the apparent, so-called passage through matter is proved in a highly elegant and compendious manner. In order to reach by the shortest way the surface of the slate, the coins must apparently have penetrated not only the walls of the box, but also about twenty millimeters' thickness of the oak table. The two slate pencils must

155

have traveled the same way in a reverse direction from the surface of the slate.

"Thirdly, by these experiments an incontrovertible proof is afforded of the reality of so-called clairvoyance, and that in a double way. The first time, with the five-mark piece, the contents of the closed box appeared in the form of a definite represented image in Slade's intuitional life; he 'saw' the numbers 5 and 1876. The second time this was not the case; but the contents were communicated to us in the form of written characters on the slate. The contents of this rectangular box must therefore have existed as imaged in another, not a three-dimensionally incorporated intelligence, before that represented image could be transmitted to us by the aid of writing. Hereby is proved, as it seems to me, in a very cogent manner the existence of intelligent beings, invisible to us, and of their active participation in our experiments."

19: THE RETURN OF
PATIENCE WORTH?

EVEN though the Ouija board is frequently danger-ous, it has on occasion produced genuine evidence. And people often begin their interest in psychical phenomena after a casual attempt to play with the Ouija has revealed startling information that arouses their curiosity.

Such a one was Pearl Lenore Curran of St. Louis. Her spirit communicator was Patience Worth, an entity who produced through her much material of literary merit. Pa-tience has been written about so often in psychical litera-ture that I wouldn't dream of using anything about her again if it were not for the fact that I have something new to add. This has never been published in a book before, although I wrote an article about it in *Occult* magazine, September, 1971.

I suspect there is a possibility that since Mrs. Curran's death Patience Worth has begun to communicate again, through a New Englander named Kenneth Taylor. Some material furnished me by Ken purporting to come from Patience is fairly typical of her writing style. Of course, no actual word-by-word comparison has been made to be sure that the new entity who claims to be Patience uses the exact vocabulary the previous Patience did. Until this is done, no one can state for sure that they are identi-cal—if you can ever state anything for sure when dealing with alleged spirit communicators.

The story of Patience Worth begins in St. Louis on an

evening in July, 1913. Pearl Lenore, the wife of John H. Curran, and her friend, author Emily Grant Hutchings, were playing with a Ouija board. Both women of culture and refinement, they had often used the Ouija before; but on the night Patience arrived, the pointer suddenly became endowed with an unusual agility, and with great rapidity it spelled out these words:

"Many moons ago I lived. Again I come. Patience Worth is my name."

As the women gazed at each other in surprise, the board continued: "Wait, I would speak with thee. If thou shalt live, then so shall I. I make my bread by thy hearth. Good friends, let us be merrie. The time for work is past. Let the tabbie drowse and blink her wisdom in the firelog."

Mrs. Curran was so impressed that she took down every word written by the new communicant, and she continued to do this as, for a long time afterward, the Ouija produced a fantastic amount of material. Before this alleged spirit entity, who said her name was Patience Worth, had finished with Mrs. Curran, many years had passed and hundreds of thousands of words had accumulated. There were numerous poems, parables, allegories, epigrams and maxims, dramas, and even novels. All these were strewn with wit and wisdom and of an intellectual vigor and literary quality unsurpassed in the literature of spirit communication. Patience's faculty of composition was of a very high order, and she could produce poetry as fast as the pointer could move across the board.

Although she has always been very wary of talking about her own lifetime on earth, Patience indicated that she was born and reared in England, and she once gave the date 1649. At that time she said she came to America with migrating Puritans, and she died in this country. This is witnessed by her knowledge of the England of three hundred years ago and the early American scene. Her language is of this period, the idiom incorporating words that are archaic, obsolete and dialectical.

It was discovered that Patience would write only when Pearl Lenore Curran was at the Ouija board and that it did not matter who the other partner was, so Mrs. Curran was recognized from the beginning as the medium. In later years Patience learned to speak through her mouth, thus eliminating the use of other instruments of communication.

Naturally it has always been suspected that Mrs. Curran's own subconscious was producing the material. But nothing in her background could possibly explain such a thorough knowledge of earlier days in England. She had never been to that country. She had only a high school education and no interest in either literature or history, ancient or modern. Neither did she personally have any poetic ability. Her studies after she left school were confined entirely to music, to which she was passionately attached and at which she was most adept.

The archaic English words with which the Patience Worth material abound were completely foreign to Mrs. Curran. Once, for instance, a line was received that read: "The cockshut finds ye still peering to find the other land."

"What's a cock's hut?" asked Mrs. Hastings.

"Nay," wrote Patience, "cockshut. Thee needeth light, but cockshut bringeth dark."

Search revealed that "cockshut" was a term anciently applied to a net used for catching woodcock, and it was spread at nightfall, hence "cockshut" also acquired the meaning of early evening. Shakespeare uses the term once, in *Richard III,* in the phrase, "Much about cockshut time," but it is a very rare word in literature and probably has not been used, even colloquially, for centuries.

Another such archaic word was used by Patience when a character in a story she was writing spoke of herself as

159

"playing the jane-o'apes." No one present had ever heard or seen such an expression. Patience was asked if it had been correctly received, and she repeated it. Upon investigation it was found that it is a feminine form of the familiar "jackanapes" and means a silly girl. Seventeenth-century English dramatist Philip Massinger used it in one of his plays, but that appears to be the only instance of it in literature.

In personality Patience was always constant and unvarying. The thing that most distinguishes her communications from those of so many other intelligences who have purported to write from the spirit world is her intellect, which is at once keen, swift, subtle and profound. So often communications have displayed a lack of intelligence; they have been largely, although with many exceptions, crude emanations of apparently weak mentalities. This can often be explained by the fact that material from spirit has to filter through the minds of automatists who are sometimes of a rather mediocre intelligence and ability. The information being received is naturally colored by its reception through a human being. Perhaps that is what attracted Patience to Mrs. Curran in the first place—she sensed in her a clear channel who would not distort her material. She may now have begun a collaboration with Kenneth Taylor for the same reason.

Aside from the dramatic compositions, some of which are of great length, most of the communications received from Patience have been in verse. Caspar S. Yost, a newspaperman who carefully investigated this case and wrote the book *Patience Worth: A Psychic Mystery,* describes this poetry:

"There is rarely a rhyme, practically all being iambic blank verse in lines of irregular length. The rhythm is most uniformly smooth . . . an intense love of nature is expressed in most of the communications, whether in prose or verse, and also a wide knowledge of nature—not the knowledge of the scientist, but that of the poet."

Patience is surprisingly familiar with the trees and flowers, the birds and beasts of England. She knows the manners and customs of its people as they were three centuries ago, the people of the fields or of the palaces. There is a spiritual significance, more or less profound, in nearly all the poems. And, Yost says, "I have been impressed with the intellectual power behind them. It is this that makes these communications seem to stand alone among the numerous messages that are alleged to have come from 'that undiscovered country.'"

One of her early poems that indicates many of these points is the following:

All silver-laced with web and crystal-studded, hangs
A golden lily cup, as airy as a dancing sprite.
The moon hath caught a fleeting cloud, and rests in her
    embrace.
The bumblefly still hovers o'er the clover flower,
And mimics all the zephyr's song. White butterflies,
Whose wings bespeak late wooing of the buttercup,
Wend home their way, the gold still clinging to their
    snowy gossamer.
E'en the toad, who old and moss-grown seems,
Is wabbled on a lilypad, and watches for the moon
To bid the cloud adieu and light him to his hunt
For fickle marsh flies who tease him through the day.
Why, every rose has loosed her petals,
And sends a pleading perfume to the moss
That creeps upon the maple's stalk, to tempt it hence
To bear a cooling draught. Round yonder trunk
The ivy clings and loves it into green.
The pansy dreams of coaxing goldenrod
To change her station, lest her modest flower

Be ever doomed to blossom 'neath the shadow of the
    wall.
And was not He who touched the pansy
With His regal robes, and left their color there,
All-wise to leave her modesty as her greatest charm?
Here snowdrops blossom 'neath a fringe of tuft,
And fatty grubs find rest amid the mold.
All love, and Love himself, is here,
For every garden is fashioned by his hand.
Are then the garden's treasures more of worth
Than ugly toad or mold? Not so, for Love
May tint the zincy blue-gray murk
Of curdling fall to crimson, light-flashed summertide.
Ah, why then question Love, I prithee, friend?

Yost points out that Patience "touches all the strings of
human emotion, and frequently thrums the note of sorrow, usually, however, as an overture to a paean of joy.
The somber tones in her pictures, to use another meta-
phor, are used mainly to strengthen the highlights. But
now and then there comes a verse of sadness such as this
one, which yet is not wholly sad":

                Ah, wake me not!
For should my dreaming work a spell to soothe
My troubled soul, wouldst thou deny me dreams?
                Ah, wake me not!
If 'mong the leaves wherein the shadows lurk
I fancy conjured faces of my loved, long lost;
And if the clouds to me are sorrow's shroud;
And if I trick my sorrow, then, to hide
Beneath a smile; or build of wasted words
A key to wisdom's door—wouldst thou deny me?
                Ah, let me dream!
The day may bring fresh sorrows,
But the night will bring new dreams.

When this was spelled on the Ouija board, its pathos affected Mrs. Curran to tears; and, to comfort her, Patience quickly applied an antidote with the following jingle, which illustrates not only her versatility but her sense of humor:

Patter, patter, briney drops,
On my kerchief drying:
Spatter, spatter, salty stream
Down my poor cheeks flying.
Brine enough to 'merse a ham,
Salt enough to build a dam!
Trickle, trickle, all ye can
And wet my dry heart's aching.
Sop and sop, 'tis better so,
For in dry soil flowers ne'er grow.

Many of Patience's poems and some of her novels were published, one novel even becoming a best seller. Besides the Yost book, her story was also carefully covered by Dr. Walter Franklin Prince in *The Case of Patience Worth*, and many writers have since mentioned her as having provided the best example of successful automatic writing.

Little else about Mrs. Curran's life or Patience's later poetry had been written, however, until I had a lucky windfall. At a bridge party in New York City in 1964 I met Dulcie Elder, who said she could lead me to some previously unpublished Patience Worth poems because her brother, Marshall Hall, had known Mrs. Curran. But I found it impossible to get in touch with Mr. Hall; he didn't answer any of my letters. Eventually I gave up my search as one more of those promising psychic clues which lead to nothing.

In January, 1966, I gave a series of lectures at the Reef Hotel in Honolulu, and Marshall Hall attended, introduced himself, and gave me an appointment for an inter-

163

view. I was fascinated by his first-hand information about Mrs. Curran and his description of how Patience had communicated through her, and I gladly accepted the sheaf of poems he gave me. Some of them were published in my *Widespread Psychic Wonders*.

Marshall Hall himself is an interesting person. He has been a world traveler, lecturer, writer and theatrical director, as well as a performer in ballet. After retiring from the theater, he became a real estate operator in Honolulu. In his early twenties he was prominent as a dancer and pantomimist, having created the pantomimic role of Prince Guidon in *Le Coq d'Or* at the Metropolitan Opera.

Shortly after that he was asked to dance an excerpt from *Scheherazade* at a party at the apartment of industrialist Herman Behr in New York City. Forming a friendship with the Behrs, Hall was often asked to visit them after that. On the afternoon of November 7, 1919, when he called by chance at their home, Marshall discovered that a party was in progress. The guest of honor was a Mrs. John H. Curran of St. Louis, who had arrived in town that day. She was said to have a certain facility with that curious object—the Ouija board. Her communicator claimed to be a spirit entity known as Patience Worth.

Hall is sure that Mrs. Curran had not been briefed about the numerous other guests, and he had dropped in by happenstance; yet everyone received messages in the form of poems which were personal and pertinent. When it came time for Patience to pay attention to Hall, she addressed him as Pierrot, the traditional pathetic figure of pantomime and ballet. As it happened, he was feeling somewhat like Pierrot at the time. After having danced at the Met, he had for a brief period been reduced to touring in vaudeville. While he had not spoken of this to anyone present, he was rather unhappy about it, and his secret depression was reflected in the poems Patience gave him.

It was the custom for each guest to take a turn at the

Ouija board with Mrs. Curran, although Patience Worth, by then, did not actually use the board to communicate. In former years it had been entirely depended on, but Mrs. Curran's mediumship had progressed to the extent that the pointer was simply kept in motion on the board as a means of concentration while the messages were actually spoken through her mouth. This fact has been mentioned in records about Mrs. Curran, but Hall told me one curious fact that I had never heard before. He said that Mrs. Curran, when being communicated through, did not enunciate words. She always spelled them out. Mr. Curran sat beside his wife and wrote down each letter as it was spoken; and in this tedious manner poems were given for every guest at the party.

When Marshall Hall first placed his hands on the Ouija board, Patience spelled out the following message for him through Mrs. Curran's mouth: "I shall sing thee a wee whit singin', for here be a twist, with a heart in his heels and a soul that follows 'em not."

Then a poem was given him entitled "Pierrot." Because there is so much material that I cannot cover it all, I find myself using only my favorites. For this reason I will quote the second poem Mr. Hall received. It was composed as if he were speaking in the first person.

The Child of My Soul

So, this is reasoning,
That I who would drive the stars
As steeds, should play at jesting,
While my soul sits, regal-throned
And frowns, and I do ponder deep
With confusions, letting my feet labor
While I create. Oh, my soul is in agony:
What shall it bring forth? I ask thee,
I ask thee, what shall it bring forth?

165

On a certain morning I shall arise
And the fetters shall fall, and I
Shall stop my feet, and I shall
Behold the child of my soul!

Presumably Patience Worth was exhausted after a party during which she provided so much entertainment. She soon excused herself politely and disappeared, leaving Mrs. Curran's lips capable of speaking only her own words and thoughts. That Patience returned on several subsequent occasions while Mrs. Curran was visiting in New York is revealed by other poems she dedicated to Marshall. At a reception at the home of the Behrs on Wednesday, November 19, 1919, he performed a solo dance. He was rewarded by his favorite poem, which begins:

To Marshall Hall

Pierrot, Pierrot!
With thy bruised toes and laughter,
Toes bruised with stumbling
And laughter covering the bruises.
Pierrot, Pierrot!

One of the most entertaining stories told to me by Marshall Hall concerned a meeting at which Patience entertained a group of celebrities, including actors Ethel and Lionel Barrymore; Rose O'Neil, the creator of the kewpie doll; Hereward Carrington, the famous psychical researcher; and poet Edgar Lee Masters. When Patience exhibited her talents at composing such fine poetry spontaneously, Masters was highly skeptical. He insisted that he could write good verse just as quickly as she, for he was rather convinced that her material must come by some normal, understandable means.

Patience took Edgar Lee Masters' comments as a challenge, and so a contest was arranged for them each to write an original poem right then and there. Masters, sitting quietly alone in a corner, chewed his pencil and thought and wrote and erased and wrote again. But through Mrs. Curran's mouth came poetry with the usual speed and polish and with never an alteration. When her verse was complete long before Masters was finished, Patience began to tease. She described the other poet's thoughts and told several pertinent facts about his personal life which no one else knew.

Some years later Mrs. Curran died and Patience was without a mouthpiece.

In February, 1969, I received from Kenneth A. Taylor a letter in reference to one of my books he had recently read. Later he sent me an anonymous poem so similar to those of Patience Worth that I questioned him about it; and Taylor revealed that for the past seven years he had been receiving, by various automatic means, communications purporting to come from our same Patience.

Typical of the poetry she produces is the following:

What Oft Sends Me?

What oft sends me thrilling—
The touch of nature blushing with the morn,
The swift and sleek stream murmuring,
The rustle of the trees, the larks bursting.

I feel a unison with all that's vibrating.
Often I sense the discord, shafting in 'gainst current,
'Gainst mutual accord, 'gainst the Master-plan.
All nature changes, and we be changelings too.

I ken the hush, the questions rising, the answers.
All hearts speak a universal language with the best,

167

The deep resonance, lifting, and the expectation—
Even the least of them ken the Master-touch.

But what of sound? Will it echo back again,
Tho ages pass and miles fly in between?
Will my earnest child, the product of my soul,
Confront me, and with its sound release

All beauty, comfort and all rising up to bliss?
I wonder, and my wonder merges with the universal
     heart
To grow and find accord, and treasure all the sounds
And all the murmurings of people searching!

Kenneth Taylor is one of two sons of a Yankee mother
and a Scottish father. Both his parents were psychic, but
they came from families who disliked any evidence of the
supernatural, so they repressed their unusual talents. Ken's
came upon him unbidden. In high school and while he attended accounting school, he had an awareness that permitted him to picture situations, analyze them, and act a
little faster than most people. Yet he says, "I was always
hopeful that I could just go on being like others, not
seeing too closely."

Later, while he was occupied with office management
and accounting in the greater Boston area, he developed
the ability to write automatically. This came about as an
outgrowth of drawing. Being artistic, he frequently spent
time sketching, and one day he had an impulse to hold the
pencil lightly and dot out a variety of forms. These resulted in pictures of the seashore, mountains and cabins
which he had not consciously instigated. If he could draw
with the help of unseen presences, why could he not write
the same way? And so he attempted to allow himself to
become a medium for communication. He then learned
that the artist who had been using him to draw was a

spirit named Mary Sullivan, who told him she was a World War I nurse killed by a shell fragment sent over by the jerries. She requested that he give his time to her in daily sessions of a half-hour, and during them she taught him, he says, to "write in the mind's eye on a white screen and finally to rely on audible communication as well."

Taylor next began to see pictures thrown on the screen of his mind. The first one, which lasted for several seconds, was of a driving northeast snowstorm. On another occasion he saw the head, face and shoulders of Christ in vivid colors, complete with thorn crown and agony. Many colored pictures have appeared to him since, mostly against an absolutely neutral grayish background.

"The people I saw," he says, "were beautifully radiant and serene, the children nicely clothed and in family groupings. Some spoke briefly; others merely gazed and smiled happily. Entities often brought others to participate in written or spoken exchange."

For the last fifteen years Kenneth Taylor has been doing research for a large nonprofit organization on such subjects as population growth and problems of town service. About seven years ago he read Caspar Yost's book about Patience Worth and "fell in love with the depth and beauty of her philosophy." He asked Mary Sullivan to bring Patience to him if it were possible, and he has became convinced that she did. Since then through him Patience has written many poems and much prose.

Once the communicant was asked, "How can I know that you are really *the* Patience Worth?"

She replied in prose: "How does one know that there is God? Yet every ripple in a stream and every swell of ocean tells of His presence. Who other than God could run the earth with such beauty and completeness? Small 'uns are we to ask: Is it He? Everywhere the answer ringeth sweet and clear: It is I. Where does the I stop and the He begin? Sweet love, had we not tasted thee, as a bee tasteth honey, would we know the sweet from the sour? Even with much blindness, we can but view all wonders as a part of us, and we a part of them, yet only in the tasting can we know life.

"Am I Patience? That I be for long years."

In the fall of 1963 Patience reminisced a bit with Ken Taylor about some of her earth experiences. Her discussion of her voyage to the Colonies follows:

"It be a merrie day, with much laughter and little foreboding, when we set sail. The ship's captain mustered us on the deck for a last look at the cliffs, falling away into the somber, silent sea. We were alone with our peril, vengeance, and our hopes. We wondered which of us would last to step ashore to a still greater unknown and to the whimsy of nature, savages, and fortune seekers."

On another occasion she described the landing, after a storm at sea: "I be telling of that mad voyage through the seas, atimes athrought the waves, and barely did we escape the crest till plunging, escaped another. The helmsman lashed him to his wheel and cried askance before the spray's cruel lashing. I be a mind to him and brought him brew while another hugged the wheel. The storm caused wrenchings to the stomach and beat us down the hatchways and along the rain-soaked aisles to safety. Oh, light that followeth after darkness! The morning revealed an encircling arm, which tendered us to harbor and to safety. On shore we spied the movement of a band of people along a ridge geeing heart's rapture in token. Scarce had the anchor dropped than many hands went overside in boats, idling in the waves. Thence ashore. What a moment to set foot ashore, scramble over the rocks, and fling a welcome to that band of people! Aye, our hearts were filled." She ended this, as she often stops writing, with, "I be a weaving. Patience Worth."

On November 27, 1963, Taylor asked Patience, "What are you thinking this day before Thanksgiving?"

She then described a scene from her early days in this country: "I be thinking of loved ones and the sounds of Thanksgiving long since silenced away.

"It was a far-off winter's night. If ye had in mind some Thanksgiving story—I am weary and spent, and not mindful of the cheery prattle and the little ones gathered for the feast, and the older ones set to their counting and settling. . . .

"The wind blew right through the cracks and crannies in the wall. The windows, if such they were, were bedded with some roughly woven cloth, to ease in a little sun if it shone, and keep out the snow bits from squirming through. The room was bare save a chair, a table, what passed for a cot, and a flickering candle placed atop the rough-hewn hearth where a pot boiled fitfully. In the corner played a child and a dog of kind unknown. It was a merrie dog with legs outspread, eyes and ears well placed, and a defiant sort of snip-away-at-the-world kind of look. The girl was wrapped in a gray shawl, more off than on, her dress a raspberry red—the only gay note. It would give you a catch in the throat to see those startled black eyes jumping for joy, through tossled black hair.

"The door opened, with a flurry of snow blanketing a figure which hurried to fasten the door with a bar against the frame. It was a slight figure, older, but with the same flashing black eyes, not quite dimmed by the wind's cruel bite. She said, 'Can ye no brush away the wet and brisk up the fire, while I be a'settin' good things to sup?' "

Ken Taylor says, "Patience is a remarkable person, loving and being loved throughout time." Her bright, steadfast and illuminating writings and utterings through him are entirely spontaneous. As to her present techniques of communication, Ken says, "I can tell when she is present by the vibrations which come to the left side of my face. Then I tune in to her wave length and she talks out her thoughts. If I go off rhythm, Patience will go back over

171

the previous phrases or stanza and pick up the lilt and swing. And she does not brook substitution or diverting from her idiom. I have learned gradually to accept Patience when she feels inclined to burst forth with poetry or comments. She follows events and thoughts very closely, and she is as intensely warm and vibrant as an old English garden."

Patience through Kenneth Taylor, exactly as through Pearl Lenore Curran, has "steadily sidestepped any reference to proof of identity, direct indication of her life settings while on the earth plane, and the direction and scope of her evolving," says Ken. Yet at the same time she has continued to show her love of life, nature, and people.

The blessing that Patience Worth brings us, through whomever she communicates, is the assurance of the continuation of life. Ken says, "She is so vibrant and eager in her enjoyment and linkage to life and in her dedication to the service of her fellows in their searching toward mutual fulfillment that she provides a benediction to all efforts to grow in psychic knowledge."

If we do not wish to believe that this new Patience is really the same Patience Worth who communicated through Mrs. Curran, or any other real surviving entity sending her loving thoughts from the spirit world, it is no matter to her, for she has a timeless existence.

"Disbelieve me, the reality of me," she says, "and you have done nothing more than to suffer me to another fifty years of boiling in my own juice."

172

20: TICKETLESS TRAVEL

THE idea that some individuals can live and function consciously for a time outside their physical bodies is startling, to say the least. But out-of-body travel is probably no more surprising than many of the other concepts discussed in this book. This sort of thing is much more commonplace than one might suppose.

Ken McCaulley of Detroit described to me his initial incident of this kind. "The first thing I was aware of was being near the ceiling of a rather large room. I could see my wife, Pat, and myself lying in the bed below, and I could detect no movement of my body. After a few moments of idly wondering what was going on, it occurred to me that I was dying; and the thought of Pat having to take care of our two children all alone was overpowering. I faced the fact that I didn't want to die and started trying to get back into my body. At first I encountered a feeling of paralysis. Then I found myself in the body, but I must have been disengaged somehow, slightly out of alignment. There was something like an explosion, a banging in my ears, and then it was all right."

Not having found his first experience all that agreeable, Ken says, "I've learned now to project only my consciousness, not my spirit body."

Robert Monroe of Charlottesville, Virginia, has recently published *Journeys Out of the Body* to give others the benefit of his many unusual happenings of this nature. In it he told about having several odd seizures in which his body would begin to shake violently or to vibrate. These occurred before he had his first actual adventure out of his body. He writes: "Some four weeks later, when the 'vibrations' came again, I was duly cautious about attempting to move an arm or leg. It was late at night, and I was lying in bed before sleep. My wife had fallen asleep beside me. There was a surge that seemed to be in my head, and quickly the condition spread through my body."

As he lay there trying to analyze what was happening to him, he let his mind ramble momentarily and thought how nice it would be to take a glider up and fly the next afternoon. Gliding was his hobby at the time. As he thought of the pleasure it would bring, he soared away into space . . . although he didn't know it. He writes, "After a moment, I became aware of something pressing against my shoulder. Half-curious, I reached back and up to feel what it was. My hand encountered a smooth wall. I moved my hand along the wall the length of my arm and it continued smooth and unbroken."

His senses fully alert, Bob tried to see in the dim light. It must be a wall, and he was lying against it with his shoulder. He immediately reasoned that he had gone to sleep and fallen out of bed. He'd never done so before, but all sorts of strange things were occurring, and falling out of bed was quite possible.

Then he looked again. Something was wrong. This wall had no windows, no furniture against it, no doors. Why, it wasn't a wall, it was the ceiling. He was floating against the ceiling, bouncing gently with any movement he made. Startled, he rolled in the air and looked down. There, in the dim light below him, was the bed. There were two figures lying in the bed. To the right was his wife. Beside her was someone else. Both seemed asleep.

"This is a strange dream," he thought. Whom would he

174

dream to be in bed with his wife? He looked closely, and the shock was intense. *He* was the someone on the bed!

"My reaction was almost instantaneous," he writes. "Here I was, there was my body. I was dying, this was death, and I wasn't ready to die. Somehow, the vibrations were killing me. Desperately, like a diver, I swooped down to my body and dove in. I then felt the bed and the covers, and when I opened my eyes, I was looking at the room from the perspective of my bed."

Bob had already been to doctors about the vibrations. Then he rushed to them again, sure that something terrible was happening to him physically, or even mentally. Eventually a psychologist friend, Dr. Bradshaw, suggested to him, "Some of the fellows who practice yoga and those Eastern religions claim they can do it whenever they want to."

"Do what?" asked Bob.

"Why, get out of the physical body for a while," he replied. "You ought to try it." And eventually Bob did, with all kinds of interesting results.

In 1952 the late Dr. Hornell Hart, professor of sociology at Duke University, in an attempt to discover how extensive such unconventional modes of flight might be, submitted a questionnaire to one hundred and fifty-five Duke students. Of these, 30 percent answered yes to the question: "Have you ever actually seen your physical body from a viewpoint completely outside the body, like standing beside the bed and looking at yourself lying in bed or like floating in the air near your body?"

Of the 30 percent who reported yes to this question, at least 70 percent remembered more than one such projection. That was twenty years ago. It is safe to say that a similar question today would probably evoke a much larger response. The widespread use of psychedelic drugs has undoubtedly caused an increase in the number of out-of-body experiences (or OOBE's or astral projections, as they are also called).

The individual who has this experience believes he is normally conscious at the time and is positive that he is not dreaming or hallucinating. His ordinary critical faculties are present, and he often has a most exciting and stimulating time.

As Charles Tart says in his Introduction to Bob Monroe's book, ". . . OOBEs are a universal human experience, not in the sense that they happen to large numbers of people, but in that they have happened all through recorded history, and there are marked similarities in the experience among people who are otherwise extremely different in terms of cultural background. One can find reports of OOBEs by housewives in Kansas which closely resemble accounts of OOBEs from ancient Egyptian or oriental sources."

It is possible for some persons to go out of their bodies at will. Four such travelers, Sylvan Muldoon, Oliver Fox (pseudonym of Hugh Callaway), Dr. J. H. M. Whiteman, and a French writer, whose nom de plume is Yram (Mary spelled backward, which leads us to suspect it might be a woman), all have published books on their personal experiences with astral projection. To this list must now be added the name Robert Monroe, whose new book brings the most up-to-date report of the subject. All these individuals have experimented endlessly, and they have recounted their experiences for the purpose, as much as anything, of assuaging the fears of those who have spontaneous out-of-the-body incidents and don't know what to make of them.

Without statistics, but with a file full of notes, I myself can testify to the prevalence of OOBE's because of the number of people who have told me about them. Wherever I lecture or make radio and television appearances around the country, I usually mention out-of-body experiences among the other curious psychical subjects in which I am interested. Afterward I receive numerous comments, telephone calls, and letters from those who state, "Thank God I hear you say that it is perfectly normal to have these things happen. I've been frightened to death that I was going out of my mind." These individuals have not spoken of their strange adventures because they do not want to be considered peculiar. So they have suffered in silence, not knowing what was happening and being fearful of illness or insanity. Because people are most reluctant to talk about such a weird thing unless they are sure they will be thoroughly understood, there is no use in telling me you have never known anybody who has astral projections. I would be willing to make a bet that at least one of your relatives or friends secretly has such experiences. And you may learn to have them yourself if you can somehow acquire the proper techniques.

Spontaneous occurrences may happen just once or twice for what seems to be no logical reason. Certain physical conditions may give rise to them. We occasionally hear of people taking anesthetics who have such an experience.

A woman I know, Joan Cartwright of Preston, Lancaster, England, took sodium pentothal in a dentist's office in 1959, and it gave rise to something she has no desire to repeat. Suddenly her mind seemed completely detached from her body. She said, "I couldn't tell you how I got up there, but the thinking part of me was up in the air . . . in space. . . . It seemed to be higher than the ceiling!" She looked down and saw herself sitting in the chair, but although she knew what was going on there, she could not actually *see* the dentist filling her tooth.

Joan was particularly impressed with the enormous feeling of aloneness she had up there, which was mentally very disturbing. Later she realized all at once that she was back in the dentist's chair again; since that time she does not deliberately recall the episode if she can help it.

Well, enough of those instances that report fright. They are not necessarily in the majority. Many find OOBE's exciting, sometimes joyful, and even frequently inspiring.

Kenneth L. Orris of Millbury, Ohio, was loading ore at Superior, Wisconsin, on a beautiful summer morning in 1945. He said in *Fate* magazine, March, 1965, "I was in the best of health, my spirits as bright as the sunshine; my enthusiasm for life was as great as a twenty-three-year-old man's could be." But he was physically fatigued, having just come off duty at six o'clock, firing a Great Lakes ore carrier. He decided to go into his cabin and rest for a while.

"Lying on my back on top of the covers," he says, "I fell into that dreamy, mystical state I so very much enjoy, and almost before I realized what had happened, I raised up and out of my body. It was so easy and so wonderful."

In that state he slipped through the steel cabin sides, out onto the deck, to watch again the loading of the boat. Then his attention was directed upward.

"My eyes went beyond the brightness of day out into the darkness of space and fastened on what appeared to be three separate stars, a large one and two smaller ones all grouped together.

"There's my star! There's my star!" he fairly shouted with the joy of recognition. His being began to race toward those stars with incredible speed; so fast, indeed, that he could feel a resistance, like air pressure, holding him back as the stars got bigger as he approached them.

Some doubts came into his mind at the distance he was traveling from his body. Had he left it for good? He didn't really want to do that. So, "With that thought my direction immediately was reversed and before I realized it I slammed into my body like a thunderbolt."

The memory of that experience is still as strong with Mr. Orris as it was twenty years ago. While different in that he visited the stars, it is typical of the exhilaration that some people have had.

For the scientific researcher, evidential experiences are preferred; and, oddly enough, there are some that do involve elements which bring genuine evidence that they have been more than merely subjective hallucinations. Being such a rational human being, Bob Monroe admits: "It wasn't until the first evidential experience which could be checked that I seriously considered these to be anything but daydreams, hallucinations, a neurotic aberration, the beginnings of schizophrenia, fantasies caused by self-hypnosis or worse." And Bob did undergo the kind of astral flight that has been labeled by parapsychologists "traveling clairvoyance" because of the ability of the astral tourist to bring back some kind of supernormal knowledge.

In the *Journal* of the Society for Psychical Research, Pierre Émile Cornellier of Paris told of an experiment conducted in 1915 with a model as his subject. She was hypnotized and asked to go out of her body and find a particular person. She said, "I see him. He's walking barefoot over cold stones."

This seemed a most unlikely statement, but it was afterward discovered that at that very moment the individual concerned was taking his first treatment of a cure which involved walking barefoot over cold stones.

We can't say that this sort of thing actually *proves* out-of-body travel. Many think it does, especially those who can do it. The fact of extrasensory travel in such instances can be discounted only if you hypothesize a highly accurate form of clairvoyance or telepathy combined with the hallucination that one has actually traveled away from his body to the destination where he procured the information. It would seem easier to admit that the individual has done what he thinks he has than to hypothesize several

179

other different things which are really not any more verifiable.

In the December, 1962, issue of *Fate,* Alice C. Hall of Provo, Utah, told about a time when her husband was working out of town in Page, Arizona, and only able to get home weekends. She said that Thursday, October 8, 1959, was wet and dreary and she was lonely and discouraged. That night the bed was cold and damp, and she lay there shivering and trying to decide whether to get up and get more blankets or to suffer it out. She missed her husband terribly as she lay there too cold and lonely to sleep. After a while, however, she thought she could feel a kind of warmth on her husband's side of the bed. She ran her hand over the sheet, and it did feel slightly warm to her.

She says, "A little later I felt impelled to reach out again and I ran my hand over the sheet in a caressing gesture. There was no mistaking it this time; the bed definitely was warm as toast." She slid over into the inviting warmth of it and in a little while was fast asleep.

She forgot about this until she and her husband were having breakfast the next Sunday morning. He stared at her in astonishment when she told him, and then he recounted the following:

"That night I was resting on my bunk in the bunkhouse at Page surrounded by snoring, sleeping men. I was so sad and lonely that I was about to chuck it all—job or no job—and come home to you right then. If I'd had my own car, that's just what I would have done." He pictured himself at home in his own clean bed with his wife sleeping beside him. "That was not possible," he said, "so I decided to try an experiment: I decided to come home for a few minutes!"

Putting his hands behind his head, with all the power in him, he willed himself home. He cast out every thought from his mind except the thought of home and his wife. He says, "After a while I stood by the side of the bed looking down at you. You were on your side of the bed, just resting, not yet asleep. I slipped quietly in beside you, and soon you moved your hand along the bed close to me. I waited and presently you did it again. I thought you knew I was there because you snuggled over close beside me. I put my arm around you and we slept."

Another example in which an OOBE brought back evidence was reported to me by Jag Sodhi, a native of India now living in St. Paul, Minnesota, and his wife verified his statements. He said that on the night of March 4, 1971, he asked his wife if he might sleep alone in the bedroom. He had a presentiment that something was wrong, and he felt that he might be able to learn what it was. All during the night, although his body was sleeping in his bed, his mind was in New Delhi with his mother. She was dying. All about her he could see her deceased relatives, who were in the process of helping her soul leave her body. He prayed in order to help her, but those with her told him she didn't need any help now. Her time had come, they said.

In the morning Jag told his wife that his mother was dead. It took five days for a letter to reach him confirming the fact that she had indeed died on the date of his astral trip.

It is interesting that in so many of our stories which bring evidence of out-of-body travel, we also seem to acquire some indication of a life after death. Jag saw the deceased relatives helping his mother's soul out of her body. Apparently it is not rare for an individual who is said to have died momentarily to have an OOBE during that interim. They often, then, describe heaven as a beautiful and blissful place where they are greeted by their beloved relatives. Sometimes it is so appealing to them that they don't want to return to earth.

Mrs. Eileen Tetu, also of St. Paul, said that in 1964 she was in a state of exhaustion after giving birth to one of

181

her large brood. She fell asleep and slept for twelve hours. During that time she found herself looking through an archway at a most beautiful scene filled with happy people. When she tried to go through the archway to join them, she unfortunately heard the words, "Not yet."

Since she wasn't allowed to accomplish that aim, she satisfied herself with just floating around where she was, observing a fascinating city filled with clean, tannish-colored buildings. She got too close to one of these buildings and started to fall down the side of it. At that moment she woke up in her body.

Mrs. Tetu is sure that this was an OOBE rather than a mere dream because she has had many adventures out of her body. She frequently visits sick friends, she says. "I try to visualize my spirit body with someone who is ill. I touch them on the forehead, and sometimes they seem to be aware of my presence."

On the morning of Thanksgiving, 1969, Eileen got up early to prepare her turkey. Then she had a glass of water and went back to bed for two hours. Suddenly during this time she discovered herself waking up in a different body. It was smaller than she and about five months pregnant. She had just had a baby two months before and had no desire to go through such discomfort again so soon. Apparently she had entered the body of a woman who was in a coma while the woman's own consciousness was probably having an out-of-body experience. Eileen was willing to help out, for she felt that she was probably being used to keep the woman's body alive and give it strength. But she had to get out of there before the time came to deliver.

As she opened her eyes, an older woman and two little boys were staring at her. They looked sad and poor. She wanted them to know she was not the ill woman she was replacing, so she cried, "This is me!" . . . not necessarily a

182

very bright remark. Then she asked, "Where are we? What town?" The woman answered, "Cracow."

Eileen told me, "I didn't even know the name Cracow; but I learned since by looking it up in my atlas that it is in Poland."

Similarly, Bob Monroe once found himself in the body of a comatose man, and again in the body of a drunk who was being supported along the street by two friends. In each case he got out fast!

A kind of OOBE that brings evidence is when one is seen by others while he is out of his body. Frederic W. H. Myers made a large collection of such cases in his *Human Personality and Its Survival of Bodily Death*. An example from this quotes Alex S. Beaumont: "In September, 1873, when my father was living at 57 Inverness Terrace, I was sitting one evening, about 8:30 P.M. in the large dining room. At the table, facing me, with their backs to the door, were seated my mother, sister, and a friend. Suddenly I seemed to see my wife bustling in through the door of the back dining room, which was in view from my position. She was in a *mauve* dress. I got up to meet her, though much astonished, as I believed her to be at Tenby. As I rose, my mother said, 'Who is that?' not (I think) seeing anyone herself; but seeing that I did. I exclaimed, 'Why, it's Carry,' and advanced to meet her. As I advanced the figure disappeared. On inquiry I found that my wife was spending that evening at a friend's house, in a mauve dress, which I had most certainly never seen. I had never seen her dressed in that color. My wife recollected that at that time she was talking with some friends about me, much regretting my absence, as there was going to be dancing, and I had promised to play for them. I had been unexpectedly detained in London."

In trying to explain such a situation, which he ran into fairly frequently in the reports of the SPR, Myers invented the word *psychorrhagy*. He writes: "When I say that

Mrs. Beaumont or Mrs. Hawkins, agents in cases cited, were born with the *psychorrhagic diathesis*, I express what I believe to be an important fact, physiological as well as psychological. . . ." The pedantic words he used were the only ones, he felt, which meant exactly what the facts obliged him to say, *psychorrhagy* being from the Greek word which strictly means "to let the soul break loose." That which breaks loose in Myers' hypothesis is not the whole principle of life in the organism; "rather it is some psychical element probably of very varying character, and definable mainly by its power of producing a phantasm, perceptible by one or more persons, in some portion or other of space. I hold that this phantasmogenetic effect may be produced either on the mind, and consequently on the brain of another person—in which case he may discern the phantasm somewhere in his vicinity, according to his own mental habit or prepossession—or else directly on a portion of space 'out in the open' in which case several persons may simultaneously discern the phantasm in that actual spot."

Others who are also scientifically oriented do not find it difficult to conceive that there is a spirit body, sometimes called the astral or etheric body, within the physical which can sometimes leave it even though the consciousness remains with the physical. This would account for the cases Myers was worried about. And if the consciousness accompanied the spirit body, it would account for those cases where an individual was aware of traveling and also was seen at a distant place.

Dr. Robert Crookall of England, who is probably the most active researcher today of out-of-body experiences, has numerous case histories of people who were conscious of being in a spirit body. They were also frequently aware of what has been described as a luminescent or silverish cord which seems to stretch from the astral body to the physical body. In *Events on the Threshold of the After-*

Life Crookall quotes one man as observing that his released double was attached to his body by a "white cord like a piece of string."

Mrs. H. D. Williams told Dr. Crookall, "On turning round, I saw a shining white cord, two or three inches wide, composed of loosely woven strands, stretching from my Soul as far as I could see back to my house."

Mrs. Clara Clayton of Nottingham wrote: "Out I came and floated above my body and found I was attached to it by a silver thread of light which was pulsating with light. I moved farther from my body and found that this cord of light appeared to stretch. Then I drew near the body again; the thread of light drew inwards toward the body. It was just like elastic. I rose once more and floated away from the body; on and on I went, but this silvery cord of light was still attached to my body and to my Real Self, a long distance away from it. It seemed that a long flight from the physical body made no difference; neither did the positions assumed out of the body, such as vertical or horizontal, alter things. This cord was alive and vibrating all the time."

Mrs. Clayton concluded her account by saying that after she returned to her body, "During the rest of the night I lay awake absorbing every detail of that wonderful experience."

On rare occasions the person who was seen somewhere else while having an OOBE was also obviously aware of it. Padre Pio, the late saintly Capuchin monk who had the stigmata, was a great one for being two places at once.

"What has always seemed to me the most impressive of all the astonishing facts about Padre Pio," writes Alberto del Fante in *Who Is Padre Pio?* "is the story of Monsignor Fernando Damiani, the Vicar General of Salto, Uruguay. . . . Padre Pio had at one time cured the prelate of a cancer of the stomach, which had made them great friends for years." Some time later Monsignor Damiani was in

Italy and, as he was advanced in age, expressed the wish to remain there so that he could die near Padre Pio. But the padre told him he was destined to return to Uruguay.

"I will visit you at the time of your death," he promised.

In 1942 the Archbishop of Montevideo is said to have been awakened by a Capuchin friar, who told him to go to Monsignor Damiani because he was dying. Beside the bed was found a note the monsignor had been able to scribble, with the words on it: "Padre Pio came." Then in 1949, when the Archbishop of Montevideo met Padre Pio in Italy, he recognized him to be the Capuchin who had awakened him. Yet, of course, the padre's body had been at his home base in Pietrelcina all the time.

Many mediums claim to have out-of-body experiences at will. I can remember sitting in a development class in Daytona Beach, Florida, once, and when the lights were turned on after the meditation, someone asked the medium if she had been traveling astrally again. She said yes, she'd been to the dressmaker's where Jackie's wedding dress was being prepared for her marriage to John F. Kennedy. She described it in detail, but to my recollection it was nothing like the gown worn a few days later at the wedding.

Even though this was doubtless a sham, I believe that some mediums have actual astral projections while they are in the trance state. I have heard none of them describe how it is done. Most of the explanations of how to accomplish this unusual feat of leaving the body are given by the writers I've previously mentioned. I would particularly recommend Sylvan Muldoon and Robert Monroe. Only a few persons imply that it might be easy deliberately to seek OOBE's. There are many complications for most first-time travelers, and even sometimes for those who do it frequently. Eileen Tetu gives the only simple suggestion I know of when she says she drinks a glass of water on an empty stomach and then goes to sleep and has out-of-body experiences.

Most habitual astral travelers agree that it isn't wise to try to cause projection by forcing yourself out of your body. Yes, I know this book is full of admonitions; but when you are playing with the mind, or consciousness, you are playing with the most important thing in your life. So handle it very carefully. There's no use taking chances with it, I always say.

Several persons who have written about astral projection warn against it for varying reasons. Muriel Hankey in her book *J. Hewat McKenzie: Pioneer of Psychical Research* maintains that excess in psychic practice is as undesirable as immoderate indulgence of any appetite, and so the careless or overindulgent participant is touted away from experimentation. She has another well-taken word of advice, one which has probably already occurred to some readers: It is surely inelegant to be an eavesdropper while you are wandering about invisibly.

"Above all," Mrs. Hankey says, "I would draw attention to the questionable ethics of entering deliberately into these experiences without sanction." She feels it particularly improper to sneak unseen into the house or room of another and spy on him, even in the ostensible interests of scientific proof of the experiment.

Besides the matter of moral conduct, there are very real dangers, according to Oliver Fox. In his book *Astral Projection* he lists them:

1. Heart failure or insanity arising from shock.
2. Premature burial. (The body of one who is astrally traveling is usually in a comatose state when he is gone. There is no doubt that on occasion it has been buried, and he has returned to find it covered with dirt and forever useless to him.)
3. Temporary derangement.

4. Cerebral hemorrhage.
5. Severance of the cord, which means death.
6. Repercussion effects on the physical vehicle caused by injuries to the astral body. (No one says the consciousness can't get into mischief while it is traveling.)
7. Obsession. (This is claimed to be a danger in any trance phenomenon or when the mind is not in complete control of the body. When the consciousness is away, spirits may play.)

Even though he warns of such appalling possible dangers, Fox would not try to dissuade any earnest investigator with a passion for truth.

"Very likely these experiments are no more dangerous than motoring," he says, "but I must confess that I do not really understand what I have been doing. It is easy to say, 'The Soul leaves the body and returns to it'; but this riddle of projection—of what actually happens—is in truth a most profound subject and hedged around with many subtle problems."

To those attempting to develop their psychic powers, this unorthodox activity is inevitably a challenge. And for those endeavoring to prove the survival of the human soul, it lends encouragement. They reason that if there is something (call it consciousness or soul) that can exist and function outside the human body while it is alive, why could it not perform in the same manner after the death of the body? Of course, this is mere conjecture so far. But who knows what proof the future will bring?

21: PITFALLS

NO one should undertake to develop his psychic powers without a clear and sufficient understanding of what is involved; and, face it, there is much to put up with that you have probably not yet considered.

Saint Paul said, ". . . the manifestation of the Spirit is given to man to profit withal." And it is true that through the development of the higher faculties an entirely new world is opened up. One must be prepared to receive new ideas and to assimilate new knowledge and therefore to re-model his preconceived beliefs, to readjust his whole system of values—in other words, to make an entirely new man of himself. Except in rare cases, the opening up of the soul and the psychic senses is long and arduous work; but beginners don't often accept what they hear about the tedious periods when nothing happens and the many difficulties to overcome before they gain command of their psychic faculties.

MacGregor and Underhill say, "All real artists or inventors, whatever their profession, are natural psychics. With the right unfoldment these people can acquire greater control over their creative minds and thus surmount many difficulties. The training of the soul's faculties, whether as a medium for communication or as a creative worker, should bring about better health and mental poise, greater willpower and more self control; it should never result in complete surrender of the personality, in abject humility or in the conceit which brooks no opposition. These two extremes, particularly the latter, are pitfalls which must be avoided at all costs; they constitute the real dangers to be met with in psychic development. In the former case the individual surrenders his personality, and when he is not master of himself, he is liable to become the prey of any spirit entity or of any general thought-current that happens along. While the obsessing entity or thought may not be evil in nature, its effect upon the weak-willed person is often deleterious. On the other hand, a person who thinks of himself and of his psychic messages as infallible is in very real danger. In ordinary life the positive and unteachable person—the egoist—is most objectionable, as a psychic he is a menace to himself and to those who take his messages literally."

The person who considers himself invariably right is incapable of knowing when he is wrong. He refuses to change course or to listen to advice from those who know the dangers he is courting. If he is too positive, he is insensitive to the truth, and if he breaks the laws operating on psychic planes of consciousness, he must suffer the consequences.

Harold Sherman warns, "Make sure you do not let your ego become inflated. If you do, you will bring your Self back into the picture, you will lose your sensitivity to a great degree, and make many embarrassing mistakes, unable to detect the difference between a genuine impression and a false one. I have seen this happen to many men and women who have developed fine sensitivity, have gained a little reputation, 'it has gone to their heads,' they have lost their humility in the face of this Higher Power, which I hold to be sacred."

In this field we all occasionally run into the braggarts who so enlarge on their achievements and abilities that they become the objects of ridicule. In fact, among those who purportedly receive communication from the spirit world there is what might be called the "I am a chosen vessel for the word of truth" syndrome. This is indeed an area in which all aspects of mind and personality are thrown into relief, so great care must be taken to see oneself as one really is, to develop strength of character, and to guard against exaggeration, whether by over- or underestimating one's powers.

The adulation some mediums achieve from their supporters almost invariably ruins them. Eventually they seem to arrive at the point where they believe that everything they say and do is so wonderful that they don't even need to bother producing genuine phenomena. A young medium in whom I have placed much faith in the past because I am sure I have seen him do very exciting psychic things has gone through many traumatic experiences in recent years, it is true. The fact remains that today what goes on when he purports to produce manifestations of a supernormal nature is laughable, it is so obviously fraudulent. That is, it would be laughable if it weren't so sad to see someone with such great potential throw it away.

Another point we must note: A person may be a fully developed medium and yet have his mind so crammed with false beliefs that his unconscious memories tinge every message he gives and all the work he does. The psychic must learn to control his own mind and to regulate his actions before he can begin to see the truth uncolored by false conceptions. The talent for mediumship has nothing to do with goodness or badness, intelligence or ignorance; like any other talent it is bestowed on the individual without regard for his principles or beliefs. "Like the rain it falls on both the just and the unjust." If he misuses his gifts, however, he will pay a terrible penalty because what he is dealing with is so basically important to mankind. He is wise if he realizes this and recognizes his responsibility.

"He who would achieve the greatest growth," say the

ladies MacGregor and Underhill, "must live in accordance with the highest principles, and maintain a degree of personal integrity whereby his true worth may be appraised. Aside from the fact that the character of the medium plays a considerable part in the value of the results he obtains, his worth as a medium will be of lesser account if he is not a sincere and true personality."

The reason so many psychics continue, year after year, to see meaningless visions and to give out inane messages is that they have not been properly trained and remain content with inferior work. Those who go to a professional sensitive for messages should demand clarity and accuracy and not be satisfied with less. This would eventually raise the level of mediumship.

MacGregor and Underhill point out that some developing mediums delude themselves by thinking they have exceptional powers if they are always conscious of spirit presences, hear voices ceaselessly repeating meaningless phrases, or see the same visions over and over again, or if they get any messages at all, whether or not they make sense. This is not true mediumship; it brings about undesirable and sometimes injurious effects, and it should be firmly repressed by exercising willpower. Nor is seeing symbols useful without being able to interpret their meaning. One must cultivate the habit of asking for and receiving an interpretation for all clairvoyant visions and demand that one's messages be pertinent and reliable.

Occasionally a woman psychic will receive messages such as that Christ is to be born on earth again . . . and to her! Or one may be told that he is the reincarnation of Jesus or of any famous character in history.

There was a young woman I'll call Lucy in one of our groups in New York City who stood up shyly one day and announced that it had been revealed to her that she was the present incarnation of Mary Magdalene. She said this modestly, almost bowing in her humility as she made

192

the statement; but she accepted it completely and began to live the role. Unfortunately she was soon so confused that she was put into an institution.

After debating about the advisability of trying to help her, her friend Anna informed Lucy of an experience she personally had at Virginia Beach, Virginia, during the days when the great seer Edgar Cayce was alive. She was sitting in the anteroom one day when a radiant girl walked out of a session with Cayce. She was so filled with joy that she spouted forth her happy news.

"I am Mary Magdalene!" she cried. "Mr. Cayce just told me."

Somehow Lucy accepted the news that Mary Magdalene was already spoken for in this generation better than we had expected, and she decided to withdraw her claim. Facing up to reality allowed her normal personality to take control sufficiently so that she was soon released from the hospital and able to resume her ordinary life.

Obviously caution must always be observed, for without it even faith can degenerate into a pitiful lack of judgment and a sentimentality which leads straight to disaster. The person who never troubles to test the accuracy of his messages, who believes that faith in his own communications is all sufficient, who never exercises his reason and judgment is bound to take numerous tumbles. Many students, and mediums, too, for that matter, tend to scoff at parapsychologists for being so objective and critical. If they would instead learn from them and apply some of their logical reasoning to the reception of all messages purporting to come from spirits, they could avoid much trouble.

Of course the incipient medium must learn to trust his spirit helpers, but only after he has proved them reliable. Even then he should add the light of reason to all statements purporting to come through him. Gullibility causes many errors. If we open our minds to hear only what we wish to believe, we run the risk of turning a deaf ear to our guides when they find it necessary to tell us something we don't care to hear.

It is also essential that the psychic learn to control his thoughts and never allow them to dwell on degrading subjects. Aspiration is the keynote to all desirable psychic experiences, but it must be an aspiration totally devoid of vanity and self-aggrandizement. One reason why we can be certain that the evolution of our higher gifts is in accordance with God's law is that in order to acquire the desired command over them and to realize them in their highest forms, we must try in all ways to be true to our highest selves.

Here are a few suggestions that will make development easier for the neophyte. First, he should never center all his attention on his development, especially if he begins to find himself too deeply involved. He should always have other work, exercise, and recreation. He should mix with people of other interests, even those who might be somewhat critical of his psychic efforts. But don't cultivate those who are actually unpleasant about it or are so closed-minded that they can't be gracious. Who needs them?

The student should do all in his power to maintain bodily fitness and mental poise. The body should be kept clean both internally and externally. Sunshine and fresh air are important. A healthy diet should be maintained. Habitual overeating is anything but spiritual.

Somehow it is difficult to envision a particularly gross or obese person as a medium, although many middle-aged sensitives are comfortably overweight. But there was at one time an extremely competent physical medium who was huge! Her name was Mrs. Guppy, although this sounds like a put-on. In her youth, when she was Miss Nichols, she had sat for some time with scientist and psychical researcher Alfred Russel Wallace and his family at their home circle. She had been particularly adept at producing apports (which are said to be objects dematerialized in one place and rematerialized somewhere else), being able to provide fresh bouquets of flowers with dew still on them and other apports into the séance room when Wallace had the doors tightly locked and the entire room under careful control. Miss Nichols' mediumship had developed so well that she became a professional later when she was married to Mr. Guppy.

One night, it is reported, a home circle was being held in the same town but with another medium presiding, and apports were apparently being produced on request. One of the persons sitting in the dark jokingly expressed the wish that Mrs. Guppy might be apported to them.

Mrs. Guppy was at that time sitting in her home some three miles distant, writing in her account book. While the company at the séance was laughing at the absurdity of the idea of her appearing there, a loud bump was heard. A match was struck, and it revealed a surprising sight. There in the center of the table stood the large Mrs. Guppy, an account book in one hand and a pen in the other, and a dazed expression on her face!

Whatever your weight problem, it is a rule never to eat a heavy meal just before a mediumistic sitting or before the development class meets. Some people even prefer to fast beforehand. If they find this beneficial to their general health, as well as to their psychic powers, well and good; if it causes overfatigue, irritability, headache, or other unpleasant symptoms, it is not advisable. And during a quiet meditation period someone's stomach rumbling because of hunger can be mildly distracting.

It would surprise you how many in the psychic field have given up cigarettes. It's the exception rather than the rule to have to tell participants in a development group that smoking is not allowed until later in the evening. Yet heavy smokers may find it hard to believe that the smell of tobacco will cling to their clothing and will scent their breath so that it may be repugnant to those sitting near them during a quiet meditation period. Afterward, of course, if and when refreshments are served, it would hardly make a hostess popular if she insisted that the "no-smoking" ban remain, for there will invariably be some who wish to avail themselves of the privilege. Over-smoking, however, just like overindulgence in liquor, hardly becomes one who is attempting to enlighten himself spiritually.

I was visited once by a woman who had just returned from an ashram in India so impressed by her guru that she could talk of nothing else. She went on and on about his spirituality and, incidentally, her own, since she had been his chela, or pupil, for a number of years. As she talked, she was smoking incessantly, lighting one cigarette from the butt of another and never once allowing her hands to rest quietly in her lap, so busy were they moving the cigarette to and from her mouth. One could not help but react unfavorably to her nervousness.

"If you have learned no more poise and tranquillity than this from your great teacher," one naturally thought, "he can't have imparted much to you." And so another convert was lost.

In *Hints on Mediumistic Development* British medium Ursula Roberts points out: "Jealousy is a fault which comes into great prominence among mediums, and innumerable circles have been forced to disband because of jealousy which arose between developing sitters."

Every medium should learn to study his own reaction to the work of others. If it is one of faultfinding, criticism, and the desire to belittle others, then beware! The seeds of jealousy are beginning to put forth poisonous tendrils, which may later choke all your good aspirations. Your reaction instead should be one of kindness and loving tolerance, and even of mutual support.

196

"Jealousy," Ursula says, "should be weeded out of the character as firmly as lasciviousness."

Lasciviousness? Yes, sex rears its ugly (if you want to call it that) head here as well as everywhere else in our modern world. Ursula says of it, "Many a developing medium has led a frustrated sex life, and it often happens that the sexual desires become stimulated during development." The wise medium, she maintains, will endeavor to transmute these urges onto other creative activities.

It is not advisable for people who have lately been bereaved to begin their development during this period; nor should those who feel the effects of a severe shock try to develop their psychic powers until they have returned to a normal condition. Those who have suffered from nervous disorders should not attempt to open up their psychic faculties except in rare instances and then only when acting under the personal guidance of a very capable instructor.

Certainly overindulgence in alcohol is not wise for a potential psychic. And even for those who enjoy a therapeutic drink before dinner, it is recommended that they forego the pleasure on the night of the development class.

It is unfortunate but true that people who are psychically sensitive are also sensitive in other areas. Mediums seem to be sick a great deal more than most people. And there is a trend, sometimes, toward their becoming excessive drinkers in their later years. No matter how psychically gifted they are, therefore, people who are more than normally interested in alcohol or in taking drugs or barbiturates should never develop until they have fully conquered the habit.

Dr. Thelma Moss of UCLA discussed her own experience with LSD in *Psychic* magazine. ". . . I think LSD lets down our defenses so that all kinds of *un*conscious forces erupt into awareness. And with so much power that many of us are overwhelmed, sometimes remaining overwhelmed, long after the drugs have disappeared from the body.

"Perhaps that's why many people have left the drugs and have gone into meditative disciplines. They can explore these fascinating dimensions of mind with more control, more gradually and more safely, with these techniques rather than LSD.

"Let me again emphasize that you don't know where you're going to land with an LSD experience. It can be absolutely terrifying—I know, I've had some real bummers."

Since psychical development is, more than anything else, the opening up of our centers of awareness, it can be seen that, whether the intruding entities come only from our subconscious, as Dr. Moss suggests, or from some other dimension of existence, they may impinge upon us to such an extent that we are appalled and horrified. So never, but never, take any hallucinogenic drugs if you are attempting to develop psychically.

One of the probably temporary penalties to be endured in the course of development is highly increased sensitivity. The great changes which are taking place in the individual affect him physically, mentally, and spiritually. In fact, no one is ever the same again after he has awakened his psychic faculties, for a big step has been taken in the progress of the individual.

"For a time, until the readjustment has taken place, one is apt to feel supersensitive and irritable; one may also experience unpleasant physical symptoms which pass off as development proceeds," say the MacGregor-Underhill team. If in the earlier stages the psychic feels a distaste for crowds, he should avoid them until he is able to protect himself from the effect of mixed conditions. It is most helpful if the sensitive can be with people who understand what he is experiencing and can surround him with healthy and constructive thoughts. It is harmful for the psychic to associate with anyone who is overanxious or fearful for him.

It may be well to conclude this chapter on pitfalls with the suggestion that people whose powers are not fully developed should never try to sense conditions in old buildings or in any spot where tragedies are known to have taken place; the morbid and sordid should always be avoided when possible until complete development has been achieved. There are definite reasons for you to stay clear of ghosts . . . and isn't that encouraging!

22: HERE THERE BE DRAGONS!

REMEMBER those antique maps of the known world, around the edge of which the unknown was labeled "here there be dragons"? That's what this chapter is all about: the very real dangers, if not actual dragons, that lurk about the periphery of mediumship.

As I've intimated before, when one learns the laws governing psychic forces, there is little or no danger in using them. Those who have bad experiences or who become unbalanced over it are the ones who dabble, never taking the trouble to observe the laws or to listen to others who know more than they. When such people open up their consciousnesses psychically, they don't always distinguish between the false and the true, and this can be the difference between success and disaster. The danger lies not in the use but in the abuse of psychic powers. Properly developed mediums should be sane, well balanced, practical and capable.

If I appear dogmatic about this, it is because there is need of extreme care, and I still run into those who refuse to believe it. They tell me, "Oh, no, I'm perfectly safe. I believe in Jesus." Or, "Nothing can bother one who is pure in heart!" I have seen these same people crack up because of the half-glimpses of psychic truth they have grasped, rushing off by themselves in an attempt to put their own ideas into effect.

It is a common mistake to think that all the warnings

apply to other people but not to you and that high motivation protects you from danger. Misses Underhill and MacGregor say, "The psychic laws are powerful and there are no exceptions to their reactions. This we know, because definite effects are caused by working with or against them. It is by comparing the experiences of the many that we have come to understand the right and wrong ways to achieve our purpose.... There are unknown planes of consciousness to be explored; forces, the effect of which must be understood; Universal Principles which must be comprehended and laws which must be obeyed; otherwise the would-be psychic is like a child playing with live wires."

It is certainly true that the forces contacted when one becomes involved more exclusively with the psychic are just as real as electricity and just as unknown in their basic principles. Yet certain laws of operation have been discovered, their reality has been proved by experiment and corroborated by experience. An example is the law of protection, that if you surround yourself with a white light of powerfully thought-out protection, you will be safe. It is easy to scoff at this and ignore it ... until one finally needs help so badly he will try anything, and then he learns that the law works.

It is time for people to begin to understand how to utilize their valuable psychic gifts—talents which lie dormant in the average person throughout his life—and it is imperative that they learn how to use them with benefit to themselves and to others. But those who start trying to develop their psychic powers without taking into consideration the known and unknown laws which govern the whole field will be inviting harm as surely as if they were sticking their fingers into open sockets.

These main dangers that I refer to as dragons are actually human beings—but they are human beings who have passed through the experience called death. Not all who

201

have died are sweet, loving relatives who wish you well. Probably most of those you will contact are the types you and I know, not the kind ever to be villains after they die. But there are a certain number of individuals who die with hatred in their hearts, or with a complete lack of spiritual values, or just with ignorance of their situation. They find themselves after death unable to comprehend where they are and what has happened to them. Not knowing that they must start to improve their lot, they wander around in a daze in the dimensions of the hereafter closest to earth . . . and they are known as earthbound. These are the ones who often try to make their presence known to those still on earth, to influence our minds, sometimes to intrude themselves on us completely. Most ordinary citizens are usually safe from them, but persons attempting to open up their awareness and receptivity to communication are particularly vulnerable. They hope to be contacted only by good spirits, but they don't know how to close out the unenlightened earthbound and keep them away.

After all, when attempting spirit contact, you are communicating with someone who is invisible. How can you be sure who he really is, no matter what name he gives? There is no possible way to ascertain who is using your body to wield the pencil or the Ouija board. It could, of course, be your subconscious mind, as most parapsychologists and psychologists maintain. It could also be spirits working through your subconscious mind, as those who have developed their psychic powers will independently insist. But if it is a spirit, which one? It may often be the enlightened and welcome one who claims to be writing. But it often may not. Frequently those who are endeavoring to communicate are told that their correspondent is Napoleon Bonaparte or Christopher Columbus or Mary Baker Eddy or Abraham Lincoln or any other historical character. If you allow these intruders to give you their messages, in the mistaken belief that you are being honored by the real spirit with the famous name, you are told a variety of stories, frequently contradictory, quite misleading, and often filled with vulgarity and profanity.

A friend of mine began to realize that she was having psychic experiences frequently, so she decided to attempt to contact her deceased parents. She used the Ouija board and then automatic writing, and she soon began to have conversations, she thought, with her loved ones. Not aware of the possible hazards of attempting to communicate on her own without having previously learned how to protect herself, my friend was soon placing herself entirely in the hands of her communicants, allowing them to control her whenever they wished to write. Then she discovered that they had control of her at other times as well. Her right hand, which she had so innocently allowed them to use for writing, began to do the most ridiculous things apparently of its own volition.

On one occasion, when my friend was sitting on a bus going home from work, her right hand was lifted with force and slapped her face brutally. She then realized that things had gotten completely out of ... hand. That is when she wisely stopped all efforts to communicate until she had developed her potentialities and learned protection.

There may be argument in the minds of many readers as to whether or not these intrusions come from mischievous spirits or if they actually originate in the subconscious, as psychologists insist. Where this comes from is important in our ultimate understanding of the overall picture, but while you are enduring the indignities, it seems irrelevant. The things are happening to you; you find your body or sometimes your mind out of control, and it is devastating.

Members of groups who sit in the proper way for development of their psychic talents soon learn how to have command over all such intrusions, and they never let them happen again. Then they are safe to continue their development, and they find themselves with such peace in their souls that their lives give evidence of their harmony and tranquillity.

They have learned, before they start meditating or on any other occasion when they may be reaching out and opening their centers of awareness, to say, "I surround myself with the white light of Christ. Nothing can harm me, mentally, physically, or spiritually."

You can do it too. Say this three times aloud, concentrating on each word. Mentally enclose yourself in a complete thought form of protection. In other words, start at the top of your head and wrap your body in the thought of protection as you repeat the above phrase. With this you can build so strong a wall that no harm can enter. Nothing can come near you that does not come from God in love and peace. Know this at all times. Thoughts *are* things, and it is very important that you who are developing realize it. It will keep you safe from intruding entities at all times.

If you are sitting with a group and have orally established the fact that you are meeting in love and peace and want no interference from any entity who does not come in that spirit, you probably will have little trouble. If anyone in your group should go into trance, entities may attempt to talk through him who do not identify themselves as anyone you know and desire to converse with. They seldom speak intelligently, giving rambling accounts of their lives, their needs, or their philosophies. Sometimes they claim to be famous people, who hardly would have anything in common with your group. The leader should ask them to leave unless they can give definite proof of who they are and why they are there. It is a complete waste of time to bother with obviously unenlightened spirits. If a really important, highly evolved entity were to

204

come, there would be such a feeling of inspiration in the room that everyone there should be aware of it.

If at any time anyone in your meetings begins to see ugly or unpleasant pictures or visions, he must insist that they go away and that whatever is causing them leave at once. If he stresses this with conviction, there is little likelihood of his having any further trouble. One learns this technique of self-protection in groups, and then when he is alone, he continues to practice it. He particularly must protect himself if he tries to communicate via Ouija board or automatic writing at home alone or with only one other. This is not recommended; and if you do it, you do it at your own risk.

A young girl who lived in my apartment building in Miami enjoyed her Ouija board tremendously, for it was like another beau to her. The entity who wrote with her purported to love her and said he intended to stay with her always. Whenever she was lonely, she could sit at her board and converse with her unseen admirer and have her morale build up. I warned her it was not a good thing to do, but who could tell her anything? She especially would not consider the possibility that her subconscious mind could be working the board, and so she gloated when one day it gave her evidence of supernormal ability.

She and several friends had gone to the beach, young men and women having a happy outing. They met a Cuban youth there and invited him to come home with them. When they arrived at my friend's apartment, they got out the Ouija board and talked to her invisible lover for entertainment. Then they decided to try to test it, and it agreed to play the game. None of the girls and boys understood or spoke Spanish except the Cuban, so they suggested that he think of a question and they would ask Ouija to answer it in Spanish. Sitting across the room from the board, he asked mentally, "How long have I been in this country?" and the board spelled out, *"Dos años,"* which was correct.

Then he asked it another, more complicated question, and it gave the right answer to that.

This was great, except that whoever or whatever was working the Ouija had a great antipathy to his girl's having any other boyfriends. Whenever a man sat at the board to work it with her, it addressed him as "bastard," "son of a bitch," and worse.

Unfortunately, this negative attitude toward her suitors began to extend to other aspects of her life. It got so that she couldn't keep a sweetheart no matter how hard she tried . . . and she was a charming girl. Something kept turning them off, although she never did find out what. When first one and then another of her boyfriends began to have accidents that incapacitated them, so they couldn't come to see her, the girl finally got wise. She asked whoever was writing to her on her Ouija board please to stop and to leave her alone. She told him that she would never converse with him again, and she kept her word, putting the board away for good. Not too long after that he apparently realized she meant it and went away, for her love life returned to its usual satisfactory state.

If, after all these warnings, you are nonetheless determined to attempt communication on your own, you must first always wrap yourself in protection. Say aloud that you are building a mental wall around yourself and your Ouija board or your paper and pencil or your typewriter and that no one who does not come from God in love and peace can enter. If you believe this firmly when you say it, you will be protected.

Often you may be told you are in communication with a parent or someone else in whom you have faith. Always ask for identifying information from whoever purports to write, and if it isn't given clearly and promptly, stop writing immediately. It is never good to ask for advice or help because if it should not come from the spirit you believe it to be, it may be completely wrong and misleading. You will probably be told to do just what you want to do. It is possible for gullible persons to be taken in completely by such misinformation and to become unsettled and confused by the conflicting data given them by intruders. If you are weak-willed to begin with, you may even be opening the doors for an earthbound entity actually to possess you, or else to influence you strongly. This is so great a danger that I cannot stress it enough. That's why it is better to sit for development in a group for some time before attempting to communicate alone. Usually then you will learn to have such excellent communion through meditation that you will have no need to try the more mechanical methods. No highly developed mediums ever use Ouija boards; and only certain ones whose special training makes them particularly useful to spirit communicators of a high type are found using a pen or pencil or typewriter to receive their messages.

Another danger of using Ouija boards has nothing whatever to do with spirits but with solid substantial forms of flesh and blood. It is gullibility, that tendency to be taken in by fraud. People who seem perfectly sound mentally can do the dumbest things when allegedly instructed to by spirits. They often seem to take all leave of their senses when they become enraptured with spirit communication.

I have before me a newspaper clipping which states, "Messages spelled out on a Ouija board directing a seventy-one-year-old millionaire to give $59,285 to 'the good angel' were caused by fraud rather than spirits, a judge and jury decided."

The story was that Miss Clara Hoover of San Francisco, the heiress to a tanning industry fortune, had brought suit against her onetime friend and masseuse, Mrs. Margaret Faulkner, who had used the Ouija board with her. Soon the board had spelled out requests for jewelry and money, ostensibly to be given to a gypsy named Yuma in an unidentified church for transmission to "the good angel." Yuma never appeared in court.

Neither did "the good angel."

23: POSSESSION

YOU may shudder at the concept of spirit possession. I did. I would not have accepted it as fact under any circumstances until I became deeply involved in psychical research and found so much evidence for it. I know better now; and I hope you will consider what I am telling you, if for no other reason than to realize that some people do need protection from the danger.

Historically, the idea of possession is nothing new. Christ drove the devils out, as you will remember. Referring to these "devils" who possess people, Canon J. D. Pearce-Higgins explains in "Haunted Minds": ". . . what we invariably find are dead, discarnate former living beings who have become 'earthbound' after shedding the body, and because of a variety of factors, *e.g.*, ignorance of the real nature of death, sensual and materialistic outlooks on life, or both, have failed to progress forward, and have remained close to the scenes of their earthly life. If they find 'an open door' in the psyche of some living individual, they enter and use the mind and body for their own ends. Why some people have open doors is a mystery, but severe illness and nervous debility, a blow on the head (very common) or some psychological trauma seems to be among the main causes.

"The case histories then appear to show that possession is a fact, and that a good many patients in mental hospitals suffering from hallucinations, hearing or speaking in

209

strange voices, or suffering from split-personalities, *may* be cases of possession who would benefit from treatment similar to that given by Dr. Wickland [Dr. Karl Wickland, a medical doctor and psychiatrist who reported in 1924 in *Thirty Years Among the Dead* how he used his wife's mediumistic ability to cure possessed patients]. Here, unfortunately, we come up against a problem, because even supposing psychiatrists were prepared to try this completely harmless experiment in 'exorcism' (for want of a better word), where shall we find the mediums who can do what Mrs. Wickland did?

"There are possibly half a dozen in the world who can do it—I know two, and both of these undertake such cases with great reluctance because of the great strain involved."

Some religions allow possession as part of their regular ceremonies. The Vodun or Voodoo of Haiti is typical of this. Of course, the entities who possess the entranced priestesses are said to be gods, or loa. But this does not necessarily mean they *are* anything more than ordinary spirits who take over when given the opportunity. Except when it is done in the name of religion or when efforts to communicate are made by those who have no knowledge of how to protect themselves, it is usually people who are particularly vulnerable or who have bad social habits who are most likely to be possessed. When any person allows his mind to become so weak and degraded that it attracts the lowest and meanest spirits—those who hang closely about the earth for nothing but sensual gratification—he is in constant danger of possession. The earthbound spirit will attempt in every way possible to take him over completely, move in, and push his consciousness aside entirely. When this occurs, the original mind in that body lies dormant until the body dies, or until the intruder's hold becomes weakened by alcohol or in some other way that dislodges him, or when he is convinced through the effort of spirit helpers or human rescue circles that he must leave. Only then may the soul of the possessed individual, which has more than likely lain dormant during the period of occupation, return to his own body and take over. Sometimes both the human and the spirit consciousness may fight for possession of the body. Some cases of schizophrenia are attributed to this.

An example of what was most likely intermittent possession is an incident that was among America's most notorious crimes. It involved wealthy, well-educated Harry K. Thaw, who had been so erratic and excitable during his youth that his parents, who had close to $30,000,000, were afraid to correct him for fear he would go insane. They didn't realize it then, but apparently he was subject to malevolent spirit influence all his life and could be taken over from time to time by wicked earthbound entities who made him do terrible things.

After Thaw reached adulthood, he would go on crazy sexual binges, half out of his head with rage. Susan Merrill, the madam of a New York City brothel, was later to testify that he kept an apartment in her house, where he sometimes ravaged girls and beat them senseless. About one occasion she stated, "I could hear screams coming from his apartment, and for once I could stand it no longer. I rushed into his rooms. He had tied the girl to the bed, naked, and was whipping her. She was covered with welts. Thaw's eyes protruded and he looked mad."

Then an attractive sixteen-year-old named Evelyn Nesbitt came from Pittsburgh to New York and joined the Follies chorus as a Floradora Girl. Soon she became the mistress of wealthy architect Stanford White. But when Thaw saw her and fell in love with her, he married her. Unfortunately, he knew about her relationship with White, and for almost three years he persecuted her for it during all his wild periods.

Once while crossing the Atlantic aboard ship, Harry K.

211

Thaw chained his young wife to the bedstead in their stateroom and whipped her with his belt for hours until she confessed that Stanford White had done to her every horrible atrocity she could dream up. The part of her story publicized was that in their love nest White had continually stripped her and raped her and made her pose naked on a red velvet swing. At the time of the trial she became famous as "The Girl on the Red Velvet Swing."

Everything Evelyn told her husband, even though he beat it out of her, he believed, and he vowed revenge on Stanford White.

The evening of June 25, 1906, was warm and peaceful until Thaw took his wife to dine at the theater on the roof of Madison Square Garden, where a light Victorian musical farce called *Mamzelle Champagne* was opening. Most of high society was there, and so was Stanford White, who sat at a table alone. Thaw walked over and proceeded to put two bullets into his brain.

One of this country's most notorious court trials ensued for seven months, hotly contested because Thaw claimed he was innocent. He admitted that a strange form of insanity took him over on occasion and made him do bad things, including killing White. Spirit possession was as little known in those days as it is today, and so it was not used as an alibi. However, Thaw described something very similar, calling it Providence. He pleadingly told the jury, "I never wanted to shoot that man. Providence took charge of the situation."

Deciding that black powers had taken temporary control over Thaw's reasoning at the time of the murder, the jury returned a verdict, "Not guilty on the grounds of his insanity at the time of the commission of the act." After several more court battles and one occasion when he escaped briefly to Canada and was recaptured, Thaw was placed in a mental institution. Nine years later he was freed. He never publicly did anything degenerate again for the rest of his life, but he apparently continued to be just as psychically prey to invisible intruders. From time to time that wild stare would appear in his eyes, his mouth would sag, and strange words would tumble incoherently from his lips.

Many of you know an individual who drinks too much and then becomes an altogether different person. You think it is the baser elements of his own personality coming out. It is more likely instead the baser elements of another personality taking over his body. When the mind is too beclouded by alcohol, its hold on the body can easily be loosened and a spirit entity may move in. Usually he continues drinking to the point of further stupefaction, and the normal processes of awakening in the morning bring the owner's consciousness back into his body. Only rarely is an alcoholic so completely possessed by a spirit that he loses his identity permanently. The intruder, benumbed by liquor, can have no greater hold on the body than the owner had, so the possession is usually a temporary thing. But while it goes on, no love for family or friends is shown because the new entity does not know them. Usually none of the virtues of the original consciousness is present, only the vices of the intruder. So if you drink to the point of insensibility, you may lose yourself to a spirit intruder because of it.

If you are a consistent drinker, yet not to the extent that you become dead drunk, you aren't likely to be possessed; but you are definitely in a position to be influenced by those entities who get a vicarious thrill out of your experiences. This is called obsession. Some chronic drinkers have long been puzzled and alarmed by the fact that something in their minds has urged them to drink even when they knew they did not really want to.

A friend of mine named Pearl, a lovely blonde, is an alcoholic When she began to study metaphysics and learned

213

about possession, she was extremely grateful to know that was part of her problem.

"I always wondered what kind of a devil could be hiding in my own subconscious mind," she said. "It frightened me to death, for I seemed powerless to keep it from ruling my actions. I thought I had a split personality and knew that if I went to a psychiatrist, he might put me away, so I suffered with it alone."

To become aware that an external force might have been prompting her to do things she knew to be wrong for her relieved Pearl's worries considerably. She told me later she had found a successful way of treating her problem.

"I tell the spirit to scram," she said. "When I get these mental urges to take a drink—not the physical needs, I understand them, but the thoughts pushing and prodding me—I tell the entity I won't listen to it. I'm very firm about it, and eventually it leaves me alone. After I showed it a few times that I'm now the boss of my life, it stopped bothering me."

Unfortunately, it came back one time when Pearl had not been drinking—at least, no more than one, she maintains. As she was driving her car, she was suddenly urged to kill herself.

"You've got to come over here with me," the voice in her mind said. "Kill yourself . . . right now! Drive into that tree!"

Somehow powerless to resist, Pearl turned the wheel and headed the car off the road and into a tree. Fortunately, she was not killed, but both she and the car were considerably damaged.

Probably her resistance to the entreating of this entity was low because she had followed his suggestions so much in the past. My communicant James gives the sound advice to take steps to rid yourself of the drinking habit the minute you begin to suspect you might be a problem drinker. No bad habit has to remain if you wish to lose it, he

214

says. But you can rid yourself of bad habits only by making an effort. And it is not possible to continue drinking to excess and then expect to lose your invisible persuaders.

The same situation exists with those who are addicted to drugs, James says. It is appalling that so many young people today are playing with the milder drugs. LSD, peyote, mescaline, amphetamines, methedrine, glue sniffing, even marijuana—any awareness-expanding or mind-changing drugs—may not be habit forming, but they are still hazardous. The dangers lie in several areas. First, the group communion is stimulating; and when you are secretly gathering with those who turn on with certain less harmful drugs, it's not easy for you to back out when your friends decide to experiment with something stronger. The second danger is more important and less realized: Whenever you open your mind wide, even to fascinating new sensations and sometimes inspiring visions, somebody may move right in. Yes, you are vulnerable to possession or obsession.

Obsession is spirit influence. Not taking over your body as in possession, the entities instead overshadow you and influence your thinking. Just as they hang onto your thoughts when they are negative and sad and attempt to make them worse by insinuating more and more unhappy ideas into your mind, so when you are on drugs they may move in on your visions and make them unpleasant instead of beautiful. It is possible that you may suddenly begin to see devils and horrible scenes or begin to think of yourself as low and degraded. These pictures and thoughts do not necessarily come from your subconscious mind, as you may think. In some cases, at least, you are not bringing out buried filth. What is happening is that you are being strongly impressed by spirits. If you allow them to influence you in this way by taking the drugs often, you may find yourself completely unable to control your mind.

For mischievous entities to move in and try to take over

215

another's mind is a vicious thing, but it is frequently done. Being aware of the possibility will help you keep it from happening. Stay away from all mind-influencing drugs as carefully as you stay away from heroin. If you wish to have happy visions, think happy thoughts frequently so that they become a habit. Then learn the proper system of meditation, and the pleasant pictures will come without any outside stimulation. And you won't be in danger of the terrible consequences of spirit influence.

Reverend T. N. Tiemeyer, pastor of Christ Congregational Church in Miami and a brilliant religious and philosophical thinker, says in "Dimensions of Defensive Prayer": "It is illogical to assume that death is a magic wand which transforms ordinary, worldly-minded people into perfected divine beings. Passing through the 'valley of shadow' merely means leaving behind the physical vehicle. To each is offered the opportunity to transfer earth consciousness to the infinite and eternal awareness. But suppose the entity rejects this privilege?

"People come in many varieties. Some are ignorant, some evil, some overly sensual, and some corroded with hatred. Since these are mental attitudes, they survive death and continue to dominate discarnate beings. Unable or unwilling to accept survival of mind or reality of spirit, they cannot move on to higher levels. Remaining as close to the material plane as possible, they may seek vicarious fulfillment, revenge, or sadistic satisfactions through those still on the earth plane.

"Thus we have a logical basis for belief in spirit possession. In Biblical days this was assumed to be fact. In the early scientific era such hypotheses were discarded as medieval superstition. Today the possibility is again being seriously considered. Not only is it imperative that such afflictions be explored, but the preventions and cures must also be perfected. In this area prayer has proved itself to

216

be the most powerful defense and the most potent corrective."

The Reverend Mr. Tiemeyer says there are many qualified authorities on mental paranormalities who believe that most cases reported as evidence of reincarnation can be better explained by temporary spirit possession. My communicant, James, agrees.

In his article Mr. Tiemeyer rather lets the cat out of the bag about my "James." He speaks of my having received communication for years from an entity who called himself James but later revealed that he was the late psychologist William James. I seldom mention this because I have no possible way of being sure the entity really is the famous William. He can be judged only by the astuteness of his communications. The paragraphs that the Reverend Mr. Tiemeyer thought most effective in James' messages on possession were the following:

"If you live for yourself alone, considering your pleasures more important than anything else, you will probably die with nothing better on your mind. You will then be an earthbound spirit. Such an unenlightened individual hangs closely around the earth for many years. If this entity is an alcoholic, he will remain close to a hard drinker, inciting him to further drink so that he can enjoy the experience vicariously. If he took heroin on earth, he still thinks of himself as a user and will live with addicts, urging them on so he can possess or obsess them when they are under drug influence.

"Negative thoughts from the earthbound can intrude themselves upon one who is worried or unhappy and make him twice as miserable. Many entities of a more malicious character know they are dead but do not know what to do about it. They continue to hang around the earth, reveling in the kind of life they used to enjoy. Sex is one of their favorite subjects as you can well imagine. The best way to keep such as these from you is to be the clean

217

living, positive thinking type who does not interest them in the least.

"If you are weak-willed and negative in your personality, they may pressure you to indulge excessively in your weaknesses, commit crimes, or even drive you to suicide. Realize that you can protect yourself. Insist orally that you will not allow anyone to influence you who does not come from God in love and peace. Affirm this often, and *believe* it."

Lewis Smith, a Reformed Jew and a group leader in the south Florida chapter of Spiritual Frontiers, effectively uses the following prayer to help possessed persons:

"Dear God, cleanse, clear, fill and encapsulate me in the white Christ light of healing and protection. Remove all negative energies and entities from me and send them to their proper plane. Then close the aura against their return and in their place put the highest and most powerful vibrations. Thank you, Father."

Those of us who write books in this field frequently receive letters from people who have run into ugly situations of this kind. Harold Sherman says he gives those who wish to get rid of possession an order that must be issued with all the force at their command: *"Get out and stay out. I won't have any more to do with you any time, anywhere. I call upon the God presence in me to throw you out. You are no more."*

I can only urge the use of this as strongly as he does.

24: RESCUE CIRCLES

WHEN the psychic faculties are opened, the individual is bound to be supersensitive; impressions made at such a time are deeper and can be more uplifting but, on the other hand, can be more disastrous in their effects than when a person is in his normal state. If a man is known by the company he keeps in this world, this is doubly true when he touches the psychic planes. The danger of drawing undesirable spirits into the aura (or causing them to cling to you) is not imaginary. A medium who contacts the lower entities deliberately is touching evil and is apt to become infected by it. We should never debase our higher gifts by using them for dishonorable or degrading work, nor should we ask our guides to do such work for us. If we have reason to believe that undesirable psychic influences are present, either in the aura of an individual or in a particular room or house, we are justified in obtaining the assistance of a developed medium, providing that he or she has a strong character and is spiritually, as well as psychically, evolved. With the aid of his spirit helpers such a one can free the individual from obsessing entities or ideas and remove the evil conditions from the room or house.

The late, great medium Eileen Garrett did a good bit of rescue work of this type, releasing unhappy ghosts who haunted houses because they knew no better. Broadway columnist Danton Walker had such a spook in his restored

Early American home in Rockland County, New York, in the 1940's and '50's. The house dated from pre-Revolutionary times, and its location, Camp Hill, got its name because Mad Anthony Wayne supposedly bivouacked his troops there, before or just after the famous battle of Stony Point in 1779.

Walker made a comfortable home of the old house but found himself unable to live in it because of the mysterious noises and unexplained activities thereabouts. You'd have thought there was an invisible striptease going on, there were so many bumps, knocks and grinds in that house. Often the iron knocker on the front door crashingly resounded when nobody was anywhere near it. One guest, who was particularly sure there was no such thing as ghosts, was awakened from a sound sleep by a violent slap in the face. He then saw a chair rocking and a shirt blowing as if in a breeze, but there was no breeze. He went away from there.

One night at Walker's request a group consisting of Mrs. Garrett, a prominent Park Avenue psychiatrist, and a few others visited the old home on a rescue mission. They brought a secretary to take notes, a tape recorder, and a photographer with an infrared camera.

Mrs. Garrett went into a trance, and her control, Uvani, spoke. He gave a long dissertation, as a sort of warming-up process; then another personality came through, and, as Walker said in his book *Spooks DeLuxe,* "then things really began to happen." The new entity, almost babbling in fright and confusion, was apparently not aware he was dead.

The story which emerged from his telling concerned a Polish mercenary who had been trapped there during some Revolutionary action. He had been chased into the house by the "big men"—apparently British soldiers—and horribly beaten. Walker writes: "His teeth knocked out (this illustrated by a grisly pantomime), his head bashed

220

in and one leg broken, he had been left there to die. He didn't die—then—but lived on for many pain-wracked days, broken in mind as well as body. And this was the spirit who was haunting my house!"

Mrs. Garrett fell onto the floor and writhed in anguish while the entity was speaking through her; but the others present talked to him and told him he had died and could be released from his pain and terror if he would just listen to the spirit helpers who were there. Apparently he finally did, and Mrs. Garrett's body was relinquished. Then Uvani returned, assuring everyone that the Polish mercenary's spirit was now set at rest and he would never disturb Walker's house again. He didn't, either.

"It is unwise for partially developed mediums to sit in 'rescue circles,' or to permit themselves to be controlled by unregenerate and debased types of spirits," say MacGregor and Underhill. Such rescue circles are occasionally held by various groups around the world, apparently without danger to more powerful psychics and with a great deal of advantage to the spirits who need to have their situation explained to them. The circle sits in the dark or near dark and the medium goes into trance. It is understood that her guides will bring in a few earthbound spirits who need to have information about their condition, where they are, and what they can do about it. When this occurs, individuals who are usually confused speak through the medium, asking all kinds of innocent questions like "Where am I?" "What is going on?"

They are usually asked who they are, and eventually it is ascertained from them that they had a severe illness or were in a bad accident or a sudden shooting or the like and then everything became confused. They don't know exactly what has happened to them and usually think they are having a bad dream. Members of the circle ask them questions and discuss their situation with them, usually convincing them that they have died but that it really isn't so bad after all. Then they are told that helpful guides and missionaries will assist them, and they are removed from the medium by the control. Such rescue circles, while they sound almost simplistic, apparently do a great deal of good.

Say MacGregor and Underhill, "Certainly there are a few psychics qualified to do this work, and their spirit guides are capable of protecting them from harm. Even when actuated by the highest motives the average psychic is not equipped to do such work. We advise those who feel drawn to help souls who are in need never to allow themselves to be controlled by low and undesirable characters. Prayer is just as effective, even though it is a less spectacular method of assisting them, and it is foolish for inexperienced people to expose themselves and others in the circle to unnecessary danger."

I have attended rescue circles in many parts of the country, and the procedures are usually similar. Rosalind and David McKnight have made a specialty of them. Their sessions usually open with several musical renditions by Ralfonzo, through Rosie's untutored hands on the piano keys. After that either David or Rosie or both will go into trance while sitting in a circle with others, who will provide power and helpful conversation for the rescue work.

David wrote me the details of how they got started with such work: "At the same time that we were getting to know Ralph, I began experiencing, also in a semitrance state, a series of personalities, many of whom were obviously disoriented or even in distress. Fortunately, Katie King, the medium with whom we were sitting, and the other development class members recognized these entities as 'rescue cases': persons who had passed over without realizing, or being able to accept, the fact that they had made this transition. As these overshadowing personalities became stronger, Katie and the class members began to talk with them, explaining to them their condition, and urging them to seek help and enlightenment from higher realms. One such case was that of Usoto, who upon his first visit explained that he had been in Hiroshima with his wife and child at the time of the atomic explosion in 1945. He stated that he was a medical doctor and had been looking for his family without success since the explosion. A scientist and a religious agnostic, Usoto was apparently unable to accept the reality of another world, following his death in the atomic blast. But now, after twenty-four years of earthbound searching for his family, he was prepared to listen to our little rescue group's explanation of the fate that had befallen him and his family and of his present condition in a new dimension. With his characteristic gentleness and dignity, Usoto stated that he would think about what we had said, and the circle gave a prayer in his behalf. On his next visit he related, with grateful tears, that he had been reunited with his wife and child just as we had promised he would be. Since that day, Usoto has been a frequent visitor, sometimes speaking to groups about his experience of being rescued, sometimes giving guidance—or just nodding in briefly to acknowledge his friendship and appreciation. As with Ralfonzo, we hope some day to find public records concerning Usoto and his family, and have collected bits and pieces of information from him as we are able for this purpose."

After David had experienced a number of rescue cases, Katie King urged him to "close himself off" to such entities in favor of receiving higher influences. However, some months later Rosie picked up this work, and they continued their rescue efforts through her. The variety of personalities and life situations which followed was "tremendous," according to David, "as we have found is the case with other rescue mediums we have since come to know. Though it is hard to select a representative case, an interesting one came while we were visiting friends who were houseparents at a private girls' school in New York State. This young couple had found that their two small children refused to sleep in what had originally been established as their room, and instead ended up sleeping in the parents' bedroom. The couple, although they told their children nothing about their doubts, suspected a spirit influence in the children's bedroom, for they themselves were aware at times of a negative force in the apartment. Thus during our visit we found ourselves in a rescue circle, hoping to establish the source of the unfriendly atmosphere. Rosie soon brought through an old man, who demanded that we get out of his house. As we talked with him, we determined that he had suffered blindness from an early age, as well as a severe respiratory condition in later life, and he was an intensely bitter and lonely person. He spent many of his last years isolated in his study, while his wife, for whom he had little love, stayed largely in other parts of the house. It appeared, from clues in his conversation (rescue work is detective work!), that he finally died of a stroke while sitting in his den, without anyone coming to his aid. However, he vehemently insisted that we were crazy for suggesting that he was dead, and he even accused us at one point of being ghosts who were bothering him. No amount of talking seemed to budge this withdrawn and angry individual, whose lovelessness was holding him down to earth. So we simply tried to love him and ended our session with a prayer that light might penetrate his lonely isolation.

"At our next rescue session, at our home, we were visited again by this lost soul, who had followed us; but he showed little progress, and again we prayed in his behalf. The next time he returned, however, he was a changed man. He understood what had happened to him and had met and been reconciled with his wife! He thanked us for having taken such an interest in him. Shortly thereafter, we learned from our friends at the girls' school that neither their children nor they had sensed any negative presence in their home since the first night the entity had been contacted."

David said in response to my request for their suggestions, "We have not really learned any very special techniques for bringing through rescue cases or for doing other forms of trance and semitrance work. Such cases can come through spontaneously or upon request. A controlling entity (doorkeeper or gatekeeper) should be overseeing the entire process so that no unwanted influences may enter or disturb the medium's body. After a prayer, we simply sit quietly for a few moments—though we sometimes now employ a yogic breath technique recently explained to us. After mind and body are quieted, the medium gradually begins to feel some of the facial and other physical characteristics of the influencing entity. Muscles, particularly in the face and neck, respond involuntarily, and often those in the circle can tell something about the entity's physical appearance or condition while on earth. Then words come into your mind, and you (the medium) speak them; or they sometimes come out almost before you are aware of them. Often there is a change in voice or a characteristic accent. All the while, you are more or less conscious of what is happening; you hear it almost as an observer. But you are also partly involved, feeling to some extent the speaker's feelings. Sometimes, toward the end of the session, you see (though your eyes are closed) a light or feel the presence of a loved one—particularly, of course, if the session is successful in aiding the rescue entity. Sometimes such an entity finds his way in just one sitting, and in other cases several—or even many—sessions are required. At the end of the sitting, the influence gradually leaves, and you sit quietly for a moment to readjust physically. If you are rested before the session, the experience is not at all tiring, no matter how

225

vigorously the entity has expressed himself. Often you feel quite awake and rested afterward.

"There are precautions which we take concerning all rescue work, however. (And we would never want to recommend in a general way that individuals attempt such work independently. It is commonly agreed that there are much more beneficial forms of communication with higher spiritual forces than trance work normally permits, such as through prayer and meditation, and we have found this to be so in our own personal experience.) Rescue circles have a very specialized purpose, which is to offer spiritual aid and information to individuals who are emotionally or intellectually disoriented following their passing out of their physical bodies. With this purpose in mind, the chances of helping such individuals are greatly increased. We therefore begin every rescue circle with a prayer for guidance and protection. In our case, we often say the Lord's Prayer and have a cross present to signify the spiritual purpose of the circle. Rescue circles should be composed of a small group of well-informed and committed persons who meet regularly and faithfully over a long period of time. When rescue work is done successfully, it is a high form of service and offers great rewards. We have certainly learned much about the problems and purpose of both this world and the next and are grateful for the opportunity to be of apparent help to some who have lost their way."

25: THE ALPHA STATE

BY going into trances yogis have been accomplishing fantastic feats for hundreds of years. So have mediums and those who meditate themselves into a state of cosmic consciousness. Until just recently scientists paid no attention whatever to such claims. Now they are investigating altered states of consciousness and their accompanying physiological states with the enthusiasm of those who have just discovered something new and exciting. They are learning how one can gain voluntary control of his brain and his internal organs, and the accomplishments of the yogis of old are being somewhat validated by hard data.

Using such scientific equipment as the electrocardiograph (EKG) for measuring heart activity, the electroencephalograph (EEG) for measuring brain activity, the electromyograph (EMG) for measuring muscle activity, the electrooculograph (EOG) for measuring eye muscle activity, audio oscillators, digital frequency discriminators, and omnidirectional tilt detectors, scientists can study what is going in inside the human organism. The technique of self-monitoring by use of these instruments is called physiological feedback, or biofeedback, and with it both those persons serving as experimental subjects and patients in therapy have a means of rather precise internal scanning. This, according to John White in "The Yogi in the Lab," "can open the door to learning (or in the case of neurosis, unlearning) physiological and psychological data previously beyond the range of their awareness."

It has been ascertained that the heartbeat, blood pressure, body temperature, and gastrointestinal activity are subject to conscious control, just as Oriental practitioners have demonstrated for centuries, as yogis lowered their metabolism while buried alive for days, or reduced pulse volume so that their hearts seemed to have stopped, or walked on fire without blistering their feet, or laid comfortably on nail points, or pierced their flesh with swords bloodlessly and with no signs of pain.

Subjects are also learning that it is possible to put themselves into various brain states at will, researchers having discovered that certain brain waves on the EEG are correlated with certain states of consciousness. The alpha, beta, theta and delta waves show a range of mental conditions from rest to high alertness. The normally conscious state is called the beta. Alpha is the inner conscious level of deep meditation or mild psychic trance. Theta and delta are usually unconscious levels.

The alpha state is one of relaxed, serene wakefulness in which floating images—but no deliberate thought—are occasionally reported. It shows a rhythmic pattern of eight to twelve cycles a second on the EEG. You can see why it is of particular interest to us—it is the state of meditation. If we can learn to get into it at will, our ESP development will be more rapid.

David Techter, in "Latest from Maimonides" in *Fate* (January, 1971), discusses the recent fascination of parapsychologists with the alpha rhythms. "Briefly stated," he says, "normal functioning of the brain produces small surges of electrical activity which may be detected with the electroencephalograph. Alpha, beta, delta and theta are terms given to various frequencies of such electrical surges. It is of interest to psychical researchers that alpha activity frequently is associated with states of meditation, which in turn are sometimes the occasion for ESP experiences.

"However, until relatively recently it was thought that the individual had no conscious control over his brain rhythms. Now a number of researchers (led by Joe Kamiya) have demonstrated that many individuals can be trained to produce alpha rhythm at will by a technique known as biofeedback. By this means the subject comes to know when he is producing alpha rhythm because a continuous EEG monitoring system activates a signal when alpha is present. Thus if a light comes on whenever the subject produces alpha rhythm he can be trained to keep this light on for relatively long intervals.

"Using this new technique parapsychologists have undertaken a variety of experiments to test the relationship between alpha rhythms and ESP experiences. The results, alas, have been mixed and even contradictory. Clearly, no one unique mental state is revealed by alpha rhythm; different subjects, or the same subject on different occasions, may experience quite varied states of mind during alpha activity."

Even when ESP isn't produced, there are various other rewards from achieving the alpha state. It is pleasant and relaxing. It helps one to meditate and also to develop more creativity. People with insomnia have learned to go to sleep at will; and withdrawal from the use of such drugs as alcohol, amphetamines, barbiturates and nicotine can be facilitated. Alpha control can be used as a learning aid because the poised nondrowsy state generally associated with it appears to expedite the recall process. It is a powerful tool for the psychotherapist and the hypnotherapist because of the possibility of training subjects to experience at will deep reveries and increased ability to visualize. It has already been proved in clinical practice that many physiological disorders can be cured by electromyographic feedback alone.

Joe Kamiya, director of the Psychophysiology of Consciousness Project at the Langley Porter Neuropsychiatric Institute in San Francisco, is doing considerable research concerning physiological feedback training and the psychophysiology of meditation.

"It is the possibility of correlating the electrical activity of the brain with the subjects' reports of their experience and their behavior which has intrigued me as a psychologist," Kamiya says, "for I feel it is a more solid approach than building hypothetical mental mechanisms on the basis of verbal reports alone."

Kamiya began in 1958 by having volunteers simply discriminate between the presence and absence of spontaneous alpha waves. He monitored the EEG and controlled the signal tone, sounding it randomly and asking the subject whether he thought he was in alpha. His subjects usually became 75 to 80 percent correct in their discrimination within three hours. As his work developed, he wondered if people could be trained to control brain waves as well as to discriminate between states. The answer was affirmative; they could turn on or suppress the alpha rhythm at will. Word of the new kind of "turn-on" spread, and Kamiya is now besieged by volunteers eager to groove their way into an instant satori.

Dr. Elmer E. Green and his wife Alyce teach autogenetics—self-regulation of internal states—in their laboratory at the Research Department, Menninger Foundation, Topeka, Kansas. In a paper titled "Voluntary Control of Internal States: Psychological and Physiological" they give credit to German researcher Johannes Schultz for bringing to the Western world a great interest in what yogis had been doing in India for some two hundred years, reported by medical doctors serving with the British Army or Civil Service there. Their phenomenal control was obtained, they said, through long practice of specific mental, emotional, and physical disciplines.

By 1910 Schultz had developed a Western system of self-regulation by combining various ideas from his medical research, especially from hypnosis, with concepts from yogic methods. Although Freud gave up the use of hypnotism in therapy because its results were too unpredictable, it occurred to Schultz that the major defect with hypnotism might lie in the fact that the patient was not in control of the situation and therefore resisted in various ways the doctor's instructions. Schultz combined the free will or volitional aspect of yoga with some of the techniques he had used and eventually developed the therapeutic system named Autogenic Training, which is self-generated or self-willed.

His procedure had a measure of success, but it takes considerable time for the subject to learn it. It was the need to shorten the learning time associated with Autogenic Training and to adapt the system for research in states of consciousness that led to the methodology used by Dr. Green. In it the autogenic development has been carried one step further by combining the conscious self-regulation aspect of yoga and the psychological method of Autogenic Training with the modern instrumental technique called psychological feedback (or the use of mechanical apparatus so that the subject can learn what his body is trying to tell him).

When the Greens use autogenics in the laboratory, their subject wears a special jacket equipped with a built-in respiration gauge, which gives a readout to one of the pens on their twenty-four-channel polygraph. Other channels record the raw EEG on the left and right sides of the brain; frequency of theta, alpha, delta and beta brain waves; muscle tension; blood volume and flow in the subject's hand; galvanic skin potential and response; and heart rate. Brain waves, temperature changes, and arm muscle tension also register as vertical bars of light on a screen in front of the subject. These light bars give him an easily understood indication of his internal physiological activity.

The Greens also worked out a way for people to practice Autogenic Training at home without any instruments, in which one must watch and listen to his body to get feedback from it. I have found the first stage of this to be very useful in producing an alpha state during meditation period. I will briefly give the outline of the entire procedure, but I wouldn't want the reader to try any more than the first part alone without a trained person to run you through the procedure.

You must first get comfortable, either by lying down on a bed with your legs out straight and your arms down by your sides, or by leaning back in a high-backed chair with your feet up on a foot stool. You sit or lie quietly with your eyes closed. Let your breathing slow down. Say in your mind, not orally, "I am relaxed . . . I am at peace . . . I am calm . . . I am relaxed." Say this over several times as you feel yourself becoming very secure and calm. Then start the exercises by thinking about how heavy your right arm is. For one minute think about your arm, *sure* that it is heavy. Heaviness is a feeling that comes naturally with sleep. It means that the large muscles are relaxing. Keep thinking very gently about your arm and how comfortably heavy it is. You must use what is called passive concentration, which means that you have to let the thing happen, not try to make it happen. If your mind tells your arm to get heavy, your arm will get heavy because it has to do what your mind tells it to do. It may take a few days for you to get the heavy feeling, but it will come if you stay with it and let it happen.

At home you should practice three times a day if you possibly can while you are learning. You will need to do it only once a day after you have learned. After you practice with your right arm for a few days, your left arm will begin to get heavy, too, when you start telling it that it is

232

heavy for one minute. Then, when both arms are getting heavy for you, start on one leg, then the other leg. Learn to listen to your body. Let it act as a feedback mechanism to tell you when you are doing an exercise correctly.

There are six standard exercises you can do at home, and I will mention them, but you must promise not to do them without further instruction, because you might do the wrong thing. If you were to say, for instance, "My heartbeat is getting slower" instead of "My heartbeat is calm and regular," you might cause your heart to stop altogether; that's why it is so important to do it correctly.

The exercises are:

1. "My arms and legs are heavy."
2. "My arms and legs are warm."
3. "My heartbeat is calm and regular."
4. "My solar plexus is warm."
5. "It breathes me."
6. "My forehead is cool, my hands are warm."
7. When you are finished with whatever part of the exercise you are doing, conclude with "My body is light and ready" and a good stretching before you open your eyes.

Using these techniques learned at the Menninger Lab, by causing their blood to flow more strongly into their arms and hands instead of into their heads when migraine headaches threaten, some students have completely overcome violent headaches which had plagued them for years. They have also alleviated long-lasting insomnia by relaxation and also by increasing the temperature of their feet at night. Through education in blood-pressure control one man conquered the symptoms of his hypertension.

However, the Greens are primarily interested in experimenting with lowering alpha frequency and increasing the percentage of theta rhythm, for theta waves predominate

233

in the final phase of Zen meditation when the masters achieve satori, deep peace and clear ecstatic consciousness and oneness with all creation ... the highest state of consciousness. For this research two more bars of light have been added to the feedback screen in the laboratory to indicate lowering alpha and continuous ten-second theta.

Dr. Green says that this research—voluntary control of alpha and theta brain rhythms—is specifically to explore "the general processes, conditions and contents of consciousness during a state of deep reverie." Reverie, he says, is a state of inward-turned abstract attention or internal scanning akin to some dreamlike states, a condition associated with low-frequency alpha and theta waves. In reverie hypnagogic-like imagery has been detected, and this is "the *sine qua non* of creativity for many outstanding people."

The state of consciousness experienced in the transition from wakefulness to sleep is called hypnagogic, and the hypnopompic state occurs during the transition from sleep to wakefulness. When they come on, you have miraculously clear, detailed, and colorful dreamlike images. I can recall experiencing a few such instances spontaneously when I saw, for example, properties for a stage setting, all in unimaginable detail, consisting of the most elaborate and expensive articles of every kind. I could see the costume brocades so closely and intricately that I could almost feel their texture. The ropes that held up the flats all were entwined with pearls ... oh, that was a magnificent stage set, all right. And a magnificent experience. I did not find it in any way useful, but it was exciting because it was so much more vivid and realistic than ordinary imagining or dreaming.

Green notes that often through hypnagogic imagery come words, symbols, and gestalts which result in brilliantly creative solutions to perplexing problems. German chemist Friedrich Kekulé's theory of molecular construction arose from a series of such reveries in which he saw atoms gamboling before his eyes.

"I saw how the larger ones formed a chain," he wrote. "I spent part of the night putting on paper at least sketches of these dream forms."

If psychics could in any way train themselves to have psi experiences at will during the alpha or the hypnagogic or hypnopompic states, as some have them spontaneously, it might revolutionize parapsychological investigation. Neurophysiologist Dr. Barbara Brown of the Veteran's Hospital in Sepulveda, California, is attempting such testing. Typical descriptions of a series of tests she has planned include "Attempt to train old and young subjects to vary the frequency of the alpha rhythm and to observe the effects on ESP scoring" and "Alpha rhythm and psi-effects."

"In five years," Dr. Brown predicts, "there will be biofeedback centers all over the country, in which people can learn all manner of mind and body functions."

Dr. Joe Kamiya, working with José M. Feola, president of the California Society for Psychical Study, Inc., undertook a pilot study to look for correlations between scores on ESP tests and amplitude levels of alpha waves. The experiment was limited to five subjects who had learned under Dr. Kamiya to change the amplitude of the alpha rhythm at will. The results from these experiments were different for each subject, but, as in many reports of parapsychological scientific testing, "no conclusions can be drawn from such a preliminary approach."

Numerous papers have been recently published in various scientific journals regarding research of the alpha state. One of interest to us was reported by Larry Lewis and Dr. Gertrude R. Schmeidler in the *Journal* of the American Society for Psychical Research (October, 1971) titled "Alpha Relations with Non-Intentional and Purposeful ESP After Feedback."

They stated: "The possibility of relating ESP to brain changes has long interested parapsychologists. Recently this interest has grown even keener because of biofeedback research, which shows that it is possible to exert direct, conscious control over brain events. Immediate information (feedback) to a person about some brain change, or apparently any other physiological change, may let him become aware of it and then produce it at will. Two questions arise for parapsychologists: Can we find a relation between EEG alpha waves, which are now being studied so intensively, and ESP? And if a person can learn by feedback to control his heart rate or skin temperature or alpha, can the same method teach him to control his psi-hitting and psi-missing?"

Fourteen subjects tried to identify and control their alpha and ESP, as reported in this paper. As to the results, "These data suggest that the relation between alpha production and ESP success is not a simple one, but will interact with such other factors as the requirements of the task or the demands of the experiment."

Among other conclusions, various analyses of the data all confirmed that when the subjects did not realize they were making ESP responses, they tended to make good ESP scores when alpha was present or was more pronounced than usual (but tended to score at chance if they showed little or no alpha). This suggests that when subjects are not strongly motivated to do well in an ESP task, a factor associated with alpha production is conducive to success. This meshes well with many laboratory findings and with the observation that spontaneous psychic experiences seem likely to occur during "between" states, when the person is not busily engaged in an activity which requires his full attention.

Today everyone is jumping on the bandwagon to find the quickest and easiest way to acquire and use the alpha state. Some are proclaiming that they can teach you mind control without the instruments that provide scientific researchers with feedback; and they may have something there. It wouldn't seem too difficult, for experienced meditators, at least. to know when they are in the alpha state, without any machines flashing colors or ringing bells to tell them so.

I, personally, am all for mind control courses. Even if they don't do all they purport to do, anything that will start people using their minds constructively is of value. They usually provide methods of auto-suggestion, of learning how to condition yourself to accomplish what you wish with your mind. In other words, the techniques for programming yourself. It is then up to the student to use them in his life situations in order to promote more successful practices and to break bad habits. After all, even to attempt to learn relaxation, dream control, concentration, memory retention, and how to correct disturbing habit patterns such as excessive drinking, smoking, overeating, nervous tension, shyness and insomnia should be of value. And if you really work at it enough to accomplish your goals, you've got it made!

Mind control courses, however, from the evidence of experienced practitioners with whom I have discussed the subject, are not going to provide you with instant ESP. There are just no quick gimmicks to produce psi phenomena. Mind control provides new techniques with which one can attain meditative states. These can be of use in meditation and development classes, causing you to be more receptive, to attain a deeper level of consciousness, to achieve helpful relaxation. But in these states you have to reach out, to be receptive, and, sometimes, to wait and wait for something to happen. It takes time and patience to develop your psychic sensibilities.

I still maintain that unless you fall on your head, have a severe fever, or do something else equally as spectacular (and with results equally as chancy), you will have to *work* to develop psi.

26: HEALINGS DO HAPPEN

MOST psychics appear to have the gift of healing to a greater or lesser degree. Even those who have not practiced to develop the healing ability may sometimes perform remarkable feats to help others.

Dr. Arthur Guirdham, psychiatrist at the Bath Child Guidance Clinic in Somerset, England, published in the medical journal *GP* an account of a sister (or nurse) who was saving lives around the hospital because of her ESP.

Once she implored the surgeon on his rounds to take a plaster cast off the fractured leg of a young man injured in a motorcycle accident. The patient looked comfortable and had no pain or temperature elevation, so the doctor ignored the nurse's request. Becoming nearly hysterical, she pleaded with him, and finally, for her sake alone, he agreed. On removing the cast the doctor found virulent and rapidly spreading gas gangrene, which would have killed the youth had he not ordered an immediate amputation of the leg.

This same woman, reported Dr. Guirdham, experiences strange vibrations in her arms, from her elbows to her fingertips, whenever she touches the skin over diseased or abnormal organs or tissues. With this ability she sometimes finds diseases unsuspected by doctors.

To me the most surprising thing about this story is that an MD admitted it and was able to get it published in a reputable medical magazine. Yet perhaps I shouldn't sound

239

so cynical. After all, in the United States we have a recently formed Academy of Parapsychology and Medicine, and that's certainly a step forward.

Although some psychics develop healing suddenly and spontaneously, as a rule those who have a tendency to want to cure others develop the ability by working with established healers . . . sort of as apprentices. Through observation and practice, it is said that almost any sensitive can become a channel through whom cleansing, healing and energizing forces can flow to those in need.

The potential healer must first recognize the fact that he does nothing except channel a power that comes from higher sources. He must be aware that these forces do not emanate from him but are obtained from an inexhaustible supply "in the sky."

New Jersey medium and healer Ethel E. DeLoach says in the *Newsletter* of the New Jersey Society of Parapsychology (November, 1971) that there is a definite technique she uses in calling on the divine healing force.

"I tune in to the universal power that instantly responds. I feel that in a moment I am in the twilight of the past when the cardinal principle was the application of religion to life and therefore to healing.

"Einstein stated it all for me in these words: 'The most beautiful and most profound emotion we can experience is the sensation of the mystical. It is a source of all true science. He to whom this emotion is a stranger, who can no longer wonder and stand rapt in awe—is as good as dead. To know that what is impenetrable to us really exists manifesting itself as the highest wisdom and the most radiant beauty which our dull faculties can comprehend in only their most primitive forms—this knowledge, this feeling, is at the corner of true religiousness.' "

It is advantageous if the person to be healed is aware of this also and adds the force of his belief to the proceedings. Reverend T. N. Tiemeyer, who preaches amazingly helpful and perceptive sermons, has explained the role of the patient thus: "God has created your physical temple to be the habitation of your mind, your will and your immortal soul. YOU ARE THE LORD OF YOUR TEMPLE!

"The mystery of the workings of man's mind, brain and nervous system has long puzzled philosophers and scientists. Now at last in this age of cybernetics with its calculators and electronic memory systems, we have found the key to the mystery. The neurological system in you, in its nature, structure and functioning is like an electronic brain, and deep within you is a Control Center.

"Man's machines are still so crude that (according to Dr. Maxwell Maltz) if you would try to imitate the capacity of the human brain with IBM products you would need one square mile of such machines, a legion of programmers, and more electricity per day than is produced in the state.

"Such is the awesome marvel of the neurological complex which is in operation every second of every day within you. Not only is there a control center and an incalculable network of communications, but in every cell of your body there is an intelligence which takes orders from and functions in harmony with this control center.

"This miraculous system computes in split seconds the chemical, thermal, nutritional, growth and elimination needs as well as the requirements of every muscle, ligament, bone, tissue and cell. All of this technical skill is still far beyond the finest electronic devices made by man, but these phenomenal calculations are recording millions of times per minute within your body, and then await to receive instructions from the control center as to what it shall do with its information.

"YOU ARE THE MASTER MIND WHICH INSTRUCTS THE CONTROL CENTER.

"Of course, even automation needs operators. There are

241

buttons to be pushed and tapes to be punched. God has supplied you with an ingeniously trained servant who is your obedient engineer at the control center. Psychologists have variously called him your unconscious, or subconscious or subliminal mind. He is a skilled operator but lacks imagination. He is an automaton. He believes everything he is told and tries to fulfill it. He does not think for himself, but blindly obeys. This control center engineer looks to you for his orders. Your thoughts are his command; your wish dictates him; your faith supplies his orders for action.

"If you think thoughts of health, wholeness and vitality, your inner mind strives with all its available resources to make your thoughts come true. As you think so you become. According to your faith so shall it be unto you." This works, as all those who have tried it know. If the patient believes and thinks constructively, the vitality of his spiritual conviction is half the battle.

Yet, oddly enough, many people who don't believe in any kind of faith or psychic or spirit healing may still be miraculously cured. There is much evidence for the sudden marvelous healing of children and animals and also of the occasional agnostic and atheist who definitely do not believe in the possibility that they might be helped in any supernormal way.

So how do we account for all this? We don't. We really don't know exactly how to understand any kind of miraculous healing. Doctors call it spontaneous remission, which doesn't explain anything. But whatever it is, you may be able to accomplish it as part of your development.

There is no channel of healing that is inferior as long as it produces wholesome and successful results. And ESP is one of the most active channels of all. Today more sensitives are developing for healing than for any other form of mediumship.

There are many instances where healing has occurred

without the intervention of a practicing healer, however. A mother may place her hand on the forehead of her son who complains of a headache, and the pain stops immediately. Sometimes love alone is sufficient, or even just friendship.

I had one slight personal experience of this nature which involved a warm friendship, nothing more—except that the apparent healer believed firmly in God's power to heal through him. While having dinner with my friend in a restaurant in New York, I mentioned to him that I had a headache. Because we were in public, he didn't follow his instinct to put his hands on my forehead or neck, but instead he held my hand for a few moments, while mentally sending me healing thoughts. The headache stopped at once. It started up again, however, just after he put me into a taxicab and said good night. I've been trying to analyze this experience. Was it just a psychological reaction on my part? Did my friend personally exude some magnetism which was effective only in his presence? Did my belief in his ability to heal maintain only when he was near?

One of my readers wrote me about the great rapport that has always existed between her mother and herself, to the extent that her mother has been able to assist her in unusual ways. This telepathic relationship between her mother, Mrs. Marjorie McCoy of Atlanta, and herself has frequently puzzled Mrs. Kathy Floyd of Riverdale, Georgia.

She wrote me: "From the time I was less than a year old, Mother would take aspirin if I had a fever and my fever would go down. She would take my laxative for me and I would be affected. As I grew older and developed asthma, my mother would occasionally take my horrid medicine rather than have to force it down my throat, and my asthma attack would soon cease."

Kathy says she doesn't know for sure how this idea occurred to her mother in the first place, and Mrs. McCoy has forgotten, but she recalls as well as Kathy does that she helped her throughout her early childhood in this way.

"Now, I don't mean to imply that she took all my medicine for me all the time," says Kathy, "but she did on enough occasions to form some sort of pattern. In anticipation of some questions you might have, my mother nursed me for the first six weeks only. After that I was bottle-fed. I have read accounts of a laxative or other drug being taken by a nursing mother and being ingested through the milk by the baby with the result that the baby would be medicated as well. I specifically asked my mother about this, and she said that the times she used self-medication for me were after she stopped nursing, and they continued until I was at least four."

The telepathic rapport between them extends to other areas besides medication. Kathy says she has vivid memories of occasions during the past six years when she would begin to feel depressed and weepy, for no good reason she knew of. She would phone her mother, even though at times they have been two thousand miles apart, and say, "OK, what's wrong?" Invariably, she would learn that her mother was unhappy for some reason or another. Also, says Kathy, "I would buy a dress pattern, and before I could use it, my mother would send me a dress she had made for me from the same pattern. When she moved back down here from Pennsylvania, we found almost every pattern she had was a duplicate of one I had bought, except for the size."

The same power of healing by supernormal means that is evident today also existed in all primitive cultures and in Biblical times. The shamans, witch doctors, priests . . . all religious leaders were also healers. Among the early Christians this was accepted as normal. To Jesus, the Twelve Apostles, and their congregations, curing the sick was just as important as preaching the gospel. The clergy were the physicians of their eras.

244

The schism between doctors and spiritual healers probably gained its greatest impetus in the thirteenth century, when Pope Innocent III condemned surgery and all priests who practiced it. Thirty years later he forbade as sacrilegious the study of anatomy and the dissecting of the human body. With this act, progress in medical science finally became divorced from the church and members of the clergy seemed to lose all interest in healing. It is only now returning. Due to the efforts of such organizations as Spiritual Frontiers Fellowship, there is a great resurgence of healing in many churches.

Because of the meditation and psychic development in many of these prayer or study groups, it is sometimes difficult to distinguish between spiritual and spirit healing, for when any group meditates regularly, psychic experiences begin to occur. So for all those who believe the results come directly from God, or from Jesus, through supplication of priests, ministers and prayer groups, there are just as many who believe that the actual healing activity comes from the same or a similar source but through the efforts of spirit doctors. Most of those who work in psychic areas (except parapsychologists, who always attempt to maintain an objective viewpoint) believe firmly that miraculous healings are caused by the efforts of physicians and teachers who have died and are working from the spirit world through mediums on earth.

A long-distance healing which illustrates that a spirit guide was somehow involved was reported by Vancouver medium James Wilkie in *The Gift Within*. One day, he says, author Allen Spraggett's wife, Marion, was worried because their baby daughter was running a high fever with a congested chest. Just then Wilkie telephoned her because his guide had told him he was concerned about the Spraggett baby's health. Wilkie was at the time some three hundred miles away and could not have known normally that the baby was ill.

245

When the medium phoned and asked about the child, Marion told him she was just on the point of calling a doctor. Wilkie replied, "No, she's fine now. My guide just healed her. Go and check again."

Marion had just been with her little daughter, and so she returned to the crib doubtfully. To her astonishment she found that in the few moments since her last check the baby had lost all her obvious symptoms and was sleeping soundly with no trace of fever or congestion. And the recovery proved lasting, Wilkie says.

Whether it is spirit doctors working through them or some more direct contact with the source, there are numerous healers in this country who are having highly successful results. Olga Worrall of Baltimore, Alex Holmes of Caro, Michigan, Kathryn Kuhlman of Pittsburgh, and Agnes Sanford of Los Angeles are but a few, and they all use daily meditation and prayer.

This, too, is the way those who seek development as healers gain greater capacity. Says Ursula Roberts in *Hints on Mediumistic Development,* the aim is to "lift the consciousness of the healer to the highest center of Healing Power. In other forms of mediumship, the aim is to establish a perfect link with the spirit operators. In this mediumship the aim is to lift the consciousness above that of the spirit operators and try to reach the Christ, or Cosmic Heart of Love. When the power flows from the Highest Center to the healer, the spirit operators will do their work and guide the healer's mediumship, but the Power will do the healing.

"The aim of the healer should be purity—pure thoughts; feelings untainted by lust; a body which is clean inwardly and outwardly! A tongue which speaks no ill—if it finds no good to say of other people, then let it be silent! Such a purified personality should be able to transmit the rays of Divine Healing Love, in such Power that swift and perfect healing of disease would transpire.

"To the developing healer I would say, 'Aim as high as you can' and just go about and serve suffering people, remembering, 'He who would be greatest among you, let him be the servant of all.' "

27: HINTS FOR HEALING

"THERE is no one way to conduct spiritual healing and there are no set rules that govern its procedure," says Harry Edwards, perhaps the best-known healer in the world today. "Every healer is individual unto himself, and the healing guides are individualists, too, so there must always be a variation in method of usage of the healer by the healing guides."

Nearly all those who become professional healers commence their ministry of healing through the development of trance, according to Edwards in his book, *The Hands of a Healer*. He, himself, did this, although, he says, "In common with many other healers, I subsequently learned that a trance state was not necessary for healing to take place. . . ."

To allow the spirit guide to take control of the mind and body functions, a state of trance is almost invariably thought necessary. Once this is attained and the healing directive is received, the personal difficulties are largely overcome, says Edwards, for the healer takes refuge in the thought that it is not he who is responsible for what takes place. It is the controlling guide instead. This enables him to overcome any natural timidity and self-consciousness in approaching a patient.

The beginning healer doesn't usually realize it, but his subconscious mind will nonetheless influence what is said and done through him. This is an important fact to remember.

"The guides make the best possible use of their human instruments," says Edwards, "but they may be hampered by the healer's subconscious conviction." It would be very difficult for the guide to induce any act or behavior that may be in opposition to the medium's beliefs. If the healer is convinced that a prelude to recovery must be "the healing of the patient's aura," then his mental awareness of what is taking place will not be satisfied until the aura is first healed. The guide, knowing this, will therefore allow the technique of aura. healing to be performed, while the actual act of curing the patient is taking place by other means. In other words, the guide tolerates the healer's weaknesses.

This is probably the reason so many healers do such weird things. It is not because the spirits who work through them demand it, but because the healers themselves have been previously so conditioned, thinking such things are necessary to healing. Thus if the healer in his development has seen the leader of the circle carry out any particular techniques, such as making passes, exaggerated hand movements such as waving them up and down, darting fingers forward and backward in spurts, blowing on the patient's body, or even the "taking away" pass and the "throwing away" pass, he will continue to do so when he goes into practice on his own. It is wild to see a healer spreading his hands and running them over the outside of the patient's body, at some slight distance away, as if grabbing out the disease. Then he makes motions as if he were violently throwing something on the floor. This way, he claims, he is throwing "lumps" of the disease away.

"This is, of course, absurd," says Edwards, and I quite agree with him, for I have seen it done. He has even known some healers to warn those present not to get in the way, as otherwise they may have lumps of arthritis or lumbago or whatever scattered over them and then they may get the illness.

It is such practices as these that tend to demean spirit healing in the minds of observers. Yet if you dare question such procedures, you are regarded by the practitioner as a heretic, for he believes they come from his spirit guides and that, by criticizing, you are impugning their reputation.

Those healers of ability and experience who have advanced to the understanding of healing science all have developed beyond the stage of needing to go into trance, according to Edwards. This is natural, for they have proved to themselves that healings take place just as effectively without the need for inducing a trance condition and certainly without the need for any dramatic contortions on the part of the therapist.

Healing without trance is far more personal and interesting and far less exhausting than healing under trance, says Edwards. "There is a very great advantage that follows healing through attunement, and not through control, and that is that the healer becomes a more conscious part of the healing act, his intelligent awareness is cultivated, his satisfaction in seeing a disharmony yield to the healing gives the greatest of all joys." Thus he is not simply a human instrument used by the spirit doctors, but he is an associate who is conscious of his guide's presence in a much higher and more refined way.

The great Harry Edwards heals not only with his "healing hands," which are guided by his spirit doctors, but also by absent treatment. *Psychic News,* London (January 2, 1971), reported that he made an actual out-of-body journey from London to help a California woman who didn't even know of his existence until she saw him.

Mrs. Amy Kees of Lynwood, California, was crying helplessly from pain and praying for surcease when, she says, "A face floated before my eyes. I asked who he was.

250

He said his name was Harry Edwards and he lived in England. His hand brushed my forehead and my migraine headaches disappeared from that day on!"

A few days later at a friend's home Mrs. Kees picked up a magazine which featured an article about Harry Edwards. She immediately recognized the face that had appeared to her after her desperate cry for assistance.

At nineteen Amy Kees was made a hunchback by a fall on a dirt road which injured her spine. After extensive surgery the medical diagnosis was "invalidism by forty"; by then she was a cripple and could walk only with crutches, suffering intense pain all the time. Her healing was only partly accomplished in that first miracle when Edwards appeared to her. Later that same night, when her distorted spine was sending fiery pain through her limbs, she struggled out of bed and onto her crutches to go to the kitchen for a glass of water. The room glowed with a great light, which was moving toward her.

"Then," she says, "it seemed to condense into a lightning bolt of pure energy. It cut through the flesh along my spine. I felt as if I'd been electrocuted." The shock was as severe as if she had undergone major surgery, and her back was straightened. During the next week, while she stayed in bed, she became aware that many spirit entities were speaking to her. The divine energy had also opened her mind and freed her psychic faculties. After this she dedicated her home as a healing center, which soon overflowed with people from all walks of life.

This Mr. Edwards, the man who is able to travel 5,000 miles in a moment when help is earnestly appealed for, has given us some very good tips for healing development. He says the conditions that must be present are love, compassion, and healing intention. Thus when supporting healers sit to give power, they are actually giving their love and sympathy, providing a radiating force and creating conditions in which the healing can take place

251

more easily and happily. The supporters can give "power" to help the healer if they will sit with their hands on their laps and seek through their minds a blending and cooperation with the effort taking place. Thus effective help can be given "through the linking-up by the physical and the spirit minds of the cooperating healer with the patient, his healer and the ministering spirit doctors."

Healers invariably have an abundance of energy, and this is often reflected in their cheerful and happy faces. "Just as one can consciously absorb these energies, so they can consciously be imparted to another," Edwards says. A healer must be conscious that in giving of his own energy and strength he may suddenly become aware of a depletion in himself.

Margaret Underhill says that the healer who understands the forces with which he is working can draw from the sources of supply and not be drained of his own vitality. But the person who is unaware of what is taking place can be used by those who seem actually to be human parasites or vampires.

"You should learn to protect yourself from the people who drain you," she says. "When you are in the presence of someone who tires you, never allow yourself to become negative or indifferent, for then you voluntarily relinquish your hold upon your forces and allow them to be drawn upon. On the other hand, never allow yourself to become flustered or angry; for it is by exercising command over your own powers that you can control their outflow."

When you feel that too much of your energy and strength is flowing to another and become aware of depletion in yourself, it is advisable to devote a few minutes to reabsorbing purposefully into yourself a fresh supply of cosmic energy by means of the characterized breathing discussed in the chapter on meditation. Then create a mental protection.

"Think of yourself as surrounded by a hard, transparent shell, at a distance of about three feet from your body," says Miss Underhill in a paper titled "Healing from Your Latent Powers." "Visualize it strongly and know that your forces cannot be drawn through this shell against your will; neither can antagonistic forces penetrate this mental barrier; while those which are beneficial and in accord with the laws of strength and harmony will have free access to you.

"Never think of this shell in a negative way and wonder whether it is a reality. Your thoughts will create it, your doubts and fears destroy it; for it is one of those realities which are intangible, but they prove the truth of their intrinsic being if used with understanding. Try this and see for yourself that it is a real protection, and you will be surprised at your results."

Patients also can benefit from this kind of positive and forceful thinking, and they should be asked to do the characterized deep breathing, knowing as they do so that they are drawing in vitalizing forces as well as oxygen.

When both the healer and the patient are in accord, there have been numerous instances of genuinely miraculous healings of terminal cases. Of course, there are also the psychosomatic cases, which are elementary for psychics. The view that we have been advocating for years, that the cause of the major percentage of human diseases arises from mental strain, frustration and soul sickness, is now confirmed by medical authorities. The tensions of modern living produce a series of stress diseases, which orthodox medicine seems powerless to cure but with which the spiritual healer has better luck. His methods differ from medical treatment in many ways, but primarily in that through his attunement with spirit guides and his psychic affinity with the patient, he can become aware of the patient's mind and soul disharmonies. There is little doubt that the reason medically incurable conditions yield to spiritual healings is that it is able to soothe mental tensions, calm fears, bring perspective and balance to the outlook, as well as to overcome the frustrations within the soul itself. As these disharmonies are cleared, the primary cause of the disease is removed, opening the way for the spirit doctors to clear the physical symptoms and effects from the body.

It is as well first to seek the easement of the mind disharmonies through the attunement of the healer with his patient, says Edwards. During this the healer can gently hold the patient's hands to enable the corrective influencing to flow more easily. Gain the patient's confidence by friendly talk, get him to "blend" with you and your healing intention. In this way he will become relaxed, and his tensions will subside. After this, carry on and seek the healing of the physical stresses.

"It is when a patient's total mind conditions become readily amenable to the corrective influencing," says Harry, "that we see what are termed instantaneous or rapid healings. Every illness of this kind is individual and there are no set rules that govern the speed of recovery."

Perhaps the most common experience is that when a healer is giving contact healing, he becomes aware of a strong heat in his hands. This is also felt by the patient as a heat penetrating into the body, but it becomes apparent only when the hands are held close to the affected part of the patient. If the hands are moved to an unaffected part, the heat sensation disappears; but as the hand returns to the trouble, the experience of heat recurs. This heat is a psychic or spirit manifestation; it is not physical. So far it cannot be measured, nor is it revealed on a thermometer.

One who is particularly aware of this heat during his healing is Charles Cassidy of Los Angeles, whom we spoke of as having discovered his clairvoyant and precognitive ability after a bout with malaria. It was many years later when he realized he was also a healer. His wife developed a throat infection that did not completely respond to medication. Finally she asked him if he would try to help her, thinking that because of his other psychic abilities perhaps he could also heal. He didn't know what to do, but he touched her throat.

"She felt nothing, nor did I," Cassidy says, "but the problem never bothered her again. I then started to try healing with other people we knew and got good results. I began to notice that at the time when I asked for this power, I could feel it coming into me from outside of my body. This came as heat or warmth with sometimes an electric sensation across my shoulders and down into my arms.

"As time has passed, this power has become very strong," he says. "At this point, *now,* in my life I can get it at any time, any place, and very quickly. It comes when I need it at all times, without any ill effects or exhaustion. This energy has some sort of check on it. I don't control it, but I do know that the greater the problem, the greater the force that comes through. I notice that if I don't work at healing for any length of time, the crown of my head becomes very hot to the touch."

Mrs. Cassidy confirmed this statement, saying that she, too, could feel the heat on top of his head at such times.

"To heal," Cassidy says, "what I do is clear my mind, ask a higher power for this force to come to me, and it does right away. It *will not* come to me if I don't have a subject to work with. I know that I am just a medium for this force—a go-between. I believe that many people could possibly do this but have never tried it. I do know that by constant work this ability improves."

The response of some persons to his healing is very sharp and dramatic. Some get complete results in one session, some take numerous sessions, but everyone gets some kind of reaction, he says.

When I visited Charles Cassidy for a treatment, I felt

the power very strongly as soon as I entered the room. Even when he did not touch me, I could sometimes know just where his hands were, as they were positioned over different areas of my body, because a feeling of great warmth exuded from them.

"Some people," he says, "become afraid when they experience a very sharp reaction. I only work with those who are at a standstill, medically speaking."

After healing many people, Charles realizes that he is an instrument used by some supernormal force to help others. He does not ask for payment for this service and supports his family by a job having nothing to do with the psychic. Because of the great demand for his healing, he may have to give up his daily work in order to see the many sufferers who ask for his aid; but unless he is funded, how will he support his family?

At present a number of experiments are being conducted with Cassidy by the Southern California Society for Psychical Research. It is good for parapsychologists to investigate healers and attempt to evaluate them and understand what makes them tick. A few good scientific reports verifying their talents will raise their prestige to the level many of them deserve.

Unfortunately, it has become too easy for any person to claim to be a healer. Anyone who wishes to make a quick, easy dollar may hang out a shingle as a psychic or spirit healer and a path will soon be beaten to his door by the many whose ailments are said to be incurable. It must therefore be admitted that there are some alleged spirit healers who are frauds pure and simple. But, for that matter, so are some evangelists. And so are some patients, who assist in the success of dishonest healers.

One woman I know of in New York City goes up to the altar at every healing service, awkwardly hobbling on crutches. She has a spectacular and dramatic healing, casts her crutches aside, and parades down the aisle cured. Her sticks have to be retrieved between healers, for she has them ready again to assist her down the aisle when the next evangelist comes to town. That woman's in show biz!

28: PSYCHIC SURGEONS

OCCASIONALLY we hear of someone, a child perhaps, completely innocent of any knowledge of healing, who is impressed to place his hand over the painfully afflicted part of an ill person and the trouble vanishes immediately. He has suddenly become a natural channel for healing forces, and he may remain so for the rest of his life.

Such a one was Tony Agpaoa of the Philippines, one of the famous psychic surgeons about whom we hear so much. Tony's healing mission began in a rice field. When a man fell and accidentally stabbed himself in the abdomen, Tony felt a compulsion to put his hand on the wound, and it was miraculously restored. Even the knife hole disappeared. At least, this is the story we learn from Tony and his myriad of followers. Although he is among the most prominent psychic surgeons in the world, there is a great deal of controversy about his abilities—whether they are genuine or fraudulent.

The first psychic surgeons to be heard from were those in the Philippines. This extremely improbable kind of surgery apparently requires no anesthesia and gives the patient no discomfort. No antiseptic preparation is made and no asepsis is observed during the operation; yet no infection results. And the patient never dies. Another idiosyncrasy of some psychic surgery is the alleged ability of the physician to cause an incision to occur without cutting, just by passing his hand over the abdomen of the patient, using his finger as the knife or scalpel. Such far-out healers are naturally looked on with great curiosity and, I must say, suspicion, and yet thousands of patients claim to have been operated on by them and to have been healed.

A number of eminent researchers have investigated these psychic surgeons with mixed reactions. Some are sure what they have seen is fraud; others are equally confident they have, at least on occasion, seen genuinely supernormal operations. And still the throngs of "healed" patients sing their praises.

In our own hemisphere we had José Arigo in Brazil, a psychic surgeon who was killed in a car crash during the winter of 1971. Fortunately, Arigo was studied thoroughly by Dr. Andrija Puharich and several other American medical men, and movies about Arigo's unusual surgery just about prove the claims. I have seen these movies several times and always force myself to look when Arigo plunges a knife into an eye socket, scrapes it around the eyeball roughly, and pulls it out with the cyst or tumor that was causing the trouble impaled on the end of it. The patient all this time is registering no more distress than he would if a fly were buzzing about him—in fact, not as much.

Dr. Puharich has his own testimony to add to the Arigo story because he underwent an operation by this psychic surgeon. Puharich arrived in Brazil with a tumor on his arm, which was benign but which lay near the nerve which controls the movements of the little finger. Because contact with that nerve could have caused paralysis of the finger, Puharich's doctors at home had advised him not to have it removed.

When they were introduced, Arigo was allowed to examine the tumor on Puharich's arm.

"Who can lend me a knife?" he asked quickly. Accepting a penknife, he opened it and then, without sterilizing

259

it, grasped the American's arm and made an incision. The flesh opened and blood started to flow. Arigo then pressed two of his fingers around the incision, and the tumor dropped out onto the floor.

It was hard and covered with blood, but it caused Puharich no pain whatever. He had thought Arigo had run his fingernail down his arm when the incision was made. Within two days nothing but a fine line remained as a scar.

Arigo's name was really Freitas. The pseudonym he adopted for his healing mission meant "the simple fellow," which indeed José was. With a farm upbringing, he could barely read or write, yet when he was controlled by the deceased German Dr. Adolfo Fritz, who purportedly performed the operations through him, he spoke in Portuguese with a German accent or else in pure German to those who could understand him. And he operated with dispatch and authority. He also wrote prescriptions by the thousands, something Arigo in his normal state would have been incapable of doing.

Dr. Fritz said in December, 1970, that Arigo would "discarnate during the first fortnight of 1971." The fatal car crash occurred on January 11.

The Brazilian press told how, when the coroner went to perform his autopsy on Arigo's body, he was astonished to find it already prepared. He said it had been skillfully done, obviously by a competent surgeon. He presumed it was Dr. Fritz. This sounds like an apocryphal story, but we can take it for what it is worth.

In 1968 Dr. Fritz said that his spirit operations would continue through another medium, Altemir Gomes, a black who worked with Arigo for several years. As far as I know, not much has so far been heard about Gomes outside Brazil. But since José's untimely death, a new psychic surgeon from Brazil, Lourival de Frietas, has begun to make news. Gordon Creighton, a distinguished

British diplomatic secretary and consul of more than twenty years' foreign service, testified to reporters of the *Psychic News*, London (June 19, 1971), that he saw several operations performed by De Frietas with unsterilized razors or knives and that no infection resulted. The cures were immediate, and no scars remained.

Something different from the ordinary psychic surgery is spirit operations purportedly performed on the etheric or astral body of the patient. The claim is that by healing the spirit body, the physical body is also healed. Harry Edwards is strongly against this because, he maintains, "It is true that a physical disharmony is *reflected* in the etheric or spirit body but it is contrary to common sense and all logic that the physical disease has its creation in the spirit body."

Yet British medium George Chapman has numberless testimonials to his successful operations, in which Dr. William Lang, a deceased ophthalmologist, is said to participate. C. J. Mistree, a Hong Kong executive, is one who has testified to a successful operation. He says a Harley Street specialist had told him imperative surgery would almost certainly be fatal, for he had an enlarged hiatus hernia that was pressing against his heart. He suffered excruciating abdominal pain, could not eat, and had lost thirty pounds in two months. An hour after he went to Chapman for Dr. Lang's operation, Mistree emerged, he said, a new man. During the operation all he felt was a strange sensation "like ether being sprayed over my body."

Dr. Robert W. Laidlaw, consulting psychiatrist at Roosevelt Hospital in New York City, recently paid tribute to Dr. Lang. After a ninety-minute discussion with entranced medium George Chapman's spirit guide, Laidlaw, who is chairman of an American medical committee which studies all forms of unorthodox therapies, said of the Lang entity, "There is no doubt I was talking to a medical man. No layman could be familiar with all the technical medical matters we discussed."

Another who practices surgery on the spirit body is Dr. William Brown of Toccoa, Georgia. When my seventeen-year-old friend Stephanie Sladon, daughter of the Paul Sladons of Coconut Grove, Florida, was eleven years old, a tall, handsome American ballet dancer performed in Miami. In worshipful adoration Stephanie joined the crowd around him outside the theater after the show was over, holding out her program to be autographed.

Instead of signing Stephanie's paper, the dancer impulsively lifted the pretty child high into the air and sat her down on top of the station wagon he had been using as an autographing desk. At that moment he was distracted by a call and hurried off, leaving Stephanie sitting high, helpless, and embarrassed, without even his autograph to assuage her. Since no one was there to lift her down from the top of the car, she jumped—and a long series of curious events began.

The next day Stephanie's knee locked, hurting terribly, and her parents realized she must have injured herself in her jump. After a few moments when they all panicked, the knee began to move again, but the extreme pain didn't let up. Finally a doctor put a cast on her because he thought the problem might be a torn ligament or damaged cartilage. After several months the cast was removed, but the ache was still there, so physiotherapy and manipulation were undertaken. Nothing helped, and for two years the child was a tortured invalid.

It is interesting that an orthopedic surgeon once put Stephanie into a hospital to operate on the knee. The night before surgery, while he was chatting with an intern at her bedside about the procedure he would use, the doctor stopped. A puzzled look came over his face and he said abruptly, "I don't know that leg well enough. I'm sending her home."

Sylvia Sladon, Stephanie's mother, looked at the surgeon questioningly, and he said to her, with a shrug, "I've done this sort of thing before." Sylvia, knowing enough to follow hunches, gladly took her daughter home intact . . . but still hurting.

Spared the operation on her physical body, Stephanie has since undergone two psychic, or spirit, operations. First, though, she was given psychic healing without surgery. A Scottish medium named Helen L. happened to visit in Miami, and Sylvia persuaded her to attempt to help Stephanie. After she had given the painful knee her attention, the ache completely disappeared for a period of three months. Helen L. had returned to her home by the time the pain resumed, and she was appealed to by letter. She replied that this time her spirit doctors thought it would be necessary to operate on the knee and they would come soon and do it.

Before this letter was received, Stephanie experienced excruciating pain for three days, and then she was better. When the letter arrived, it was realized that Helen's doctors had evidently already been there in their invisible presences and had proceeded with the operation. This was said to be surgery performed on her spirit body by spirit doctors without the intermediacy of a medium. After this occurred, for a period of five months the knee was in perfect shape and Stephanie was able to participate in all the school activities she'd been deprived of for so long—even dancing.

Spirit doctors are only human, or so they maintain. Apparently they, too, are sometimes able to achieve only partial success. Or perhaps only a part of Stephanie's condition had been corrected. Anyway, at the end of her five months' reprieve she again began to have intermittent pain in her knee and now also in her lower back. Because she and her parents had been so encouraged by the success of Helen L.'s spirit associates and were convinced that help could come from invisible sources, they began to search for another psychic surgeon who might be able to assist them.

This brings us back to Dr. Brown of Toccoa, Georgia, whose spirit doctors perform what he designates as "etheric" surgery. When the Sladons talked to him briefly, he diagnosed Stephanie's case differently than anyone else had, saying that her main trouble was from several vertebrae in her spine that had been crushed when she jumped from the station wagon. (This was then confirmed by a medical man who examined and X-rayed her back.) It was therefore decided to let the girl undergo etheric surgery, and an appointment was made for the Sladons to spend several days at the medium's Georgia clinic.

As Sylvia described the surgery, it couldn't have been more fascinating. Stephanie lay on her stomach on an operating table, awake but unaware of what was occurring because her body was not touched at any time by the medium. Her parents watched closely as the man's hands manipulated in the air over her body, without making contact with her. When it is realized that this medium was in a trance and his eyes were tightly closed the whole time, it can be seen that this in itself was a tour de force.

"The whole thing appeared to be the most fantastic pantomime," Sylvia told me. "A number of different spirit doctors were supposed to be using the medium's body, alternating in their possession of him according to their specialty. One was an anesthetist, one did surgery, and so on. They talked through the medium's mouth, and his hands continually moved in all the operating-room procedures. Yet, of course, there were only invisible instruments used."

Sylvia had been a premed student and used to observe operations in her college days, so she was able to identify the various processes. It was easy to determine when they gave Stephanie a hypodermic, when they reached into the instrument tray and selected a scalpel, made the incision, inserted retractors, clamped hemostats. And then they threaded invisible needles and sutured the invisible wounds. Sylvia and Paul watched entranced.

Two incidents seemed to lend authenticity to the super-normal aspects of the phenomena occurring, in addition to the fact that Stephanie was healed. One was that Paul Sladon was asked by one of the spirit surgeons to take his daughter's pulse from time to time and report to them. Before the invisible anesthetic was given, the pulse was perfectly normal. By the time the operation started, the pulse rate was so low that Paul could not even feel it.

The parents observed that part of the surgery was in the area of Stephanie's left hip, although it was her back which was supposed to be involved. After the activity ended and the child was sleeping it off, Sylvia asked the doctor privately what had been going on concerning her hip. She was informed that bone had been withdrawn from it to use to rebuild the crushed vertebrae. Stephanie, as I've said, did not know what was being done to her. She had been told that although it was her etheric body that had undergone the operation, she would have a reaction of shock and pain to her physical body for several days. She was prepared to experience this, and she wasn't disappointed. The thing Stephanie could not understand when the pain began to bother her was that it was not only in her back.

"Mommy, my left hip hurts," she kept insisting. Because Stephanie did not know anything about the hip operation, Sylvia and Paul felt that her complaint was evidence that something had actually occurred there as the surgeon had indicated by his actions.

After several days the child had recuperated enough to go home. This last operation was performed on July 2, 1968, and Stephanie became a new girl after that. No more knee aches, no more backaches, not even headaches. She is as happy and lighthearted as she used to be and at present is enjoying a year's schooling in Switzerland, the fantastic change in her personality and physical well-being due entirely to the fact that she no longer suffers constantly.

It must be confessed that all spirit surgery is not always successful. I have talked to people who have had operations at Toccoa who were healed for a short time and then found their original complaints returning. I have talked to those who believed they saw tumors or gallstones removed from their bodies by Philippine surgeons and yet were no better off afterward. I have also talked to a woman who was cured of a terrible complaint of years' duration by Tony Agpaoa and swears by the authenticity of his operations. It is all very confusing and also highly challenging.

Whether we believe in surgeons who can operate on etheric bodies, or spirits who can perform healing through mediums, or a God who allows persons with enough faith sometimes to be healed, we almost have to admit that occasionally something dramatic and, yes, miraculous, does happen.

29: GROWING INTO LIGHT

"ISN'T it absolutely tragic that people can for one brief moment glimpse the awesomeness of eternity and then go back to the same pattern of life?" Reverend T. N. Tiemeyer of Miami asked in his sermon "He Is Risen, So What?" "Isn't it totally unbelievable that today worshipers will say in their hearts, 'There is no death, man lives on,' and then tomorrow go back to living as if this life were but a candle flame to be snuffed out permanently. How can you explain Christians facing the most sensational news, the most startling fact in history and yet remaining unperturbed and returning to plodding in the shadows of oblivion? How can the multitudes sing today, 'He is risen,' and tomorrow say, 'SO WHAT?'

"It should make a startling, revolutionary difference in your life. You are a living soul; you have a Christ potential; you have eternal life now. You have no beginning and no end. Once you discover that the real you is an indestructable mind and spirit temporarily sheltered in a physical body but capable of surviving without it, once you discover that, it throws the whole business into focus and, for the first time, Jesus makes sense and God has meaning."

This, of course, is what should happen to the person who attempts to develop his psychic faculties. You cannot sit long for development and not become convinced that there is a life after death and that it is possible to commu-

267

nicate with spirits. Then your whole perspective changes for the better. As Mr. Tiemeyer said: "As soon as you see that man is mind and spirit, together called soul, and soul has no color and no nationality and owns no money and lives by the same laws of consequence and restitution, you develop for the first time that sense of relatedness because you are travelers on the same road, and because you are all groping, are all lonely and are all seeking the light. I am convinced that if man by science ever makes a break-through to prove survival of personality, or if mankind by sheer faith sincerely accepts it, that will not only be the greatest advance in human relations, but the only logical basis for bringing an end to war and a beginning of a kingdom of heaven on earth, with peace and goodwill among men."

In an interview with *Psychic* magazine (October, 1971) astronaut Edgar D. Mitchell, of the Apollo 14 moon flight, the only man ever to perform psi experiments from outer space, was asked, "Do you feel that experiencing mystical or psychical states helps a person become more selfless?"

Captain Mitchell replied, "Yes, I do, provided that a person then develops a rationale for the experience and a philosophy that compels him to be selfless for his own happiness. People have to be motivated to do something, or they won't do it. And in my opinion, the truth one finds when looking for the explanations of psychic events provides the motivation, by requiring the development of a philosophy that compels a person toward a more selfless self in order to achieve his own happiness."

We are taught almost from birth that we live in an orderly universe in which specific effects always result from specific causes. Without causes there can be no effects. Yet when we first begin to observe and to experience psychical phenomena, we find results for which we cannot learn the

268

causes—indeed, for which there seem to be no possible logical causes at all. As long as we try to study these results without attempting to understand or accept the fact that the cause in most cases comes from another dimension of existence, we are faced with situations that are not in any possible way explainable; and we are in a morass of uncertainty until we finally accept the reality of conditions not as they purport to be but as they actually are. Then we can begin to face reality on its own terms.

Psychic Sidney Porcelain said in the *Newsletter* of the New Jersey Society of Parapsychology, "Even those people who are interested in parapsychology sometimes express reluctance to make use of pychic powers." Evidence of knowledge gained without the usual means of communication scares them. The possibility of precognition causes them to avoid looking into the future lest it contain tragedy or misfortune. Yet, Sidney says, "Those who are afraid of ESP can be reassured by the beneficial results of practical usage; the warnings against fire and earthquake, accidents and questionable business ventures; the healing of physical ailments and the prescription of remedies; the awareness that cements human relationships, the marriages saved and the lives maintained through psychic advice."

Many others have written of this also, of the changes in their lives once they accepted the reality of psi and its application to them. As example of this, Margaret Underhill says in *Your Infinite Possibilities*: "It is extraordinary how I am always led to the right place, or to the right people. I could cite dozens of incidents such as this, which have occurred since I began to cooperate with guiding spirits. I am never led astray; the guidance is so wise and beneficial, and it occurs so frequently that I cannot attribute it to coincidence. Previous to the psychic work my luck was in the other side of the balance. I do not think that my good fortune is due to luck, but rather to my willingness to cooperate with spiritual entities whose wisdom is far greater than my own."

Gladys Osborne Leonard puts it another way in *Brief Darkness*: "To some people God seems to be a long way away and this feeling discourages them from making any attempts to reach him in prayer or thoughts. In such cases communication with individual souls who have passed into the beyond is of inestimable value because sooner or later such contact leads us to a recognition of the divine creator, a power behind the wonder and comfort of our personal intercourse with those whom we have known, loved and trusted during their earth lives and who may seem to be much more real to our human hearts than a vague and impersonal God whom we have never seen with our physical eyes. I have met many atheists and agnostics, who through the mediumship of the séance room have found the God whose existence they doubted. The realization that love has persisted beyond the grave in a personal sense opens out the possibility and later the certainty that it also exists in a greater and more infinite form. When this knowledge leads them still further, that is to a consciousness of the Plan, then life on the earth plane, with its problems and difficulties can be faced with an inner peace and greater courage than has ever been known before. We find that 'all things work together for good' in a way that is impressive indeed."

There can really be no doubt of this. It is testified to by too many people, myself included. Your entire life changes for the better once you accept the truth of spirit help. It doesn't always go to the extreme for us that it did for Alice Barnes, however; but if we can bring ourselves to believe her story, no extreme is apparently too great, no feat impossible, if we but have confidence in our spirit guides and accept their assistance.

When I first heard Alice's story in the fall of 1966 in Seattle, I found it difficult to believe. I have come to know Alice well since then and to be impressed by her sanity, her serenity, her objectivity, and her well-rounded approach to psychical phenomena. She is what you might call an upper-middle-class, attractive, rather heavy-set woman in perhaps her early forties, with the most beautiful eyes I have ever seen. She and her husband, who is a nonprofessional healer, have been into psychical study for many years and are firm believers in the help it is possible to receive when one keeps his channels clear and his contacts with his spirit associates open. I now believe Alice's story because I believe in Alice. It's as simple as that.

Her account of the weird incident goes like this: "On a morning in September, 1965, I drove my husband to work as usual and was on my way home heading north on Richard's Road in Seattle. Suddenly around a curve immediately ahead of me came two cars heading south, abreast on the road. In its correct lane was a tan station wagon. Passing it on the curve, and going about sixty miles per hour in a thirty-five-mile zone, was a big black Mercury.

"As I was driving along, I had been mentally conversing with my spirit masters. Now, almost paralyzed with fright as the Mercury hurtled toward me in my lane of traffic, I cried out, 'You guides better help me!'

"I could see the man in the station wagon throw his hands over his face, sure that a collision was imminent. There was absolutely nothing I could do to keep from being crashed into . . . no way I could move to avoid it. I didn't have time to throw my car into reverse and try to back out of the situation. Anyway, my hands were frozen on the steering wheel and my foot was frozen on the brake. I could only think that here was my moment of transition into the next world.

"Just then, however, my car was picked up and moved back to a spot which was sufficiently out of the way so that the Mercury had space to get by. All I knew was that the trees were suddenly going by in the wrong direction, and then my car was sitting still by the side of the road. The Mercury sped down the highway.

"The man in the station wagon stopped across the road, got out, and came over to me. Tears were running down his face. I was still paralyzed with fright; but as he came up to my car and spoke to me through the window, my first reaction was to say, almost calmly, of the Mercury driver, 'He must have been late for work!' Then I, too, began to cry.

"The driver of the station wagon, in workman's clothing, walked around my car and came back to tell me there was not a scratch on it. By then he had calmed down enough that he was able to discuss with me what had happened. He said, 'Your car was picked up off the road and carried back. Did you know it?'

"I told him that was what I thought had happened. I began to observe my situation. My car was not in reverse gear; it was still in the forward position, so the backward movement could not have been of my own doing, that was certain."

Alice regrets, and so do I, terribly, that she didn't have the presence of mind to ask her witness for his name, his address, and his signed testimony of the events he observed. After a few more moments, when we marveled together at the miracle in which we had participated," she says, "he left, and I drove shakily home, thanking my masters all the way. They explained that because I was talking to them at the time, the contact was already established and they were able to go into immediate action to save me. They said they would have come anyway, had they not been so close when I called to them; but in that

272

event, although they would have been able to save me, the car would probably have been damaged."

Here is one woman who accepts the "awesomeness of eternity" and lives her life accordingly. Would that we all could achieve the same.

BIBLIOGRAPHY

ABARBANEL, ALBERT, "Are Aborigines Psychic?" *Tomorrow* (August, 1961).

A.R.E. News, October, 1971.

BORZYMOWSKI, ANDRZEJ, "Experiments with Ossowiecki." *International Journal of Parapsychology,* Vol. VII, No. 3.

BROWN, ROSEMARY, *Unfinished Symphonies.* New York, William Morrow & Co., 1971.

CHASE, JOANNE, *You Can Change Your Life Through Psychic Power.* New York, Pocket Books, Inc., 1960.

CLARK, GLENN, *The Man Who Tapped the Secrets of the Universe.* St. Paul, Minnesota, Macalester Park, 1946.

COOK, ELLEN, *How I Discovered My Mediumship.* Chicago, Lomar Press, 1919.

CORNELLIER, PIERRE ÉMILE, *Journal,* Society for Psychical Research, Vol. XXI.

CROOKALL, ROBERT, *Events on the Threshold of the After-Life.* Moradabad, India, Darshana, 1967.

DEL FANTE, ALBERTO, *Who Is Padre Pio?* U.S.A., Radio Replies Press Society, 1955.

EDWARDS, HARRY, *The Hands of a Healer.* Surrey, England, Healer Publishing, 1959.

EDWIN, RONALD, *Clock Without Hands.* Indian Hills, Colorado, Falcon Wing Press, 1956.

Fate, July, 1971; March, 1965; December, 1962.

FLINT, LESLIE, *Voices in the Dark—My Life as a Medium*. London, Macmillan, 1971.

FORD, ARTHUR, *Nothing So Strange*. New York, Harper & Bros., 1958.

———, *Unknown but Known*. New York, Harper & Row, 1968.

FOX, OLIVER, *Astral Projection*. New Hyde Park, N.Y., University Books, 1962.

GARRETT, EILEEN J., *Adventures in the Supernormal*. New York, Garrett, 1959.

GREEN, ELMER E., and ALYCE, "Voluntary Control of Internal States: Psychological and Physiological." *Journal of Transpersonal Psychology* (1970).

GREENE, GRAHAM, *A Sort of Life*. New York, Simon & Schuster, 1971.

HANKEY, MURIEL, *J. Hewat McKenzie: Pioneer of Psychical Research*. New York, Helix, 1963.

HERBERT, BENSON, "Séances with Dr. R. G. Medhurst." *Parapsychology Review* (November-December, 1971).

HEYWOOD, ROSALIND, *ESP: A Personal Memoir*. New York, E. P. Dutton, 1964.

HOLLAND, JACK H., "Let Us Look at Extrasensory Perception." *Parapsychology Periodical* of the California Parapsychology Foundation.

Journal of the Society for Psychical Research (March, 1966).

KIMAYA, JOE, "Operant Control of EEG Alpha Rhythm," *Altered States of Consciousness* by Charles T. Tart. New York, Wiley, 1969.

LEAF, HORACE, *Death Cannot Kill*. London, Max Parrish.

LEONARD, GLADYS OSBORNE, *Brief Darkness*. London, Cassell, 1931.

———, *The Last Crossing*. London, Cassell, 1937.

———, *My Life in Two Worlds*. London, Cassell, 1942.

LEWIS, LARRY, and SCHMEIDLER, GERTRUDE R., "Alpha

Relations with Non-Intentional and Purposeful ESP After Feedback." *Journal,* American Society for Psychical Research (October, 1971).

LONG, MAX FREEDOM, *Growing Into Light.* Vista, California, Huna Research Publications, 1955.

MACGREGOR, HELEN, and UNDERHILL, MARGARET V., *The Psychic Faculties and Their Development.* London, LSA Publications, 1934.

MCGRAW, WALTER, *The World of the Paranormal.* New York, Pyramid Books, 1969.

MONROE, ROBERT, *Journeys Out of the Body.* Garden City, N.Y., Doubleday, 1971.

MYERS, FREDERIC W. H., *Human Personality and Its Survival of Bodily Death.* New Hyde Park, N.Y., University Books, 1961.

Newsletter, American Society for Psychical Research (Spring, 1970).

Newsletter, New Jersey Society of Parapsychology (November, 1971).

Occult, September, 1971.

OSTRANDER, SHEILA, and SCHROEDER, LYNN, *Psychic Discoveries Behind the Iron Curtain.* Englewood Cliffs, New Jersey, Prentice-Hall, 1970.

PATANJALI, *How to Know God: The Yoga Aphorisms of Patanjali.* New York, New American Library, 1953.

PEARCE-HIGGINS, J. D., "Haunted Minds." *Spiritual Frontiers* (Summer, 1970).

POLLACK, JACK HARRISON, *Croiset the Clairvoyant.* Garden City, N.Y., Doubleday, 1964.

PRINCE, WALTER FRANKLIN, *The Case of Patience Worth.* Boston, Boston Society of Psychical Research, 1922.

PROGOFF, IRA, *The Image of an Oracle.* New York, Garrett, 1964.

———, *The Symbolic and the Real.* New York, Julian Press, 1963.

Psychic, April, 1970; August, 1970; October, 1971.

Psychic News, London, June 19, 1971; January 2, 1971.

RAUSCHER, WILLIAM V., "The Mystical and the Psychical." Publication of Spiritual Frontiers Fellowship, Evanston, Illinois.

ROBERTS, URSULA, *Hints on Mediumistic Development.* London, Aquarian Press, 1956.

SHERMAN, HAROLD, "Pastoral Uses of ESP." *Spiritual Frontiers* (Winter, 1970).

———, *Your Mysterious Powers of ESP.* New York, World, 1969.

SMITH, SUSY, *Confessions of a Psychic.* New York, Macmillan, 1971.

———, *Widespread Psychic Wonders.* New York, Ace Publishing, 1970.

———, *The Enigma of Out-of-Body Travel.* New York, Garrett, 1965.

STEVENSON, IAN, "Sensitives, Scientists, and Clergymen." *Gateway* (November, 1965).

TECHTER, DAVID, "Latest from Maimonides." *Fate* (January, 1972).

TENHAEFF, W. H. C., "On the Personality Structure of Paragnosts." *Proceedings* of the Parapsychological Institute of the State University of Utrecht (December, 1962).

TIEMEYER, T. N., "Dimensions of Defensive Prayer." *Spiritual Frontiers* (Autumn, 1971).

Time, October 18, 1971.

UNDERHILL, MARGARET V., *Your Infinite Possibilities.* London, Rider & Co., n.d.

WALKER, DANTON, *Spooks DeLuxe.* New York, Franklin Watts, 1956.

WHITE, JOHN, "The Yogi in the Lab." *Fate* (June, 1971).

WILKIE, JAMES, *The Gift Within.* New York, Signet, 1971.

WILLIAMS, SOPHIA, *You Are Psychic*. Hollywood, California, Murray & Gee, 1964.

WISE, CHARLES C., JR., "A Meditation on Meditation." *Spiritual Frontiers* (Autumn, 1971).

WOOD, ERNEST, *Yoga*. Baltimore, Penguin Books, 1959.

YOGANANDA, PARAMAHANSA, *Science of Religion*. Los Angeles, Self-Realization Fellowship Press, 1967.

YOST, CASPAR S., *Patience Worth: A Psychic Mystery*. New York, 1916.

ZOLLNER, JOHANN C. F., *Transcendental Physics*. London, W. H. Harrison, 1880.

Index

279

CAST YOUR OWN SPELL, by Sybil Leek. The best-kept occult secrets of the ages can be yours now. A book that has been needed for a long time. But, not until Sybil Leek has any witch, male or female, let the general public know their secrets of sorcery. For centuries they have kept their trust, sometimes even suffering martyrdom rather than betray it. But, Sybil Leek, the Queen of Sorcerers—a reputable and authentic witch—has agreed that it is time now, in this new age of Aquarius, to drop the veil and let everybody know how to cast a spell. Easy-to-follow instructions will amaze and delight every person who ever wanted to try his hand at occult magic.   **P012—95¢**

STAY YOUNG WITH ASTROLOGY, by Frank J. McCarthy. Now for the first time a renowned astrologer reveals the formula for lasting youth hidden in YOUR own Sun Sign. Every Sign of the Zodiac has its own special youth-giving secrets. Now, revealed for you—whatever your Sign is the way to remain full of life no matter what calendar age you reach. It has long been known and accepted that the stars have an incredible influence on the kind of person you are—but what is little known is that they can help you to enjoy a healthy, youthful, sex-filled life right through your golden years.   **P016—95¢**

SCIENTIFIC ASTROLOGY, by Sir John Manolesco. Finally, the inside truth about astrology! Here is a clear, authoritative and absorbing look at a very old subject, one that has long been fascinating to both fans and cynics. It is a most unique exploration of an influential force at work on all of our lives. Sir John's book gives outsiders an inside look; the whole truth about astrology: the information necessary to evaluate any given astrological source.   **P176—95¢**

DREAM-SCOPE, by Sydney Omarr. Here, from the man named "Outstanding Contributor to the Advancement of Astrology," is a revolutionary method of tapping the world of dreams, of viewing them both in the form of written words and pictures. DREAM-SCOPE allows each reader to embark upon adventures

To order see page 288

previously confined to the world of sleep. All the mysteries of dream interpretation are revealed, permitting the reader to "see" his dream as he never could before—but always wanted to. From cover to cover, DREAM-SCOPE is a dream of a book.

P185—95¢

BEYOND THE CURTAIN OF DARK edited by Peter Haining. This is probably the most representative selection of horror and fantasy stories ever to appear in an American paperback. All the giants of the genre are included: oldies like Poe, Hawthorne, Bierce and Lovecraft, and current favorites like Bradbury, Sturgeon, Asimov, Highsmith and Kuttner. And there's Harold Lawlor, Fred Brown, Bill Morrow, Mary Shelley, August Derleth, Joe Le Fanu, and many more. Here are axe murderers, blood-sucking creatures, monster-makers, devils and demons, vampires and vultures, and all the weird and nameless horrors loved by all.

P138—$1.25

FIRST CONTACT, edited by Damon Knight. Here are ten masterpieces of science-fiction and fantasy dealing with man's first encounter with alien creatures from outer space. With all the benefits of our science and history we earthlings still seem to find it impossible to communicate effectively. What is to be expected when our people make contact with creatures or intelligences from other worlds? Perhaps the answers to our problems are to be found in these prophetic and exciting stories from the imaginations of such masters of the game as: Leinster, Sturgeon, Asimov, Henneberg, Kornbluth, Heinlein, and H. G. Wells.

P062—95¢
